# Say When

## ALSO BY ELIZABETH BERG

# Say When

# ELIZABETH BERG

**ATRIA** BOOKS

New York  London  Toronto  Sydney  Singapore

**This Large Print Book carries the
Seal of Approval of N.A.V.H.**

**ATRIA** BOOKS
1230 Avenue of the Americas
New York, NY 10020

ISBN: 0-7434-5132-5

First Atria Books large-print hardcover edition June 2003

10  9  8  7  6  5  4  3  2  1

**ATRIA** BOOKS is a trademark of Simon & Schuster, Inc.

For information regarding special discounts for bulk
purchases, please contact Simon & Schuster Special Sales at 1-800-
456-6798 or business@simonandschuster.com

Designed by Jaime Putorti

Printed in the U.S.A.

for Howard Jonathan Berg

# Acknowledgments

· · · · · · · · · · · · · · · · · · · · · · · · · · · · · · · · ·

Many thanks to Annic Antolak and to Rod Riemersma for telling me what it's like to hire Santas and to be one.

My editor, Emily Bestler, sure knows how to make a girl feel appreciated. Thank you, Emily. Her assistant, Sarah Branham, is enthusiastic, pleasant-voiced, and always ready to lend a hand—my thanks to you, too.

My agent, Lisa Bankoff, and her assistant, Patrick Price, are supernovas on my team, and it is my distinct pleasure to once again thank them for **everything.**

Cathy Lee Gruhn and Marisa Stella handled a bazillion details and spared me from doing same.

I spent a long time in a downtown Chicago post office one winter day, reading letters to Santa. They were an inspiration, and I thank the hundreds and hundreds of children who wrote them. I will never let another Christmas season go by without the pleasure of sifting through those piles of soulful entreaties. The experience was enough to make me wish there really was a you-know-who. It was enough to make me pretend **I** was you-know-who, for many of those children whose letters I read. I got the presents, and my partner, Bill Young, delivered them. Thank you, Bill, for that, as well as for the many other things you do to enrich, stabilize, inform, comfort, and inspire me.

Grateful thanks to my wonderful girlfriends, who help me in all ways on all days: Barbara Ascher, Elizabeth Crow, Phyllis Florin, Judy Markey, Mary Beth McAvoy, Marianne Steenvoorden, and Marianne Quasha.

And to my dog, Toblance Floyd Ripkin: You and me, pal.

To understand is to forgive, even oneself.

—Alexander Chase

# Chapter 1

· · · · · · · · · · · · · · · · · · ·

Of course he knew she was seeing someone. He knew who it was, too. Six months ago, saying she needed a new direction in her life, saying she was tired of feeling helpless around anything mechanical, that she had no idea how to even change a tire, Ellen had taken a course in basic auto mechanics—"Know Your Car," it was called. She'd come back the first night saying it was amazing, she'd had the admittedly elitist idea that mechanics were illiterate, but this one was so well-**spoken,** and he'd walked into the classroom carrying a pile of **books** he'd just bought—hardback! Mostly new fiction, she'd said. But also Balzac, because he'd never read him.

"How do you know?" Griffin had asked.

"Know what?"

"How do you know he's never read Balzac?"

"Because he told me. I had a question after class and then we just started talking. . . ."

"What was your question?"

She stared at him, a tight smile on her face. Then she said, "My **question** was about the battery."

"But what about it?"

She looked down, embarrassed. "I wanted to know how you clean it. Okay?"

"Why didn't you ask me?"

"Oh, for—"

"No. Why didn't you ask me? I could have told you."

"Because," she said, slowly and deliberately, "it never came **up** between us. It came up because I am taking a **class** about **cars.** And I had a **question** for the **teacher.** Jesus, Griffin. What is this?"

"Nothing," he'd said. "Forget it."

Griffin didn't forget it, of course. Week after week, he'd watched Ellen dress for class, each time paying more attention to herself: fresh eyeliner just before she left one week, a more deliberate hairstyle the next, a lingering scent of perfume in the bedroom the night she'd gotten ready for the last class—the ridiculously expensive perfume Griffin had given her for her last birthday, for the record. He felt helpless against her drift toward another man, felt as though he were standing around stirring change in his pocket when he should be waging an earth-pawing kind of war. But the truth was that from the time he'd married her ten years ago, he'd been waiting for something like this to happen. She was always just beyond his grasp, in one way or another. He supposed, actually, that her cool reserve was one of the things that attracted him to her.

She couldn't be serious about this obvious attraction to someone else. She was nearing forty, that was all. He would let her have this, this secret relationship, this thrilling little romance. Let her and Mr. Goodwrench meet for coffee and have moony-eyed discussions about Mary Oliver and Pablo Neruda and Seamus Heaney, all of Ellen's precious poets. Let her talk until she was finally exhausted by all that **"so much depends upon a red wheel-barrow"** crap, by all those supposedly deep thoughts written by people who were undoubtedly a bunch of first-class hypocrites. Ellen seemed to think her pale gods spent all of their time sitting at their desks in rapturous torture, scribbling away with quill pens, when in fact they were probably mostly standing around scratching their asses and contemplating the contents of their refrigerators just like everybody else. It might actually be a relief for her to have someone to talk about that stuff with, so she would finally stop trying to make Griffin swoon over it—though lately she'd been pretty good about not asking him to read anything.

She wasn't sleeping with the guy, Griffin was sure of that. She would never do that.

He leaned over her now and looked at her, her hair splayed over half her face. She was not a beautiful woman, but Griffin had never met anyone who appealed to him more. She exuded an earthy sensuality made more attractive by the fact that she didn't know it. "I love to look at you," he sometimes told her. "You're just . . . perfect." "Oh, God, Griffin," she would say. "Stop."

She moaned slightly in her sleep. Griffin lay his hand on her shoulder, then slid it down her back and onto her palm-sized sacrum. When she was in labor with Zoe, he'd given her a back rub against the awesome waves of pain. When he'd felt her sacrum, he'd thought it was the baby's head and had yelled, "It's **coming!**"

"Ohhhhhhhhh, really?" Ellen had moaned. "Really?"

"Yes, it's **coming,**" he'd said, for a good forty-five minutes or more, until the doctor came in and informed him that he was not feeling the baby's head at all. They'd chuckled together over his erroneous assumption.

Ellen had gotten furious. "This isn't **funny!**" she'd said.

The doctor had winked at Griffin. "Pain pretty strong, Ellen?"

He was met with a nearly palpable silence.

"She's doing really well," Griffin said, then added proudly, "She hasn't had any medication!"

"Well, it's too late for that now, anyway," the doctor said.

"Why don't both of you just shut up?" Ellen said, and the doctor had winked again. "She's in transition," he'd whispered to Griffin. He patted Ellen's foot, and left.

Now, eight years later, Ellen seemed to be in another kind of transition. She was preoccupied: bereft-looking when she thought Griffin didn't see her, guarded when she knew he could. Twice he'd heard her on the phone when he came home, saying hurriedly, "I have to go." She wouldn't talk to him, not really, except to fill him in on necessary bits of business about Zoe, about what bills needed to be paid next, about who would take the cat to the vet.

It all made sense now.

Well. You had these times in a marriage, everyone knew that. You just waited them out, that was all. Griffin kissed Ellen's cheek lightly, then got out of bed to get his robe. It was Sunday. He'd make coffee and hash browns, eggs over easy. Zoe would sleep late, she always did, and Griffin and Ellen would sit at the kitchen table and read the Sunday paper together as usual. Maybe they'd find something on sale and go and buy it. He sat on the bed to put his slippers on.

"Where are you going?" Ellen asked sleepily.

He turned to look at her. "Downstairs."

She said nothing.

"To make breakfast."

"Stay here, okay?"

**Sex?** Griffin thought, and felt his penis leap up a little in anticipation.

He took off his robe and slippers and got back in bed. God, how long had it been? Ellen put her arms around him, her head beneath his chin, and sighed heavily. Oh. Not sex, then.

"You know something's going on, right?"

He stopped breathing.

"Right?"

He shifted his weight, checked, for some reason, the time. Ten after eight. "What do you mean?"

"Griffin, don't do this. We have to talk about it."

He said nothing, waited. She started to say something, then stopped.

"What," Griffin said.

"Oh, I don't know how to do this!" She sat up. "Look, I'm . . . Okay, I'll just say this: I'm in love with someone. And I . . . want a divorce. I'm sorry."

He lay back against his pillow, closed his eyes.

"Griffin?"

He didn't respond.

"I'm sure you're aware that I haven't been happy for a long time." Her voice was light, false. "And I don't have to remind you that—"

He opened his eyes. "Jesus, Ellen."

"It was **never** right between us, you **know** that."

"No, I don't know that."

"Right. I knew you'd make this difficult."

He laughed. "As opposed to what?"

"What do you mean?" Some color was rising in her face. Her voice shook.

"Difficult as opposed to **what?** This is supposed to be easy? You drop this **bomb,** and it's supposed to be easy?"

"Be quiet! Zoe will hear!"

"Your concern for our daughter really moves me. Let's get a divorce, but let's be **quiet.** Let's make it **easy.**"

She would not look at him. Her mouth was a pale, straight line.

"Well, I won't make it easy for you, Ellen. Do what you have to do. But don't look to me to help you."

He got out of bed and went downstairs. He felt curiously light, emptied out. Numb, he supposed. Protected by a specific kind of anesthesia. Well, here's what: He'd make coffee. Just like always. Six cups, Bed and Breakfast blend. He'd make the same Sunday breakfast he always made. The cat, Slinky, came into the kitchen, meowing, and he fed her. One and a half packs, tuna flavor. He turned on the faucet, and then, for just a moment, gripped the edge of the sink.

Behind him, he heard Ellen come in and sit at the kitchen table. She watched him for a while as he made the coffee, as he got out the frying pan, the potato peeler. Then she said quietly, "I thought at first I could just have an affair."

An affair!

"I felt restless, crazy, really sad, and I thought . . . Oh, I don't know, I thought if I did that, maybe I'd feel better, maybe I'd feel **something.** But I got deeply involved with this person. I fell in love with him. I wanted to talk to you about it right away, tell you . . . well, tell you who it was and everything. But then I figured you knew anyway." She hesitated, then asked, "Did you?"

"Did I what?"

"Did you know?"

He came to the table, sat down opposite her. "I knew you were seeing someone, Ellen. Yes."

She looked down at her hands, rubbed at one thumb with the other. "I want you to know I was really careful, okay? We used—"

**We.** "What the hell difference does it make, Ellen? Can you remember the last time you had sex with me?"

"Well, that's what I mean, Griffin! It's been so bad between us for so long. We're like . . . brother and sister. And with him, I feel I've finally found something I've always wanted, but never knew I could have."

Griffin stopped listening. He watched Ellen's mouth moving, her hands pushing her hair back from her face. He looked at the top button of her nightgown, half opened, half closed. He saw the thrusting motions of another man, entering his wife.

He looked out the window. It had begun to snow; huge, quarter-sized flakes waltzed lazily downward. To catch a flake like that on your tongue would feel like receiving communion. Ellen had seen this, too, he was sure of it. But suddenly neither one could remark on it. Nor would either of them awaken Zoe to see it.

The last time he saw snow like this was on a winter day many years ago, when he and Ellen were students at the University of Illinois. He lived in a dorm; Ellen lived in a tiny, slanted-floor apartment. Her roommate, Alexandra, was a sullen girl with long, greasy red hair. She wore only black, wrote lines of obscure poetry in a ragged journal, rarely spoke except to read her poetry out loud, and believed that wearing deodorant was giving in to the system. "Why don't you get another roommate?" Griffin would ask, and Ellen would always shrug and say, "She pays the rent. I don't think I could find anyone else, anyway."

On that long-ago winter day, Griffin went to Ellen's apartment with a sprig of lilac for her. Alexandra opened the door. "Lilacs!" she'd said. "Where did you ever find lilacs?"

"At the florist's," Griffin had answered, stepping into the apartment, thinking, **Where else would I get them?**

Ellen had come into the room fresh out of the shower. "What have you got there?" she'd asked, adjusting the towel she had wrapped around her wet hair.

"Lilacs," he'd said proudly, handing them to her.

"Oh, my God. **Now?"**

He nodded, feeling suddenly foolish. He'd paid twelve dollars for this single sprig, which now lay wilting inside the cellophane.

"Well . . . **thank** you," Ellen had said, laughing. She'd put the sprig into a wine-bottle vase, set it on the kitchen table. "Lilacs in January!" she'd said, and it seemed to Griffin that she was more bewildered than charmed. A fortune teller he'd once visited on a dare from Ellen had told him, "You're not too good with the ladies. You do everything wrong."

Ellen's mouth was still moving; she was explaining, pleading. Of course she had slept with him, he thought. How could he have deluded himself so? How many times had the two of them done it? How many ways?

She was saying something about Zoe now, about how they needed to keep her routine as stable as possible. Griffin forced himself to pay attention. "She needs to stay in the same house, in the same school. I've thought about this a lot, Griffin. And since I'm the one who stays home with her, it only makes sense that you be the one to move out."

He felt his stomach tighten, his heart begin to race. The coffeemaker beeped, signaling its readiness, and Ellen got up and poured two mugs. She set one in front of Griffin, one in front of herself. Griffin watched the steam rise up and curl back on itself, then dissipate. He said quietly, "I'm not going anywhere."

"Pardon?"

"I said, I'm not **going** anywhere. I'm not moving."

She nodded. "I see. Well, **I** can't. I have to be here to take care of Zoe."

Griffin pictured his daughter, a redheaded tomboy who would grow up to be a redheaded beauty who would knock the stuffing out of any man who crossed her. "All right, you can stay, too," he told Ellen.

"Griffin. One of us has to go."

He picked up his mug, took a sip. "Well, let's see, now. It isn't going to be me. You try to figure out the rest, Ellen. And from now on, call me Frank. I don't want you to call me Griffin. That's what my friends call me."

He went outside to get the paper. A world of news, not one bit of it about her. Or **them.** When he came back inside, Ellen had gone. He picked up her full mug, dumped the coffee down the drain. Then he got out the potatoes and began to peel them.

# Chapter 2

· · · · · · · · · · · · · · · · · · ·

On Monday, Griffin got through two meetings before he let himself think of anything. Then, asking his assistant, Evelyn, to hold his calls, he closed his door and sat at his desk with his head in his hands. The thought came to him that he needed to go home, he had to go home. And then he remembered that home was not home any longer. He folded his arms on top of his blotter, lay his head down, and closed his eyes.

Ellen had gone out early on Sunday afternoon, telling Zoe she was going to A Stitch in Time, a store she knew Zoe hated. Still, she'd asked if Zoe wanted to go with her. For a moment, Griffin thought Ellen might actually be telling the truth, might really be going to the fabric store. But when Zoe declined her invitation, she'd looked straight at Griffin, her head raised high, defensively. **You see?**

**You see how easy it's been? How could I help it when it's been so easy!**

Zoe had eaten breakfast, complimenting her father on the perfect crispness of the hash browns, and then had gone out to build a snow fort with the neighborhood boys. Except for the ten minutes Zoe returned to gulp down a peanut butter sandwich, Griffin had had the day alone. Some of the time, he spent unashamedly going through Ellen's drawers. He found nothing he was looking for—no letters, nothing that looked like a gift, no incriminating evidence. It was all inside her, in the ways she'd changed. Little things—or perhaps not-so-little things—that he had simply ignored.

Ellen had returned at dinnertime, and they sat with Zoe at the kitchen table eating take-out Chinese, tight-lipped and silent. At one point, Zoe asked, "What's the matter? Don't you guys like this?" Later she'd asked, "What's **wrong?**" "Nothing," they both said, together. She'd shrugged, then asked if either one of them knew one word, just one word, of Chinese. No, they'd said. Zoe said, "Me neither. I **guess.** But was it, like, the very first language? Or something like that? Wasn't it symbol writing first?" After neither Ellen nor Griffin answered, she said, "Whoa, you guys are **crabby!**" and left the table. She did not open her fortune cookie. None of them did.

At 8:30, Ellen helped Zoe get ready for bed, then went to bed herself. An hour later, after a half-hearted attempt to get through **Business Week** and **Forbes,** Griffin came upstairs and leaned against his bedroom doorjamb, his arms crossed, his hands in loose fists. The room was lit softly by a paper lantern of a moon, a deep yellow orb that seemed hung directly outside their window, exclusively for their benefit. **Ellen,** he thought, and the name seemed to him to hold everything he might possibly want to say to her. It was a request, an apology, a sweet claim. He looked at her lying on her side of the bed, looked too at the space she had left beside her. That was his side, because he was her husband. And she was his wife.

Quietly, slowly, he lay down beside her. She was turned away from him. Asleep? He listened to her breathe for a while and decided not, the rhythm was wrong. And anyway, he could feel her awareness, feel her listening to him. "Ellen," he whispered. "Can we talk?"

She turned over, her face full of relief. **"Yes."**

He looked fully at her, saw her eyes (near-sighted), her nose (once, out on a date when she was in high school, the guy asked if she'd broken it, humiliating her so much she feared letting anyone see her profile for years), her mouth (the first lipstick she ever wore was tangerine lip gloss, a sample stolen from a drugstore), her dimpled chin (something she used to pray would turn into a "normal" chin), her small ears (plagued by infections until she was ten—her mother used to get up with her in the middle of night and bring her into the kitchen for an orange to comfort her). I **know** you, he wanted to say. Do you know how well I know you?

He wanted to remind her that she had been in the ocean for the first time with him, that it was he she'd turned to with amazement saying, "It tastes **salty!**" He wanted to tell her that he provided her with excellent health and dental insurance, that it was he who had made her finally understand how airplanes stayed in the air—science was not her strong suit. They were so familiar to each other, he loved her so much, and she wanted a divorce? No. She **said** divorce, but she meant something else. She was confused. This . . . illness had come over her, the last several months. Together, they could cure her.

He wanted to suggest something: Saturday night dating. Yes. They'd hire a standing sitter, and every Saturday night, they'd go out somewhere. Chicago was a fabulous city; there was so much to do— they'd take advantage of the fact that they lived in Oak Park and could get in and out so easily. He was sorry he'd ignored her complaints about almost never going with her to see the ballet, or plays, or concerts, or even enough movies. Maybe she'd like to try opera; he'd be willing to try opera. Or if not exactly opera . . . No! He would be willing to try **opera.**

He'd make an effort to go out with other couples; Ellen was right when she said they needed to make friends. He'd send her flowers on a random Thursday, he'd pay attention and nod at all the right times when she told one of her interminable stories about—well, anyone would agree—about not much. He'd tell her how he **felt** about the sunrise, about the headlines, about the new neighbors down the block, about the barely discernible change in her hairstyle. He'd stop leaving the lid up—though Zoe liked it, claiming that she, too, liked to stand to urinate. Oh, he would do everything, he would do everything she wanted, maybe her demands weren't so much after all. He'd read **poetry** with her, all right? Maybe he'd amaze her with his insights; he wasn't so insensitive as she thought, he could be just as sensitive as the next guy, if he wanted to be. And she'd be so **glad,** in the end, so happy they'd stayed together.

He cleared his throat. "Ellen. I love you so much."

She started to cry. He thought perhaps this was a good sign—it was her way of saying she loved him, too. He tried to take her in his arms, but she pushed him away, saying, "No! That's not going to work! **Please,** will you please just **listen** to me!"

He moved away from her, and she sat up, yanked a tissue from the box beside the bed, wiped her eyes. "Look, I know this came out of the blue for you. But I've been thinking about it for so **long,** Griffin."

For so long! For **how** long? The fall afternoon last year when he was raking leaves, and looked up to see her standing at the window looking out at him (and he gaily **waved!**)—then? The last time they made love? When they sat watching **The Sopranos** together and he passed her the popcorn bowl, giving her the last bite even though he wanted it? On Zoe's seventh birthday, when he found Ellen crying in the kitchen and she said it was because their daughter was getting so old? Was she in fact mixing the batter for Zoe's cake and thinking, **Oh, God, I can't stand my husband, I want a divorce?** Unwillingly, he remembered a day shortly before their wedding when Ellen told him they shouldn't go through with it, she didn't really want to get married—that that's why it had taken her ten years to agree to it. He'd put it down to nervousness. As he did her taking a stiff drink in the bride's room before she walked down the aisle. He'd forgotten about it almost as soon as it happened. But he remembered now.

"Griffin?"

"Frank."

"What?"

"Call me Frank." He sat up, straightened his shirt. Damn it, he'd have to learn to iron.

"Stop playing games, Griffin."

"Call me **Frank.**"

She stared at him. "Fine. I will call you **Frank.** Okay? I will call you Frank." She fell silent.

Griffin waited a while, then asked impatiently, "So what did you want to say?"

He would handle whatever she said. Whatever she said, he would handle.

She took in a deep breath. "Okay. I told you this morning that I was in love with someone."

"Yeah, the grease monkey. Congratulations on your lofty standards."

"Well, I'm certainly not going to defend him to you, **Frank.**" She looked away, envisioning her lover, Griffin thought. What did he look like, anyway? What did he have?

Ellen rubbed her forehead, sighing. "I don't know what to say to you. What do you want me to say to you? I mean, I care about you. I really do. I don't want to hurt you. I'd just like you to **understand,** so that we can cooperate."

He considered this, pursing his lips, thinking. Then he asked, "How long have you been fucking him?"

Her hands dropped from fidgeting with her hair into her lap. "Oh, God. I might have known."

"What?"

"That **that** is what you would choose to focus on!"

"Oh, excuse me. Perhaps I meant, What does he think of postmodern fiction? But I don't think so. I think I meant, How long have you been fucking him?"

She closed her eyes for a moment, then opened them and looked sadly at Griffin. "A few months or so, I don't know."

"You don't know? You don't **know?** Oh, I think you know, Ellen. A romantic like you? I think you know the exact day, hour, and minute that you began. I think you could tell me every delicious detail about how you undressed, who was on top, every single thing he did to you—and you to him, too. Go ahead, pretend I'm one of your girlfriends. Oops, I forgot. You don't have any." It was true. Ellen was painfully shy and had always had trouble making friends. In the three years since they'd moved to Oak Park, the only "friend" Ellen had made was Louise, the waitress whose section she always requested when she went to the Cozy Corner, a local coffee shop. When Griffin once suggested she go out somewhere with Louise, or invite her over to their house, Ellen had quickly said no.

"Why not?" Griffin had asked, and Ellen had gotten up and walked away from him, saying over her shoulder, "I'm sure she has a lot of people to do things with." But he had seen it: Ellen was afraid.

Now, offended at what he'd said, her voice hardened. "What is the point of this, Griffin?"

"Call me—"

"No! I'm not going to call you Frank! I have always called you Griffin and I'm not going to stop now!"

"Everything stops now, Ellen."

"What does **that** mean?"

"You'll see." He turned over, closed his eyes, and, unbelievably, felt himself falling asleep.

In the morning, Ellen hadn't gotten out of bed. Griffin had gotten Zoe off to school, telling her that Mommy didn't feel well. Then he got in his car and drove to his computer consulting firm. Same route as Friday. Same exact route. Same radio station. His life belonged to him.

Evelyn knocked gently on his door. Griffin jerked his head up, pushed around some papers on his desk. "Yes?"

She opened the door, stuck her head in, spoke softly. "I'm sorry, Mr. Griffin, I know you said no interruptions. But your wife is on the phone. She told me to tell you."

"Uh huh," he said. "Okay." He wanted his face to look normal. How did he used to look when she called? He smiled at Evelyn, nodded, and she nodded back, closed the door.

He picked up the phone. "What."

"Meet me for lunch. We have to talk."

"Sorry, can't."

"Yes, you can."

"No, I **can't.** I have an important lunch meeting." He did not.

"Griffin, I don't want to live with you any longer. We have to do something about that."

He looked out the window, saw the trucks going by on the nearby freeway. After they graduated from college, he and Ellen had hitchhiked across the country, a romantic tribute to the sixties. Griffin had even let his hair grow long and wore an old Army jacket. At one truck stop, a massively overweight but quite muscular driver who'd had too many beers took an instant dislike to Griffin. "What are you supposed to be?" he'd asked. "You a hippie?"

"No, no—just a captain of industry like yourself, Slim," Griffin had said, and the driver had gotten up and moved rapidly toward them, his fists clenched. They'd run out of the place, terrified, and then, when they were far enough away, fell down laughing. That night, they'd lain out in their sleeping bags looking up at the crowded stars in the Montana sky. "It's so . . . big," Ellen had said.

Griffin smiled. "Yeah. That's why they call it 'Big Sky Country,' Ellen."

She was quiet for a while. Then she said, "Sometimes when I see things like this, like how big the sky is, I just feel sad. I don't know why."

Her voice had sounded so young, like a little girl's. Griffin remembered the photo he'd once seen of her as a pigtailed seven-year-old, one braid twisted nearly comically away from her head, her bangs cut crookedly. In her eyes was a shyness, a soft vulnerability that had made him run his finger down the side of her child's cheek, that had made his chest ache with his desire to protect her. Here was that child now, wrapped up in the body of a woman he'd decided he wanted to be with forever.

He'd pulled her close to him that starry night, kissed her face everywhere. Three times they'd made love that night. Three times—under Venus, under Orion, under the filmy gauze strip of the Milky Way—he'd lost himself inside her.

And now Ellen was standing in their kitchen holding the phone and telling him this impossible thing as though he would go along with it. Well, he wouldn't. He would not.

"I told you before, Ellen, and I will say it one last

time. I am not moving. I am not going anywhere. Period."

"Well, fine, Griffin. Then we will as of this moment begin leading separate lives. Consider us . . . roommates."

"Right."

"And I have plans tonight. I will feed Zoe dinner early, and as soon as you come home, I will be leaving."

"Have a good time. What are you going to wear?"

She hung up. He slammed the phone into the cradle and then picked up the picture of her that he kept on his desk. He removed it from the frame. Maybe it wouldn't tear easily—maybe he'd need scissors.

The paper gave easily when he started ripping, but then he stopped, put the picture back in the frame, and put the frame back where it had been. Exactly.

# Chapter 3

• • • • • • • • • • • • • • • • • •

Ellen looked beautiful. She was wearing a black silk blouse with her jeans, and a lot of silver jewelry Griffin hadn't seen before: hoop earrings, a bracelet, a ring with a large blue stone that she wore on her middle finger. She looked young. She met him at the door, saying, "You're late. Zoe needs a bath. Her homework is done." Then she squeezed past Griffin and went out to the car. She checked herself briefly in the rearview mirror, adjusted her bangs, and was gone. Why had they ever agreed that having just one car was the p.c. thing to do? What if he and Zoe wanted to go out? It was too cold to walk to town, and too short a distance to take a cab—Griffin would feel like a jerk asking for a ride four blocks away. He went to the window. There went Ellen, down to the end of the block, where she signaled, then turned right. Where was she going?

"You have lipstick on your teeth," Griffin said softly.

"What?" Zoe called from the kitchen.

"Nothing—just saying goodbye to Mommy." Griffin came into the kitchen and sat at the table. "What are you eating?"

"Ice cream. Ice cream soup, I like to make it soup." She stirred industriously, and Griffin watched her. Abruptly, Zoe stopped stirring and looked up. "Dad?"

Here it comes, Griffin thought, and was grateful when the phone rang. "Hold on a second," he told Zoe, and answered it.

There was a pause, and then a man's voice said, "Ellen, please."

Griffin turned his back to Zoe. "She's not in."

"Oh. Well . . . could you tell me when she left?"

"Why, certainly. Just now. Two minutes ago. Two and a half. Whoops, two minutes and forty seconds."

". . . Right. Okay, thanks."

"Hold on," Griffin said. "I'll be glad to take a message. Now, which one are you?"

"That's all right. No message."

"Is this Jeffrey?"

"No, it isn't."

"Mark, then."

The man hung up. Griffin listened to the dial

tone while he said, "Uh huh . . . Yes, all right. I'll be sure to tell her. . . . You bet . . . You're welcome!"

He hung up and sat down again, drummed rhythmically on the tabletop with his knuckles, raised his eyebrows up and down at Zoe. "So! What are we reading before bed tonight?" His voice was too loud. He stopped his drumming, asked more softly, "Same one as last night, about the White Sox? Or have you come to your senses and want to read about the Cubs?"

"Who was that on the phone?"

"Someone for Mommy."

"What did they want?"

"Something about the PTO."

"What about it?"

Griffin stood up, pushed his chair hard into the table. "I don't **know,** Zoe! They just said to tell her they'd call back, okay?"

"Sorrrrreeeeeee!" She looked down, stirred her ice cream halfheartedly, then pushed the bowl away. "I'm done."

Griffin sighed. "I'm sorry, Zoe. I had kind of a bad day at work. Hey, how about we go over to Mickey's for a gyros and fries?"

She looked at him. "I just **ate,** Dad."

"Oh—right! What did you have, anyway?"

"Soup and sandwich."

Griffin opened the refrigerator. "Uh huh. Sounds

pretty good." Yogurt, silken tofu, English muffins, a head of lettuce. What the hell was there to eat?

"Where did Mommy go?"

He stiffened. "Well, what did she tell you?"

"She said 'out with a friend.'"

"I guess that's where she went, then."

"Yeah. I guess. Well, I'm going upstairs." She scooped up Slinky and was gone.

Griffin sat at the table and took off his tie. He had to remember some things. Don't take it out on the kid. Bring home dinner. Was he supposed to bring home dinner? He guessed so.

Fine. He would bring home whatever he felt like. For tonight, it looked like . . . He checked the cupboard, pulled out a can of bean and bacon soup, put it back on the shelf. He took out the Cheerios, poured a bowlful, and ate it standing up at the sink and looking out the window into the backyard. Zoe's tree house needed some work—the floor was sagging dangerously. In the spring, he'd put a new one in.

Griffin finished his cereal, pulled a Sam Adams out of the refrigerator, and sat at the table to drink it. That had to have been him on the phone. Had to have been. How dare he call when Zoe was home? And where **did** Ellen go? Why didn't she take her phone? She always took her phone, but there it was on the counter in its charger. Forget her "divorce" crap—what if something happened to Zoe? How would he reach her? What the hell was the matter with her?

He went to the bottom of the stairs. "Zoe!"

No answer.

"ZOE!"

The sound of footsteps, and then there was Zoe at the top of the stairs. **"What?"**

"Did Mommy say **where** she was going?"

"Nope. Hey, Dad, can you play this computer game with me? It needs two."

"In a minute."

He went back into the kitchen and sat at the table, thinking. She didn't say where she was going because it was to his place. To his stylish bachelor pad in Wrigleyville, complete with espresso maker, charcoal gray sheets and towels, and a Bang & Olufsen stereo system. Track lighting, maybe even a real leather sofa. Because this was a mechanic with style: This was a man who **read.** He'd kiss her when she came in—he'd **French**-kiss her when she came in, then put down his three-thousand-page novel and say, "My darling. My love." Ellen loved that shit. They all loved that phony shit. Why did they all love that phony shit, didn't they know it was phony? Didn't they know it was step one in the Let's Get Laid game? Griffin could call her those endearments; he could do that if it was important to her. He never had, because he respected her too much. He assumed that she was beyond needing such vacuous come-ons.

But Mr. Crankshaft. He'd use them all. **Lover. Honey.** He'd say, "Does he know where you are, babe? Did you tell him where you were going?"

She would shake her head, smiling.

"Good," he would say, and kiss her again.

He would make dinner, and Ellen would help. She'd take over making the salad, of course, save him from all that fussiness. She'd be all womanly and careful and cute—a strand of hair falling across one eye as she sliced the tomatoes. He would gently tuck it behind her ear, kiss her again. My, didn't making dinner take a long time when you were so in love! When you had found what you always **wanted** and never knew you could **have!** You might have to fuck each other between courses, you were so blissful! Between bites!

Mr. Smooth would say—obliquely, of course—how nice it was to have a woman around the house. Wouldn't want to push too hard, too fast. So to speak. He would seat her at his dining room table, and, with a flourish, put before her a plateful of linguini in clam sauce. "Oh, this is so **nice,**" Ellen would say. "We only use our dining room for folding laundry, you know? For paying bills. Griffin's just not **comfortable** eating in the dining room." Mr.

Crankshaft would pointedly refrain from commenting. What a good guy, to let pass such an obvious opener to Griffin's myriad faults!

There'd be plenty of good wine to go along with the meal so as to loosen Ellen up, she always needed to be loosened up. Although maybe with him she didn't.

Griffin threw his empty beer bottle in the recycling bin, then put his bowl and spoon in the dishwasher. Yes, first they'd eat, each finding at least one opportunity to feed the other, to slide their fingers in and out of the other's mouth, slowly. Then they'd retire to the bedroom and screw one another's brains out, and then Ellen would get up and get dressed and come home and get in bed with good old Griffin.

Oh, no, she wouldn't.

"DAD!" Zoe called.

"COMING!" He wiped off the counter, threw the sponge in the sink. He turned out the light in the kitchen, then all of the lights downstairs and on the porch. He put the chain locks in place on both the front and back doors, then went upstairs to his daughter.

At eight o'clock, he ran bathwater for Zoe, then sat on the toilet seat to talk to her as she washed. Zoe draped the wet washrag carefully across her head, then asked her father, "Who am I?"

Griffin shrugged. "Beats me."

"I am the grrrrreat . . . I am the Great Buffalo**hoho!**"

"Pleased to meet you."

"YES!"

"To what do I owe the honor of this meeting?"

Zoe stared at him. "Huh?"

"What brings you here, Ms. Buffalohoho?"

"Oh. A meeting."

"I see. With whom?"

"With all my tribe in the worrrrlllddd!" She pointed at Griffin. "You are under my supreme command!"

"All right."

"And I command you . . . I command you to get me two Oreo cookies."

"Later."

Zoe gasped. "You dare to defy the great—"

"Later, I promise."

He didn't want to go back to the kitchen and turn any lights on. Just in case.

Zoe stretched herself out full length in the tub. "Hey, Dad."

"Yes?"

"Could I sleep in the bathtub some night?"

"I think you'd get pretty cold. Plus you might fall asleep and get water up your nose." Or drown. In a distressing but utterly reflexive parental way,

Griffin pictured dragging a blue-faced and lifeless Zoe out of the water.

"I don't mean sleep in **water.** Just in the **tub."**

"Don't you think you'd be pretty uncomfortable?"

Zoe made one of her goofy, elastic faces, rested her chin on her raised knees. "Noooooo."

"Why not?"

She jerked upright. "Because! I'd bring pillows! And blankets!"

"Why do you want to sleep in the bathtub?"

"I don't know. It's cozy."

She knows, Griffin thought. Even if it's unconscious, she knows. And she's scared, and she's seeking comfort in the goddamn bathtub. He imagined Zoe dreaming her young girl dreams behind the shower curtain, soothed by the white walls that rose up straight and smooth and dependable, walls that did not ever change, and that kept her from falling out of something meant to hold her securely. Goddamn Ellen.

Griffin stood and undressed to his boxers. "Coming in!" he yelled, and then, while Zoe giggled excitedly, Griffin stomped around in the bathtub, splashing mightily, until fully half the water had spilled over the side.

Zoe covered her mouth. "You're going to get in so much trouble, Dad!"

"Oh, yeah? With whom?"

"With Mom!"

"Oh, you think so, huh?"

"Yeah!"

"I don't think so." He sat down and leaned against the back of the tub, his arms behind his head. "Ahhhhhhhh!"

"Your underwear's all wet, Dad."

Griffin feigned great surprise. "It's not!"

Zoe giggled. "Is too. It's **soaking!**"

"Ah, well. It'll dry." Suddenly, Griffin's heart was breaking. "It will dry."

"What's wrong, Dad?"

Griffin looked over at Zoe, at her washcloth sliding off the top of her head. He reached out to straighten it, then said, "Well, I'm very sad. Because I am missing something at this moment— at this otherwise perfect moment with you, Ms. Buffalohoho—I am missing the **one thing** that would make my happiness complete. And do you know what that one thing is?"

"Oreos?" Zoe asked hopefully.

"NO! NO! **Not** Oreos! Cigars! Do you have any?"

Zoe smiled, shook her head.

"Smoked 'em all up, huh?"

**"Dad."**

"Well, I'll tell you what. Tomorrow I'll get a big box of real stinky ones, and you can sit in the bathtub with me while I smoke one."

Zoe grimaced happily. "Mommy **hates** the smell."

"Yes, I know she does."

"And also she says if you splash water on the floor, it wrecks the ceiling in the living room."

"Uh huh."

"Does it?"

Griffin shrugged. "Not if you know how to fix it. And I know how to fix it." He looked at Zoe, at her small, wet chest, her overly long eyelashes bejeweled by water droplets, her stick-out ears that their pediatrician had once gently suggested needed correcting. But neither Ellen nor Griffin nor—most important—Zoe saw them as a problem. Her ears were just her. She was a beautiful child. Griffin swallowed. "You know I can fix anything, right?"

"Yes."

"You believe that?"

"Yes."

"All right, then."

Zoe stood. "I want to get out, now." She shivered. "I'm freezing."

They lay in Zoe's bed and read two chapters from her book, taking turns, as usual. Then Griffin reached over to turn out the light and kissed the top of Zoe's head. "Good night, Zops."

Zoe yawned. "Good night. When's Mommy coming home?"

Griffin stood. "Don't know. Pretty soon."

"Will it be eleven o'clock?"

"I said I didn't know, Zoe! Now go to sleep!"

"O**kay!**" She leaned over, reached under her bed, and pulled out her ancient panda bear. Then she lay back down, her eyes shut tightly in angry compliance.

Griffin sat on the bed beside her. "Hey, Zoe?"

"I'm **sleeping.** You said go to **sleep.**"

"I think you're right. I think it will be eleven o'clock."

Zoe opened her eyes, studied Griffin seriously. "Okay."

"All right?"

"Yes." She closed her eyes, turned onto her side away from Griffin.

Griffin closed Zoe's door halfway, as she liked it, and started down the hall for his own bedroom. Maybe it would be eleven. Maybe not. Whatever time it was, though, he'd know.

# Chapter 4

· · · · · · · · · · · · · · · · · · ·

He dreamed that Ellen died. She died and then she came back and was sitting on the stone bench they kept near the bird feeder in the backyard. She was see-through: Griffin saw the outline of the branches of the bare rhododendron behind her. He stood before her in his overcoat and galoshes, weeping, and she, dressed in a filmy white gown, waved her hand as if to shoo away his grief. "Stop it," she said. "Look what I've brought you." She held a glowing blue bowl, filled with multicolored stones.

"What is it?" he asked.

"Just **look.**"

He stared into the bowl.

"Well?" she asked, smiling.

"Aren't you cold, Ellen?"

She stopped smiling, looked away.

He stepped closer, full of an awful longing that stole his breath, that made his fingers ache. "Ellen," he said softly. "Tell me what it's like."

She looked up at him, her face full of bitterness. "It's nothing like what you think," she said. "Not at all." She stood up, started walking away.

"Will you call me?" Griffin asked.

She turned around. "You know I can't do that."

"You can. I won't tell anyone."

She smiled sadly at him, then disappeared. He stared at the space where she'd been until he became aware of a knocking sound. It was Zoe, standing at her bedroom window, knocking at the pane and gesturing at something moving up into the sky. She knocked and pointed, knocked and pointed at something Griffin couldn't see. She was smiling.

Of course the knocking in his dream was Ellen at the door. He jumped up quickly, then remembered, and looked at the clock. One-thirty. All right. He tried to muster up some righteous anger, but the dream was still alive in him, so that after he came down the stairs and undid the chain lock he said simply, "Sorry. Forgot."

She didn't look at him. She squeezed past him, hung up her coat, threw her purse onto the chair in the living room, and went upstairs. Griffin stood by the door, thinking. What had he intended to do? Confront her with the lateness of the hour. Tell her that she could not sleep in the same bed with him. Insist that they had to speak to Zoe, together. He had thought of telling her she had to move out, too, but now he was barefoot and in his pajamas, feeling the biting draft that leaked under the front door and wanting only for Ellen to say she'd made a terrible mistake, she was so sorry, she was back.

He went upstairs and heard the murmur of voices coming from Zoe's room. "Someone from the PTO called," Zoe was saying. "Daddy took the message."

"Okay, sweetie," Ellen said. "I'll get it tomorrow. Thank you. You finish your water and go back to sleep, all right?"

Griffin moved quietly to stand outside his daughter's door. Ellen was kneeling next to the bed, for a good-night hug. He saw the smallness of Zoe's arms around her mother's neck and remembered when Ellen was first handed her—streaked with blood, beaten ugly by birth, fists clenched tightly and trembling with newborn outrage. Griffin, his hands in his pockets, had leaned over to peer into Zoe's face. "Looks like a boxer," he'd said.

Ellen—impervious, bedazzled, had stared into Zoe's eyes saying, "Oh, it's you. It's you!" She'd wept happily, rocked her baby in an instinctive and entirely unself-conscious way. She'd kissed Zoe's tiny forehead, stroked her hair. Griffin had watched all this, fascinated by the spontaneous emergence of a person he didn't know. He'd felt a momentary pull of intense jealousy—to be admired by her so! When the nurses told Ellen it was time to give Zoe to them, she'd laughed and said, "Don't be ridiculous." She'd kept the baby beside her every moment except when she showered—and then it was only Griffin she'd let hold her. The nurses, eyebrows raised, talked about her—yes, most mothers fell in love with their babies, but **this!** Ellen paid no attention to them.

Zoe had gotten a cold when she was only three weeks old. Ellen slept on the floor beside her crib at night, called the pediatrician so many times during the day that the beleaguered doctor finally called Griffin at work, begging assistance. "I think it's that she's afraid the baby might die," Griffin tried to explain, but the doctor said no, he didn't think it was that. He'd seen that before, he understood and was sympathetic to that; this was something else altogether. It seemed that Ellen didn't want Zoe to experience any discomfort whatsoever. It wasn't that she thought she was in grave danger: Her **nose** must not be stuffed. She must not **cough.** Apparently she wanted the world to be remade for her daughter. Really, if Mr. Griffin could not have a talk with his wife, he'd be forced to tell them to find another doctor.

So Griffin had told Ellen she had to stop calling the pediatrician, and Ellen had burst into tears. "Well, what are doctors **for?**" she'd asked, and Griffin had understood that she really meant it. "They are for really sick children, Ellen," he'd said gently, and she'd said, "Oh. All right." Then she'd looked up at Griffin with a face full of pain and said, "She's too important. I don't know how to manage a love like this."

But she had learned. She'd gotten better. And now she was simply unequivocally **there** for Zoe. Zoe knew it, too, and Griffin was convinced that it was one of the reasons she was such a good kid— everybody liked Zoe, everybody said so.

"I love you, too," he heard Ellen say, and then she came out of Zoe's room. She started when she saw Griffin, and then the surprise left her face and was replaced by something close to hatred. She went downstairs, and Griffin followed her. He sat at the kitchen table opposite her. "It wasn't the PTO that called."

"I know. It was Peter."

"Mr. Points and Plugs."

"Peter."

"Ellen, we have to talk about some things."

She laughed. "As I've been saying."

"Where were you tonight?"

She got up and went to the refrigerator, then closed the door without taking anything out. "Actually, mostly driving around, by myself," she said. "I was trying to figure out what to do, what to say to you to make you understand, how to get you to sit down and just listen."

"Well, here I am."

She sat down, leaned in toward him. "Are you?"

"Yes. I am. We need to decide what to tell Zoe. She knows something's up."

"What do you mean? What happened?"

"Come on, Ellen. She just knows something— nothing definite. She can sense it. Kids always can."

Ellen sat quietly for a moment, then said, "Oh, I'm so sorry about this, Griffin. If I could make myself feel differently, I would. But I can't help it. I feel . . . like another person with Peter. Alive, you know?"

"Meaning you felt dead with me." He laughed. "Is that it?"

She said nothing.

"Is that it, Ellen?"

"No. No, that's not . . ." She reached across the table, touched his hand. "I didn't feel **dead** with you, I just . . ." She leaned back in her chair. "Griffin. I'm going to turn forty years old and I have never . . . Look, I never believed in romantic love. Not for me, anyway. I never felt it. I **wanted** it, though. I'd watch all those sappy movies and feel this incredible **yearning.** . . . I didn't think I'd ever get to feel those things inside myself. But when I met Peter, there was this instant—"

"Zoe wanted to sleep in the bathtub."

"What are you talking about? Why won't you just let me try to explain—"

"Frankly, I am not interested, Ellen. I could not care less about you and your greasy paramour. I told you, just do what you have to do. I don't want to hear about it. What matters to me is Zoe. We have to tell her why things around here are going to change. And they are, Ellen. For one thing, I'm going to be going out, too."

She frowned. "What do you mean?"

"I mean **I'm** going out, too. We'll alternate nights. If you think I'm going to baby-sit every night while you live out your soap opera, you're crazy. But we have a job to do together, and that is Zoe. She gets to have a mother, and she gets to have a father. I'm not leaving; I'm not going to move into some sterile apartment with dime-store silverware and cardboard-box end tables so that you can be conveniently rid of me. I am Zoe's father, and I won't be relegated to seeing her on fucking weekends, Ellen. I will stay in her life, every day, and I will stay out of yours. Aside from Zoe, any-thing we do from now on is our own business, and not each other's. You want to be divorced? Fine, presto! we're divorced. It is done—right here, right now, because I say so. All the rest of the stuff is a formality that we will get to in time." He stood up.

"Griffin, sit **down.** I want to **talk** to you."

"I'll tell you something, Ellen. I'm getting a little bored hearing about what **you** want. And I'm tired. I'm going to bed. You don't tell me what to do any-more: That's the first thing. You don't ask me for anything. And we will both talk to Zoe in the morning." He turned to leave the room.

**"Wait** a minute!" She stood up, grabbed his arm. "You can't just leave like this, goddamnit! We have to have some **plan."**

Griffin frowned. "I just told you the plan. If you don't like it . . ." He didn't bother to finish. He went upstairs, flung back the covers angrily, and got into bed. He heard Ellen come upstairs, rummage around in the linen closet, then go back downstairs. "Fine," he said aloud. "Good." And then quietly, experimentally, **"Bitch."** The word echoed inside him, a mournful reverberation that emanated from behind his breastbone and would not stop.

Hours later, he was still awake. He'd felt, standing over Ellen at the kitchen table, that he finally had things under control. That, now that the shock of first hearing the news had passed, he was actually relieved at the prospect of getting rid of her—even at moments of extreme adoration, he'd realized she was a royal pain in the ass. Oh, yes, he'd realized that. Ellen took the concept of "high-maintenance woman" to another level entirely. He wanted a low-maintenance woman, one who would sit and watch a Bears game with him and drink real beer and realize that sex was about giving as well as taking. Ellen made him nervous, she always had. She was ungrateful and mean-spirited.

But now he lay in the darkness thinking about what her life was like. What did she do every morning after he left for work? What did she think about? When had he stopped knowing about her? When did Ellen the individual get replaced with Ellen, my wife, as in Ellen, my car?

At four-thirty he went downstairs to stand beside the sofa where she lay sleeping. He heard her breathing, recognized the familiar pattern. He thought of a time Ellen told him about a game show where the host asked husbands to try to identify their wife's hand—they could see nothing else of her. Most of the men couldn't do it. "Could you recognize mine?" Ellen had asked, and he'd shrugged, irritated—he didn't like questions like that, what was the **point** in asking questions like that? "No, but . . . could you?" she asked again and he'd said . . . yes, he remembered this exactly, he'd said, "I don't know, Ellen. Probably not. How would I? It's a **hand.**"

He sat on the floor beside her, whispered, "Ellen?"

She slept on.

"Ellen, what is happening? What is happening, here? I've loved you for twenty years." He reached out to touch her, then pulled back his hand. Perhaps she had heard him. Perhaps she would sit up, pull him to her, and laugh and cry simultaneously, saying, "Oh, God, Griffin, can you believe what we almost did? We must be so much more careful."

But she did not awaken. He went back upstairs slowly and lay in bed until the sky lightened. Then he went downstairs to make coffee.

The noise awakened Ellen, and she came into the kitchen. She stood there, her pajama top buttoned one button off, her face lined with fatigue. He felt, in spite of himself, sorry for her. He smiled. "Good morning."

Her eyes teared and she walked toward him and they embraced—out of habit, for consolation, to steady each other for the day ahead, Griffin thought. He buried his face in her hair, squeezed it in his hands, then let it go.

# Chapter 5

· · · · · · · · · · · · · · · · · ·

A t work, he leaned back in his chair for a moment to rest his eyes and promptly fell asleep. Evelyn woke him up when she came into his office. "Here's the— Oh! I'm sorry! I was just bringing you the files you asked for. I didn't mean to—"

He held up his hand, stopped her. "It's all right. I didn't get much sleep last night. Do you ever have those nights?"

Evelyn nodded solemnly. Griffin saw the cars in the parking lot outside his window reflected in her bifocals. She was inordinately dependable, never missed a day. She wore mostly pink or gray polyester outfits that were a tribute to modesty. When Ellen once suggested he give her a popular perfume for Christmas, he'd ended up regretting having done so. Evelyn had blushed and looked down, thanking him profusely. She'd rewrapped the gift to take it home. From then on, he'd given her coffee assortments, gift certificates to bookstores and theater complexes. He often wondered how old she was, but didn't feel he could ask her. "Somewhere between fifty and one hundred," he'd told Ellen.

"What do you do when you can't sleep, Evelyn?" he asked now.

She all but pointed to herself, unaccustomed as she was to being asked a personal question by her boss. Then she said, "Well, I read the Bible. The good parts."

"Uh huh. And what are they?"

Drawing herself up with a kind of dignity, she said, "Some of the passages are so like poetry, and they just make me feel better, Mr. Griffin."

Ah. He'd offended her. He hadn't meant to.

"You like poetry, Evelyn?" He tried for a certain sincerity and apparently found it, for Evelyn answered him readily.

"I do!"

"Mary Oliver, people like her?" Griffin asked, thinking, **Please don't ask me anything about her.**

"Oh, yes, Mary Oliver is wonderful, of course. But there are so many! Why, go to any bookstore, find the poetry section, pull any book down, and you're sure to find **some**thing that . . ." She smiled.

"You know, my favorite book of poetry is one I found at a garage sale. Ten cents for the most lovely collection. Poems about hummingbirds, and voodoo queens, and the streets in New York City. All in one place! I'd be happy to lend it to you, if . . ." She trailed off, unsure of herself now.

"I'd love to take a look," Griffin said. "Maybe you could bring it in to work sometime."

"Tomorrow!"

Griffin forced a smile, then picked up the files she'd brought in.

"Would you like me to hold your calls, Mr. Griffin?"

"Not necessary," he said. "Nap time's over."

He reviewed the papers he'd been given, made a few calls, spent a good forty minutes answering e-mail. Then he picked up the picture of Ellen, sat back in his chair and looked at it. Her forehead was slightly damaged from him tearing the paper—an erratic line moved from her hairline down to one eyebrow. He'd expected to be overwhelmed by pain looking at the photograph, but the truth was, he felt nothing. He remembered when his mother had called to tell him about needing a mastectomy. Her voice had been soothing, calm, and Griffin remembered thinking, **How can she talk? How can she be telling me all this and not be beside herself?** Now he understood. After a while, pain simply stopped. It was as though your mind was able to create a firewall beyond which it would not let you venture. You had to have a break from your anguish, or you'd go crazy. It was the psychological equivalent to fainting when physical pain became overbearing.

He tried to look at the picture as though he'd never met Ellen. She wasn't so hot. A certain asymmetry of the eyes. Smile crooked. But endearing, nonetheless, with absolutely perfect teeth. And her legs (not shown), they were pretty damn good. And her breasts . . . His hands began to shake. The thing about the firewall is that it dissolved sometimes, and the pain came back, just like that. Anytime. Anywhere. He stood up against its force, strode out past Evelyn's desk. "Lunch," he said, and she nodded without comment. It was 10:37.

He drove to the nearby shopping mall and parked in the very last row, a necessity even though Christmas was many weeks away. Every year, people vowed not to give into the mania, and every year they did anyway. Well, he didn't mind. He needed the exercise. Maybe he'd join a gym and get into terrific shape. He turned off the ignition, started to slip his gloves on, and then stopped, looking at his wedding ring. Why was he still wearing it? Ellen had taken hers off. Not that this was unusual: Ellen took off her ring every night, and often forgot to put it on during the day. When Griffin had complained about this, she'd said, "Oh, don't feel bad about that! I'm married to you whether I wear a ring or not. You know I don't like wearing rings. They bother me." It was true. Ellen liked other kinds of jewelry, but she'd never liked rings. Funny, then, that she'd had that big one on the other night. Maybe Mr. Camshaft had given it to her. Maybe he had handed her a beautifully wrapped little package and she'd opened it and said, "Ohhhh, it's beautiful! But you know I can't wear it."

Now she could. And now Griffin took off his ring and threw it into the glove compartment. He remembered sitting next to a man on a plane, watching the guy store his wedding ring in a small compartment in his briefcase just before they landed. When the man saw Griffin watching him, he'd smiled, only a little embarrassed. "Might get lucky," he said. Griffin had wondered, if he took off his ring, would he be approached by one of the hungry-looking women who frequented hotel bars? He had never tried it, had never taken off his ring, in fact, since the day Ellen had put it on his finger. He looked at the place on his finger where the ring had been: no evidence of anything ever having been there. Amazing, in its way.

He put on his gloves, started to close the glove compartment, and then stopped. Why leave the thing in there? Why let Zoe be searching for napkins or salt and find it and say, "Hey, Dad, what's this doing in here?" Why not just throw the ring away, and then, if Zoe ever noticed it missing, say he'd lost it?

He took the ring, closed the glove compartment, and got out of the car, locked it. He imagined throwing the ring in some mall trash can, amid boxes from Cinnabon and paper cups half full of Coke, amid hamburger wrappings and dirty Kleenex. No. Beside him was an empty field, the snow melted from it, the grass brown and flattened. He flung the ring into the field, watched it land. Then he put his hands in his pockets and headed for the nearest entrance. Cold out here. It was fucking **cold** out here! Why hadn't they moved to California, as Griffin had wanted to do, years ago? Because Ellen had wanted the seasons, that's why. Because Ellen had found the changes in nature necessary, instructive. She'd rejoiced every time the first leaf turned, the first snow fell, the first lime green shoot came up in the garden. It was tiresome, her outsized joy at such commonplace events. Although Zoe liked it. Zoe liked **her.** Griffin couldn't move to California with Zoe; Zoe loved her mother.

At a hot dog stand inside the mall, Griffin bought a chili dog, then sat on a bench to eat it. Music was playing: Elvis's "Blue Christmas." He watched shoppers pass by him with lists, mostly women, a lot of them pushing strollers with sleeping children. He saw a few older couples, men who looked as if they wished they were home, and women who looked determined to find everything they were looking for **today.** Against the wall by the bathrooms, he saw a teenage couple kissing. The boy had blue, stand-up hair and multiple piercings on his face. His pants had what seemed to be yard-wide bottoms and hung well below the waistband of his underwear. The girl had a long blond ponytail, glitter on her face, and wore skintight black pants and a pink, short-sleeved blouse that looked a few sizes too small for her. Their coats lay in a pile beside them, under a bag from Sam Goody. They'd bought music to kill by, no doubt. Rap songs about extreme disaffection and plans to exterminate 90 percent of the population. But they parted as Griffin passed by them and smiled so sweetly at him he could only smile back.

Outside of Sears, an attractive young blond woman sat at a large table, reading a paperback book—Carl Hiaasen, whom Griffin also liked and whom Ellen never read. HELP SANTA, a sign next to her said. He leaned against a store window a few yards away, watching her, finishing the mint chocolate chip ice cream cone he'd bought. Then he walked over to her, cleared his throat.

She looked up. My. She really was attractive. He smiled at her, and she discreetly checked his ring finger, then smiled back. Amazing, it was true. He hoped he looked all right. He couldn't remember what he'd put on that morning, and he couldn't check now. He hoped his cowlick was down.

"What is this?" he asked. "Something for charity?"

She shook her head. "No, I'm taking applications for people who want to play Santa. We start next week, and we still need a few more guys."

"So, what do you do? Sit in one of those eight-foot chairs and give away candy canes? And get your picture taken every twenty seconds?"

"It's reindeer antlers we're handing out this year— and candy canes, too, of course. But yes, you sit in a chair and be Santa. A lot of people find it very rewarding. Of course, you have to really like children."

"I really like children."

"Uh huh."

"So . . . maybe I'd be interested. How much do you have to work?"

"We ask for a minimum of four hours a week. Most people work a little more than that, especially as it gets closer to Christmas." She tossed her hair back. Flirting? She wore large diamond studs. A soft gray sweater, probably cashmere.

"Well, I could definitely do four hours a week. Probably more." What the hell. This would give him something to do on the nights he "went out." And Zoe would get a big charge out of Griffin being a Santa. Only last year she'd stopped believing, with much regret, Griffin thought. Zoe used to write to Santa all year long, "just to keep in touch," she'd said. She could help educate Griffin about all the latest toys—though baseball and boy toys were her major obsession, she occasionally played with more feminine things—she certainly liked her cotton candy maker. This could be a good "father-daughter" project, note absence of "mother."

"Tell you what," the woman said, handing him an application. "Why don't you fill this out? No obligation." Nice woman, Griffin thought. Just a nice way about her. And she liked him, he could tell. He could ask her out right now—ask her to go to dinner with him. Some time.

He filled out the brief application, requesting the 6–10 slot on weekdays. "Oh, good," the woman said, when she saw the hours he'd asked for. "Not many people want that time." She put his application on the bottom of the pile. "Someone will call you after the background check. I hope you'll decide to give it a try—it's a lot of fun. I'm one of the photographers who takes your picture every twenty seconds, by the way—and I work the same hours you requested."

"Good," Griffin said, backing away, smiling. "I hope I'll see you, then."

He started toward the exit, remembering a quote he'd seen recently. Where was it? Some magazine, in some doctor's office. What it had said was that once a firm decision was made, the universe would accommodate you in the direction you'd chosen. Some New Age crap. And yet.

Just before the exit was a Toys "R" Us. Griffin stood before the window, looking at all the things displayed there. Easy-Bake Ovens and plastic soldiers. Barbie dolls and baby dolls. PlayStations. LEGOs and micro-scopes. Large boxes of art supplies, complete with easels. It could be a lot of fun to be a Santa, to feel invested with such magical powers. He'd always won-dered what kind of things kids said to Santa.

What the hell, he'd try it; he could always quit if it didn't work out. Besides, he liked the looks of that woman. Why not take advantage of spending a little time with another woman, see how it felt? It might encourage him to start dating, and that might make him feel a whole lot better about what was happening with Ellen. He could date blondes; he was tired of brunettes. He could date easygoing, lighthearted women, who did not stand before win-dows staring out at nothing, who were not so thin-skinned as to weep for half a day over a baby bird fallen from a nest and killed by the cat. He'd find a really good woman, younger than Ellen, and when the time was right, he'd introduce her to Zoe.

And then he landed. He came back down to earth, and saw Zoe as she'd been at the breakfast table that morning when he and Ellen had carefully explained that they were going to be spending a lot of time apart, because they were going to be trying something new. They wanted to "grow."

"What do you mean?" Zoe had giggled. "You're already grown!" Worried, then, she'd asked, "Aren't you?"

Ellen had looked briefly at Griffin, just the tiniest bit of anxiety in her face. Then she'd said, "Well, grow in a different way, honey. Grow in our minds and in our hearts and in our souls. Grow on the **in**side."

Zoe had said nothing, and so, despite Ellen's insistence that they keep this announcement very short and very simple, she'd continued talking. "We have been thinking that it's not a good idea for people to spend so much time together all the time, even when they're married. Remember last summer, when you played with Jack Franklin every single day and you guys got so tired of each other?"

Zoe shrugged. "I guess. Are you and Daddy tired of each other?"

"No," Griffin said, quickly. "No. It's not that. It's . . ." He looked at Ellen.

"It's so we can have time for other things, too, Zoe," she said. "Like . . . our hobbies."

"What hobbies?"

Ellen shifted in her chair. "Well. Like sewing. You know I like to sew, right? I'd like to take a class in quilting."

"Oh. Robbie's mom made him a quilt. Robbie Benderhurst."

"Did she?"

"Yeah, and it had **flowers** on it. When you make one for me, don't put **flowers** on it."

"I'd never do that."

"What will you put on it?" she'd asked, her face full of such uncompromising belief and faith in her mother that Griffin thought he might weep.

Ellen smiled, full, Griffin thought, of her own kind of anguish. Then she reached over and touched Zoe's face. "If I make you a quilt," she said, "it will be full of stars and cars."

"Hey, that rhymes!"

"Yes."

"Put in some . . . hats and cats."

"I'll put in some whales and some sails."

". . . I don't like boats, Mom."

"Hmmmm. Well, I'll put in whales and tails . . . of puppies."

"Put in darts! And farts!"

"Zoe," Ellen said. And then, "Better finish up, honey. Time to go to school."

Zoe gobbled up the rest of her cereal, then put on

her coat. Before she went out the door, she turned back to ask Griffin, "What's **your** hobby, Dad?"

"Don't know, yet!" he'd said, full of a false cheer.

Well, now he knew. Searching for a new woman, that would be his hobby.

Griffin headed back toward Sears. "I wondered," he'd say, casually. "Would you have time to go for a cup of coffee with me? I have some questions about the job."

When he got there, though, she was gone, her chair pushed neatly under the table. He could look for her, he supposed; she might be eating lunch. He looked at his watch. Better go back to work.

At the car, he stood looking out at the field where he'd flung his ring. He shouldn't have done that. He'd bring it home, put it away. He might want it someday. For something.

He went to the area where he thought it had landed. Nothing. He walked in concentric circles around that spot. Nothing. Then he dropped to his hands and knees, combed through the grass. Gone. **Hey, look what I found! Cool! Think I can hock it?**

He got back in the car, started the engine, and turned on the heat full blast. His knees were wet; he was freezing. He turned on the radio, tapped his hands on the steering wheel to the rhythm of "Jingle Bell Rock." And then he turned off the radio and stared straight ahead at a November sky so devoid of color it looked to have been erased. In the distance, he saw a quivering chevron of Canadian geese. He would stay here to watch them fly by; he had always found them beautiful. But they were moving away from him, disappearing even as he watched.

# Chapter 6

• • • • • • • • • • • • • • • • • •

The porch light was off when he came home—he had trouble getting his key in the door. When at last he opened it, he poked his head into a dark house. "Zoe?" No answer. He wiped his feet on the mat, came in and shut the door, hung up his coat. "Ellen?"

He went into the kitchen, turned on the light, and saw a note on the kitchen table:

**Griffin:**
**Oak Park Hospital—Zoe fell. 4:30.**

He raced back out the door, drove the six blocks to the hospital, left his car directly outside the emergency entrance. As soon as he came into the waiting room, he saw Ellen sitting in an orange plastic chair against the far wall. She was holding her purse in her lap, staring into space. Then she saw Griffin and stood up, smiling. "It's okay; she's all right; they're just ruling out a minor concussion. They took her for an X ray—her arm hurts. They don't think it's broken, but they're just making sure. She's all right, thank God."

Over the intercom, Griffin heard a request for him to move the car immediately; he was blocking the emergency lane.

"Go ahead," Ellen said. "I'll be here—she won't be back for a while—they just took her down."

"What **happened?**"

"She fell out of the tree house. You'd better go and move the car."

"What was she doing up there? It's winter!"

Ellen shrugged. "I don't know."

"Why didn't you **call** me?" he asked, and she said, "Move the car, Griffin. I'll talk to you when you come back in. She's all **right.**"

Griffin found a parking place close by, then ran back inside. Now Ellen was standing by the door. "Come over here," she said, leading him to a deserted alcove full of vending machines.

"Why didn't you call me?"

"Griffin. Lower your voice."

"Don't you—"

"I didn't call you because I didn't want to take the **time.** I didn't know how badly hurt she was. I just wanted to get her to the hospital. I figured I'd call you from here when I knew what was going on."

"But you **didn't** call me."

"I **did.** I called your office, and Evelyn said you'd gone. Then I called your cell just a few minutes ago, and there was no answer."

"I left it in the car. I came in the house, I saw the note and I— What was she doing up in that tree house, Ellen? Why weren't you watching her?"

She stared at him. "I don't watch her every second she's outside, Griffin. I didn't know she was going up in the tree house. Why did the **floor** come apart? Why don't **you** keep that thing **safe?"**

Now neither of them spoke, until Ellen finally said, "Look. It's nobody's fault. Let's go back out there—she'll be back from her X ray soon."

They sat down, not looking at one another, not talking, until a white-coated young man appeared in the hall, saying, "Mrs. Griffin?"

"Here," she said, standing, and she and Griffin walked quickly toward the man.

"I'm her father," Griffin said. "Frank Griffin. I'm her father."

"Yes. Well, your daughter's arm is fine. No breaks."

"Are you the doctor?" Griffin asked. This man couldn't be a doctor.

"Yes, I'm Doctor Quasha."

"You're . . . a full doctor?"

The man smiled. "I am."

"Are you a specialist?"

"I'm not, but I can assure you that your daughter doesn't need one. Let me bring you back to her."

Griffin followed Ellen and the doctor into a small examining room. On a cot that made her look even smaller than she was, Zoe lay on two pillows, her arms crossed over her belly. "I'll be right back," the doctor said.

"Hi, Dad," Zoe said, and Griffin moved over to take her hand.

"How are you doing, sweetheart?"

"Fine."

"Anything hurt?"

"Just my head. And my arm. And my leg, a **little.**"

"What were you doing up in that tree house, Zoe?"

"I don't know."

"Don't go up there anymore until I fix it. I saw the other day that the floor was rotting." Beside him, he felt Ellen stiffen. "I'll **fix** it," he said, for the benefit of both her and Zoe. "But don't go up there anymore until spring, all right?"

"I'm not."

"Well, don't."

"I'm **not.**"

Dr. Quasha came back into the room, carrying a metal clipboard. "So, Zoe. How'd you like to spend a night here at the Hotel Hospital?"

"Why?" Ellen and Griffin asked together, and then came Zoe's pale echo: "Why?"

The doctor smiled. "Strictly routine. Just need to do a twenty-four-hour observation."

"Can't we do it at home?" Ellen asked.

"It's better if she stays here. You can bring her home at this time tomorrow."

"I'll stay here with her, then."

"I will, too." Griffin said quickly. He resented Ellen saying it first. He would have said it first if he'd only been given the opportunity.

"You're both welcome to stay," the doctor said. "Unfortunately, we only have room for one cot in the room."

"I'll stay," Ellen said.

Griffin moved closer to Zoe. "I will, too."

Ellen looked quickly at him, then away. "Why don't I go home and get some things for you to do?" she asked Zoe. "What would you like me to bring you?"

"**I** don't know."

"A surprise, then," she said. "I'll be back."

When Ellen got back, Zoe had been sleeping for

about half an hour. She signaled to Griffin to come outside into the hallway. "God. Scary, huh?" She smiled.

"Yes." His eyes moved over her face. Zoe's mom—they looked alike.

"I guess these things happen all the time—we're lucky we've never had to bring her to the ER before."

"I guess."

"I think every boy in her class has been here. Miles Altman broke his wrist last week. Jason Burns was in here for stitches after he cut himself. And—"

"It's not okay, Ellen."

She stepped back from him, crossed her arms.

"What are you talking about?"

"If you're not going to take better care of her—"

Her face hardened. "Don't you dare, Griffin."

"Don't I dare what?"

"You know what. You **know** what." She turned away, started back for Zoe's room.

"Ellen!" Damn it, he was sorry. He hadn't meant to do that. They were just starting to . . . to what? To come back together? No. No, they weren't, and he knew it, and that's why he'd said that. To hit back.

# Chapter 7

. . . . . . . . . . . . . . . . . .

A few days later, Griffin stopped for Kentucky Fried Chicken on the way home. It was his night to be home with Zoe, who was still basking in the increased parental attention her hospital visit had afforded her. Ellen's and Griffin's anxiety had tempered somewhat, since they'd had to set Zoe (and thereby themselves) straight on the fact that her fall hadn't been **that** big a deal. She'd apparently told the kids at school she'd been unconscious and was rushed to the hospital, and her teacher had called Ellen, concerned because one of the other kids had said Zoe had been in a coma—did she have juvenile diabetes?

Griffin got a deluxe order—all white meat. He got extra biscuits, because Zoe liked them for breakfast. But when he walked in the door, he smelled dinner cooking. Ellen was in the kitchen, making gravy. He stood still for a moment, watching her, the chicken warm against him. "You made dinner?"

She nodded, her back to him.

"What'd you make?"

"Pot roast."

"Uh huh. Do I get any?"

She turned around, dripping whisk in hand. "Griffin, I don't know why you insist on overdramatizing things. If I make dinner and you are here, of course you can have some." She gestured toward the chicken he was holding. "Unless you want **that.** I don't care."

"I got this because how in the hell am I supposed to know from one moment to the next what's going **on** around here, Ellen? One night I come home and there's no dinner. The next time there **is** dinner."

Ellen walked past him, stood at the foot of the stairs. "Zoe!"

A crashing sound, then, "It was **nothing,** Mom, it's **okay!**" And then, ". . . Yeah?"

"Dinner."

Ellen walked past Griffin again and began putting things on the table: Butter on a flowered saucer she had found in an antiques store when they went to New Orleans, just before Zoe was born. A.1. sauce and catsup for Zoe to make the "dream sauce" combination she put on virtually everything. Ellen poured milk for Zoe, water for

herself. Griffin might as well have been invisible
except that Ellen had, in a fit of generosity, put a
plate and silverware on the table for him. Griffin
set the bucket of chicken on the table, and when
Zoe skidded into the kitchen, her sneakers squeak-
ing, he pulled the lid off and said, "Hey, look, Zoe—
your favorite."

Ellen stood motionless. Then she said, "The pot
roast is for dinner."

"Or chicken," Griffin said. "Which would you
like, Zoe?"

Zoe slid into her chair, surveyed the food. "How
come we're having both?"

"For fun," Griffin said. "Want some chicken?" He
took his fork, pulled out a piece. "Here, you like the
breast." He laid the chicken on Zoe's plate.

Ellen, silent, took her place at the table, placed
her napkin on her lap.

"I like pot roast better," Zoe said. "Do I have to
have both?"

"No," Griffin and Ellen said together. They
looked at each other, then away. Griffin put Zoe's
chicken back in the bucket. "I'll tell you what. Let's
just save this for lunch. It's great for lunch, right?"
He put the chicken in the refrigerator, then sat
down again at the table.

It was quiet for a long moment. No one helped
themselves to anything. Then Zoe looked at her

hands and said, "Oh. I forgot to wash." She pushed back her chair. "Oops! Sorry."

"For what?" Ellen asked.

**"Scraping.** You always tell me not to scrape because it scratches the wood. And I always forget."

"Ah. Yes. Well, that's right. Remember next time."

"Okay." She headed for the downstairs half bath, turned on the water.

"Don't do this, Griffin," Ellen said quietly.

"Do what?" He loaded his plate with meat.

"You know exactly what I mean. Don't make it worse."

"Pass the gravy. Please."

Zoe came back and sat down, began piling food on her plate. "Are you excited to meet my teacher, Dad?"

"What do you mean?" He looked at Ellen. "Are we meeting her teacher tonight?"

"Oh. Yes. There's a little get-acquainted confer-ence. You know, that ten-minute thing they do. We're scheduled for . . . it's seven-forty, I believe."

Griffin put his fork down. "When did you find out about this?"

She wouldn't look at him. "They sent home a note with Zoe the other day. It's not a big deal, Griffin. I don't think we both even need to go."

"I'm going."

"Well . . . you know, I thought **I** would."

Griffin looked at Zoe, busy preparing her sauce. "I'll go, too."

"I didn't call a sitter."

Zoe looked up. "I don't **need** a sitter."

"Yes, you do."

"For **ten minutes?**" She looked at Griffin. "Dad, **do** I?"

"Zoe, I want you to do me a favor, okay? My shoes are killing me. Would you go up and get my slippers for me?"

She shrugged. "Okay."

After Zoe left the room, Griffin reached over to take hold of Ellen's upper arm. "Let's get this straight. **Anything** about Zoe is done together. **Anything** that comes up about her, you tell me. As soon as you know it."

She pulled her arm away angrily. "Stop it! I forgot to tell you, that's all. I didn't withhold it intentionally. I've had a lot on my mind."

"Zoe comes before those things."

"I know that!" She cut her pot roast into small pieces, then smaller.

"Here, Dad." Zoe handed him the slippers, sat back down at the table, and looked from one of them to the other. "What's wrong with you guys?"

Ellen stared down at her plate, shook her head.

"Bad day at work," Griffin said.

"Again?" Zoe asked.

"Yeah," Griffin said. "Again."

"We'll be gone about twenty minutes," Ellen told Zoe as they were leaving. "You can call us, or you can call next door if you need anything. Karen knows you're alone. You know her number, right?"

Zoe sighed. "Yes."

"What is it?"

Zoe recited the numbers in an exaggerated monotone. "All right?"

Ellen nodded. "Don't do anything but your homework. Don't—"

"I **won't,** Mom!"

"You won't what?"

"I won't do **anything** but my **homework.** But Mom, can I just do one other little thing?"

Ellen pulled on her gloves, checked her watch. "What?"

"Can I play with matches?"

Ellen didn't laugh, though Griffin did. She hesitated, as though she might stay home, and Zoe pushed her out the door. "Go! I'm all right! Jeez, Mom, you always think I'm such a baby!"

Ellen closed the door, tried it again to make sure it was locked. Then she started off down the sidewalk, moving quickly. "I don't think we should leave her alone."

"She's fine."

"She's only eight."

"She's **fine.**" Griffin looked up at the clear sky. It was cold, but pleasantly so. "Nice night," he said.

Ellen sighed. "Look. I'm sorry I didn't tell you about this conference. I really did forget."

"Yeah, all right."

They walked on, their strides matching. Behind one of the windows they passed, an old lady stood in her housecoat, looking out at the street. She would see them and think they were fine, Griffin thought, a nice young couple out for a walk.

"Zoe likes her teacher this year," Ellen said. "I'm surprised, because she's really strict. She took away Zoe's baseball cards the first day, for trading in class. But then she gave them back."

"Yeah, well, Zoe gets along with everyone."

Ellen smiled. "I know she does."

Griffin stopped walking. "Ellen . . ."

She kept on. "We don't have time, Griffin."

He caught up with her, and they walked the rest of the short distance to the school in silence. In the space of two blocks, Griffin thought of several things he wanted to tell Ellen. About how much colder it was going to get over the next few days, and didn't Zoe need a new coat? That this morning he thought he'd seen signs of his hairline receding—was it? He wanted to tell her what Evelyn had said about reading the Bible when she couldn't sleep, and he wanted Ellen to wonder aloud about that. He was sure she would. Ellen could take a piece of information like that and use it to create a whole scene. She might say about Evelyn that she saw her in a blue flannel nightgown, propped up on one pillow, her bedside lamplight falling onto delicate, see-through pages. Yes, she would say something just like that, talk about Evelyn's thin lips moving as she comforted herself with those ancient stories. The place would be marked by a ribbon, perhaps. Evelyn's knees would be raised. Or would they? Without knowing, Ellen would know.

He wanted to ask Ellen if she could think of a verse that actually might provide comfort to a sore soul. The weighty announcement from the angel to the virgin? The more poetic version of the world's beginning? He wanted Ellen to tell him what she imagined the rest of Evelyn's bedroom to look like, the rest of her house, with its kitchen cupboards and its linen closets, its arrangements of furniture and figurines. Were there plants in ceramic pots? Handwritten letters on a hall table? Was there a cat? A newspaper delivery every morning? The old Ellen would have told him, and he, assuming that kind of verbal fantasy would always be available to him, would have mostly ignored it. He saw that, now. He saw, too, how much he had actually enjoyed those rich musings, and he saw how Ellen's imagination had inspired him. Without her stories, he would lose his own.

Mrs. Pierce was the kind of teacher Griffin liked best: middle-aged, bespectacled, dignified; clad in a brown tweed skirt, a cream-colored, bow-tie blouse, and a brown cardigan sweater. Griffin couldn't see her shoes, but surely they were brown pumps, well broken in, with creases on the outside and something from Dr. Scholl's on the inside.

She was seated at her desk in a corner of the classroom, two chairs facing her. As Ellen and Griffin came in, she stood up and smiled.

It always seemed so strange to Griffin to be in a classroom at night. The room was too quiet; the lights seemed more yellow than usual. The children's desks were lined up neatly, expectant looking, all but inhabited by the spirits of those who claimed them during the day. Colorful workbooks were stacked in one corner. A tan-and-white guinea pig stared blandly through the walls of her glass cage. Zoe said she bit everyone. Her name, according to a sign taped onto the cage, was Queenie, but Griffin happened to know that the kids called her Meanie.

Mrs. Pierce extended her hand. "Mr. and Mrs. Griffin? I'm Zoe's teacher, Mrs. Pierce. Won't you please sit down?" Her voice was clear, strong, and she looked them in the eyes. Griffin sat straight before her, kept himself from bouncing his knees. She was the kind of teacher who inspired one's best posture. Ellen, Griffin noticed, was sitting straight herself, her knees pressed together, purse centered on her lap.

"Thank you for coming," Mrs. Pierce said. "This is, as I'm sure you remember from past years, just a brief conference. We'll have a longer one in January. But this is an opportunity for us to meet, and for me to answer briefly any questions you might have about Zoe. A wonderful girl, by the way—quite the baseball fan!"

"Yes," Griffin said, smiling.

Then it was quiet. Griffin looked at Ellen. She always handled things like this, she'd think of what to say next. She'd find out what they needed to know, and she'd tell Mrs. Pierce what she needed to know about their daughter. Zoe was a tomboy, yes, but she was also sensitive—very much aware of others' feelings. She seemed to have a great interest in history—had Mrs. Pierce noticed that, yet? You had to make sure Zoe understood the math—she wasn't one to ask questions.

But it looked as if Ellen was not going to say any-thing. She sat quietly, staring at the floor. Griffin was about to say that Zoe really seemed to be enjoying school this year, when Ellen suddenly looked up and cleared her throat. "I wonder if this would be a good time for us to let you know . . . to tell you about some changes that are going to be occurring in Zoe's life."

Griffin looked quickly over at her. She couldn't be! It wasn't this official yet. But then he heard Ellen go on to say, "I have told my husband that I want a divorce."

Griffin leaned forward, spoke quietly. "Well, we haven't actually decided anything yet. Formally. I have no idea why my wife—"

"Griffin . . ." Ellen broke in.

**"Ellen."**

She looked back at Mrs. Pierce. "I'm sorry. I just thought you should know that we've decided to separate. I know these things can affect a child's performance in school."

Mrs. Pierce nodded slowly. "Yes, they certainly can."

Had she sighed, saying this? Griffin wondered. Had he heard her sigh? He looked into her face for some sign of disapproval, but she gave nothing away.

"So far, she seems to be handling everything all right," Ellen said. "We haven't mentioned the word divorce, but she does know we'll be spending time apart."

"So you've moved out, Mr. Griffin?"

"Not yet," Ellen said, at the same time that Griffin said, "No."

"Well." Mrs. Pierce looked at her watch. "I'm sorry to seem insensitive, but we don't have very much time. These are very short conferences. If you would like to schedule another—"

"That's really the main thing I wanted to tell you," Ellen said. Her voice caught, and she stood. "I wanted you to know so that . . . I just thought I should tell you."

Mrs. Pierce nodded. "Yes. I'll let you know right away if I see anything of concern developing."

Ellen started to leave, then turned back, waited for Griffin.

He said nothing, stayed seated. Ellen left the room.

"So." Mrs. Pierce closed Zoe's folder. "Was there something else, Mr. Griffin?"

Something else? How about what they'd ostensibly come for? How about that? Griffin looked around the classroom, at the gigantic blue-and-brown globe, at the pencil sharpener on the wall. There was the alphabet over the blackboard, cursive this year—Zoe hated the capital **Q** and adored the capital **C.** A bulletin board was covered with wild-eyed turkeys, drawn from the outlines of the children's small hands. Zoe's was the one in the middle—Griffin saw her earnest scrawl across the turkey's breast. She'd given the bird long eyelashes and high-top sneakers like the ones she wore.

"Mr. Griffin?"

"Yes," he said. "I was just . . . I wondered, what are they learning about?"

She hesitated for a moment, then said, "Well, they've just begun keeping nature journals; they're looking at how trees change in the winter. They're working on fractions. They've just begun a biography: **Jackie Robinson.**"

"I'll bet Zoe likes that."

Mrs. Pierce smiled. "It was her suggestion. She was quite persuasive."

"Do they have recess every day?"

"Oh, yes."

"Zoe ever play with any of the other girls?"

"No. But she is kind to them, and I think they like her."

"Okay." He stood up. "I guess that's about it, Mrs. Pierce, except for one thing. Couldn't you have expressed a little outrage?"

She stared at him, blinked.

"Couldn't you have registered just a little disapproval?"

Oh, what was the matter with him? He was going crazy. Mrs. Pierce stood calmly before him. He showed her his upturned palms, a gesture half apology, half bewilderment. "I'm sorry." His voice was so quiet, he wondered if she'd heard him.

"That's quite all right, Mr. Griffin."

"I guess I'm just pretty upset."

"Yes. Well, these things happen. They surely do."

"How do the kids . . . How do they come out of it?"

Now she did sigh. "For the most part, they seem to do all right. They seem to recover—children are remarkably resilient, as I'm sure you know, and divorce has become so common. I won't say they're not affected by it, though. I won't say that. The best thing is if the parents can just be civil to each other, if they can just—" She looked beyond him into the hall, smiled and nodded. "I'll be right with you," she called. Then, to Griffin, "I'm so sorry. My next parent is here. I think you know what I was saying. But now I really must move along."

Par**ent,** Griffin thought. That being one. Perfect. He walked past the woman coming in. She was smiling, normal-looking, ringless. She was fine.

He found Ellen in the hall, waiting for him. "I can't believe you did that," she said.

"Me? **Me?!**"

Griffin pushed hard at the double doors leading out of the school. They walked half a block in angry silence. Then Ellen stopped. "Griffin, maybe I shouldn't have . . . But I was just trying to be responsible! You won't listen to me when I try to tell you why this happened. You won't help me make any plans for the future. You want to ignore everything and hope that it will all go away. But this divorce is going to happen. And it's **important** for Zoe's teacher to know. She can help her!"

"Why don't **we** help her, Ellen? For God's sake, this is Zoe we're talking about! You're her mother, I'm her father. Why don't we help her? You didn't even ask her teacher what Zoe does in school!"

"She actually tells me, Griffin. Every day."

". . . She does?"

"Yes."

"You know about their nature journal?"

"Yes. They're learning about chlorophyll."

"Did you know they're reading **Jackie Robinson?**"

"Yes, Zoe suggested it."

He was stunned. "Why don't I know this?"

"I think she told you about **Jackie Robinson,** Griffin. I think maybe you just don't remember."

She was not angry anymore; her voice was soft, forgiving. He sighed, shook his head. "Oh, God, Ellen. I guess I . . ."

She nodded, close to tears again. He thought she looked beautiful—no makeup, her hair in a loose braid. He liked her best like this, but she never believed him when he told her that. Times when she would get dressed up, her makeup magazine perfect, he would dutifully compliment her, but he didn't really like her that way. He felt he couldn't see her, that he had to change the way he spoke to her until she came home and washed. He liked it when her nose peeled in the summer. He liked when she came into the bedroom to change into her pajamas at night, pulled her spaghetti sauce–stained shirt over her head and complained about having eaten too much. Sometimes she would slap her belly and sigh as she stood in front of the mirror. Once, he put his arms around her when she was doing that, and he told her she was the sexiest woman alive. She pushed him away, but she was smiling a little. It was that night she let him hold her long enough that he felt he'd finally reached some distant place inside her. In the morning, they were back to being familiar strangers.

Now he put his hands on her shoulders and looked into her eyes. "Do you remember our first date? I took you to see **Gone With the Wind** at the campus theater; you'd never seen it. And when we came out, you were so upset you sat down on the curb and threw up. I sat right beside you. All these people were going past, and I wasn't the least bit embarrassed. I rubbed your back, and I just adored you. Where are you going to find another love like that, Ellen?"

She swallowed. "What I found is . . . It's not a love like that, you're right. It's different. But it's what I want."

"But . . ." He sighed, stepped back from her. "Well, then why'd you make me pot roast, Ellen? You know it's my favorite thing. I mean, why are you telling me you want a divorce, and then making my favorite dinner?"

"Zoe asked for it, Griffin. It had nothing to do with you." She spoke softly, with regret. Maybe she was sorry to have to say what she was saying. But probably not. Probably she was just tired of telling him over and over again that the way she felt about him was not the way he felt about her. It was simple, really. Simple and common and awesomely painful. Surely he'd hit the bottom soon, and stop falling.

He stepped away from her, struggled for some kind of composure. "Go on back home," he said. "I'll be back in a while." She nodded, pulled up the collar of her coat, started walking. "Tell Zoe we can read double chapters tomorrow," he called after her.

"Okay." She didn't turn around. She walked straight ahead, sure of where she was going.

Griffin walked back to the school, out onto the playground. He sat in a swing, pushed himself gently back and forth. These swings had bucket seats—plastic, with big, round holes in them. Not as good as the wooden seats he'd had in his elementary school, the paint faded to no color at all, the chains salty from excited hands. He used to pump until he could go no higher, until the chains began to buckle in on themselves. Then he would yell **Geronimo!** and bail out onto the soft earth below him. He argued with his friends about the origin of the word—one of them insisted it was Japanese. Eventually, Griffin gave up on trying to persuade him otherwise. It didn't matter; the point was the jump, not what you said while doing it.

He blew out his breath before him, watched the little cloud dissipate into the night air. He thought of a time when he was a little boy and was in love with some tin soldiers he'd seen in a toy store. His parents told him they wouldn't buy them; they were antiques, and outrageously expensive. But he'd loved them, and he used to stand by the glass case, aching to just touch them. He'd thought his parents were fooling, that on some grand occasion he would get that set of soldiers, but he never did. One would think he might have learned something from that experience, but apparently he had not. Here he was, sighing before the glass case again. He sat in the swing, thinking, until he grew too cold, and then he started walking. He counted ten blocks east, ten blocks south, ten blocks west, and then started for home.

The shade in Zoe's room was pulled, the light still on. Ellen should put her to bed. It was past her bedtime. Her mother was being careless, letting her stay up so long. Her mother was being careless and her father was out wandering around in the dark.

Griffin got in the car and pulled nearly noiselessly out of the driveway. Anywhere was fine. Anywhere was better than going home.

# Chapter 8

· · · · · · · · · · · · · · · · ·

He took Lake Street and headed west. He'd see what happened. He'd let himself do anything he wanted; he'd practice being free. Maybe he'd start smoking cigars in the house. Definitely, he'd use only dishes that could go in the dishwasher—the hell with antique saucers for butter plates. He knew of a man who'd thrown out all the living room furniture after his wife left him, then put in a pool table. Nice move.

At a stoplight, the car shimmied, then stalled out. It started right up again, but Griffin was nervous now. What the hell **was** that? He knew the names of things under the hood of a car but had never been too confident about mechanics in general. Was it safe to go far? Maybe he should call Ellen for a telephone diagnosis. Being a graduate of Mr. Wonderful's class, she might be able to tell him whether the problem was minor enough to ignore. If not, she could call Points and Plugs himself. "Peter, darling," she could say. "You know how my idiot husband knows almost nothing about cars? Well, he's out on Lake Street having trouble. Do you think we should go and get him?"

"Sure," he would say. "Whatever it is, I'll fix it for him. I'll give him a discount, too." Then, his voice silky and intimate, he'd say, "Aw, hey. I feel kind of sorry for him, you know?"

"I know," Ellen would say, sighing. "Me, too."

"Pick you up in five minutes," Peter would say. "And bring Zoe—I got her a toy today. 'The Invisible Car.' I'll teach her everything, so she doesn't end up like her putz father."

"Oh, she'll **like** that," Ellen would say, and Zoe would. She'd work with him, assembling the thing. She'd—

**Enough.**

Off to the right, just ahead of him, Griffin saw a diner. There were no cars in the parking lot, but the neon OPEN sign was on. Griffin pulled in, started to turn off the ignition, then stopped when he heard a song come on the radio. It was one of his favorites, an oldie: "I Only Have Eyes for You." He sat still, staring out the windshield and listening. He only had eyes for Ellen. It was true, he didn't want anyone else. Not once, since he'd met her. But why?

None of his friends had ever particularly liked her. His parents took a long time warming up to her, and Griffin thought they wished their son had married someone a little different, a little more . . . well, could they say it, did he mind? **Normal.**

The only friend that Ellen had in college was a fellow misfit, a nervous gay man named Laurence who seemed unbearably sensitive, who was overwhelmed by simple tasks like registering for classes—Ellen went with him to do it, told Griffin later about how she had made a game of it for him. Laurence had died a few years ago of AIDS—Ellen had wept, reread all his letters, and then never spoken of him again. The only person Griffin knew of who really liked Ellen was Zoe. Ellen was her mother, of course, but it was more than that. Zoe saw Ellen, because Ellen let her.

Griffin turned off the radio, cut the engine, thought of the last time he and Ellen were in bed together, before he knew anything—the night before the morning she told him. That was when he still thought their life together was secure. When, despite its oddities, it was comfortable to him, reliable and dear. That was when the thought of his wife was an anchor and not a chest-sized thorn.

That night, Ellen had wanted some hand lotion, but she was too tired to get out of bed and get it. So she asked Griffin, "If I guess the number you're thinking of between one and ten, would you get me the lotion?" He'd looked at her. **What?** "But you can't cheat," she went on. "You can't tell me I was right if I was wrong. We have to follow the honor system."

He'd put down his magazine. "Ellen. If you want the lotion, I'll get you the lotion."

"Oh," she'd said. "Okay. Thank you." Then, when he'd given it to her, she'd said, "Thanks. But was four the number you were thinking of?"

He smiled at the memory. Well, that was why, he supposed; that was why he cared for her. He **liked** her oddness, her clumsiness, even, most times, her outrageous and misplaced sensitivity. When they first moved in together, Ellen had a shy dog named Shawna, a collie mix who ate her dry dog food delicately, one piece at a time. Griffin had an overweight beagle called G.M. for "Garbage Mutt." True to his name, G.M. ate anything, at any time, with no sense of delicacy, ever. Griffin once found Ellen sitting on the floor watching the dogs eat, her hands folded in her lap, her face full of sadness. He'd sat beside her, asked gently, "What happened?" He'd been thinking that her father died— he'd been in the hospital at the time. He thought she'd say, "You need to take me to the airport right away." But what she said was, "Shawna used to eat so nicely. But now she eats just like G.M."

He'd refrained from saying, "Ellen. Jesus. So what?" and instead sat down beside her, put his arm around her. A blue velvet ribbon held her hair back. She smelled subtly of a rich perfume Griffin loved, and through her blouse, he could see the outline of her lacy bra. **Later.** He sat with her as she solemnly watched the dogs finish eating. Ellen was right—Shawna had started eating just like G.M. And after the food was gone from the bowls, they'd started fighting over the spilled pieces that had fallen between.

That night, after Ellen and Griffin had gone to bed, he'd asked her gently why the way the dogs ate had bothered her so much. He was postcoitally benevolent, practically glowing—he would make an effort to **really understand** her.

She moved closer to him, lay her head on his shoulder. "I don't know why it bothered me so much," she'd said. "I don't know! I guess it's because I wish it had gone the other way, that G.M. would have started being neat. I mean, why do things always have to go **that** way?"

"Beats me," Griffin had said. "Maybe it's a law of physics or something."

"That's another thing! How can you have any hope in the face of such pessimism? Order always progressing to disorder!"

"Who said that?"

"I don't remember. But it's true." She'd raised her head, looked at him. "Don't you wish you could talk to God, sometimes, Griffin? You know, get in a shot while you're still alive and walking around the planet having to put up with everything you had nothing to do with?"

"Do you believe in a God you can talk to, Ellen?" he'd asked tenderly.

"There isn't?"

As if he knew.

**Oh, Ellen.** He'd tightened his arms around her that night, and she'd put her head back under his chin and said, "I know how weird I am. I do. I'm sorry. But you know what happens? Everything just . . . gets to me. Everything. Even the beautiful things, they hurt. And I don't get it, I mean the whole thing. I don't **get** it."

He'd kept still, gently pushed her hair back from her face—just at her temple, which she liked, he knew that she liked that. And then she'd suddenly gotten up on one elbow and asked, "Do you know what a hum job is?"

He'd laughed, astonished.

"No, but do you?"

**"Ell**en . . ."

"Is it a blow job and you hum while you do it?"

Again, he laughed. "I **guess.**"

"Let me try," she'd said.

Later, as she slept, he lay awake beside her, staring at the ceiling and thinking about what she'd
said. He wanted to wake her up and say, "We're not
supposed to get it. We're just here. And we have
each other—doesn't that help?" But he didn't wake
her. For one thing, her answer might be no.

He cut the engine and went into the diner. There
was a twenty-something-year-old woman at the end
of the counter with the newspaper spread out before
her, doing the crossword puzzle. She barely looked
up when Griffin sat at one of the stools. "Help you?"

"Just coffee, please."

She put a tan mug in front of him, filled it.
"Anything else?"

He looked at the desserts in the glass case behind
her. "Rice pudding any good?"

"Nope."

"Is anything back there any good?"

She turned around, surveyed the cakes and pies,
the glass goblets of Jell-O and pudding. "The apple
pie's all right."

"All right. That, then, à la mode."

She served it to him, then went back to her
crossword puzzle. Griffin took a bite of the pie.
"This is awful."

The waitress shrugged. "It's better than the rice
pudding."

Griffin pushed the ice cream off the pie, ate it in three bites. Ellen made wonderful apple pie, and she always made cutouts of apples and leaves from the extra dough to arrange artfully on top. She made great rice pudding, too. **Stop.**

"How's the crossword coming?" he asked the waitress.

She looked up. "Sorry?"

"Just wondered how the crossword puzzle was coming."

"What's an eleven-letter word for 'argument'?"

Griffin thought for a minute, then said, "Altercation."

"Oh, yeah." She wrote it in. Then she stood back and stretched, arched her back like a cat would. "I hate doing these things. I mean, you do all this work and what do you get?"

"Satisfaction," Griffin said.

"From what?"

"From filling in all the blanks."

"That doesn't give me any satisfaction."

"Why bother, then?"

"I don't know. It's something to do until closing time."

"When is closing time?"

She looked at her watch. "Twenty-three minutes. And twenty-six seconds."

She looked at him frankly now, as though seeing

him for the first time. Raised an eyebrow. Was this an invitation? She walked past him, intentionally slowly, Griffin thought, and he watched her fill the salt and pepper shakers. She had a very nice figure, her youth visible even in her back. It had been so long since he'd been with another woman. He had a hard time remembering it. Was it . . . Peggy something? Was that the name of the last woman he'd slept with before Ellen? Yes, Peggy Swenson. She was auburn-haired, studying to be a pharmacist, came from a big farm family in Minnesota. She was nice. Boring, but nice. Piano legs. She'd wept when they parted, said that she'd thought they'd made such a nice couple.

He looked at the waitress's legs. Very nice—long, muscular calves, trim ankles. She wore hot pink shoelaces in her waitress shoes. She turned back to him, smiled. She had sprayed her bangs into a kind of startled, stand-up style, and pulled the rest of her blond hair into a ponytail. She was wearing a lot of makeup—black mascara that clotted her lashes into irregular spikes, a purplish color of lipstick unlike anything Griffin had ever seen in nature, blotches of blush high up on her cheeks. It was too bad, really—she was kind of pretty beneath all that. He stirred what was left of his coffee, tried to imagine her naked. Her breasts were large, and they would be high and perky. She'd have a flat belly, no stretch marks. Blond pubic hair? He saw himself on top of her, her mouth open in pleasure, maybe moaning a little.

"More coffee?" He started, looked up. She was standing right next to him now, only a young girl, really; somebody's daughter, wearing a tacky watch with fake diamonds.

"Yes, please," he said, and realized with horror that he was feeling close to tears.

"You're feeling bad, huh?"

He nodded, examined his thumbnail, tried to remember some spectacular plays in the last Bears game he'd watched.

"Yeah. I knew it as soon as you walked in here." She put the pot back on the burner, turned it off. Then she took off her apron and came to stand in front of him. "It's all over your face."

"I suppose."

"What's your name?"

"It's Griffin. Well, it's Frank. Frank Griffin, I go by Griffin."

"You married?"

"I'm . . ." Was he? "Well, I guess I'm separated."

"You guess?"

"My wife wants a divorce, so I guess I'm getting divorced."

"But you don't want to."

"No. I don't."

"Well, you're half the team, pal."

"Right."

"You are!" She reached under the counter for a rag, started wiping the counter clean. "You'd better get her back, before she finds out the dirty little secret. You know what the dirty little secret is?"

Griffin shook his head.

She leaned in closer. "You need us more than we need you."

"I see."

"It's true. Women always do better than men after a divorce. After the dust settles. My mom thought she'd die when my dad left. But now? Whoa, Miss America! Date-o-**rama!**"

Griffin said nothing.

She put down her rag, came closer. "Aw, I'm sorry. I didn't mean to make you feel bad. I can tell you're a nice guy. But it seems like guys never appreciate girls 'til we're gone. Am I right? Find me a woman who gets flowers **after** marriage, you know what I'm saying?"

"I do." He took out his wallet, suppressed an impulse to show her his photo of Ellen—a great shot of her sitting on the front porch, shading her eyes against the setting sun. Her hair loose about her shoulders. Shorts and a T-shirt. Bare feet.

"Listen—don't pay me for that sucky pie, okay? On the house."

"Thanks." He put down a ten. "Keep the change." He stood, put his coat on.

"Hey, thanks a lot!" she called after him. "You really are a nice guy!"

Barbara's Books was still open. He parked the car and went in, nodded a greeting at his favorite employee there. Thomas was a handsome black gay man, disarmingly honest, unfailingly friendly. "Hey, big man," he said. "What are you doing here?"

Griffin had no idea why Thomas called him "big man," but he didn't mind it. It was nice to think that someone thought of him that way. Made him feel important.

"I'm looking for a book of poetry for Ellen. Can you show me where they'd be?"

"Of course." Thomas came from behind the counter and led Griffin to the poetry section. "Is it her birthday?"

"No. This is just for a surprise."

Thomas looked at Griffin over his shoulder. "Aren't **you** nice."

"So who do you like?" Griffin asked, looking at the rows of slender volumes.

"I like **Jackie Collins** best," Thomas said. "You know I love **her.** But let's see what I might recommend to you here." He studied the titles, then turned to ask Griffin, "Are you sure you want poetry? Has Ellen ever read Jackie Collins?"

"I'd really like to get her poetry."

Thomas put one hand on his hip, the other to his chin. "Hmmmm." He pulled down a fat paperback. "Here you go, here's a good one. Pablo Neruda. Love poems."

"Maybe something more . . . subtle. Maybe by a woman."

"Sharon Olds?"

"Is she good?"

"Oh, sure." He handed Griffin another book. "Here's one a lot of folks really like. Marie Howe, **What the Living Do.**" Another customer came in, and Thomas said, "Just look through them all, hon. See what catches your eye. Poetry's so sub**jective.**"

Griffin selected several books, then went over to the window seat and began flipping through them. **Huh.** Not as inaccessible as he'd thought. On the seat a bit down from him, a woman unself-consciously stared at him. When Griffin looked up, she smiled. "Hi." She was about forty, husky-voiced, hard-looking, though quite beautiful.

"Hi."

"See anything you like?"

"I'm just starting to look."

"I'd be glad to help you. What have you got over there?'

"I'll be fine," Griffin said, returning to the book he held.

"I'll bet I could make things easier for you. Why don't I—"

"No thanks."

"Well, excuse **me**," the woman said. She got up to leave.

Griffin watched her walk out the door. How did women walk in those high heels? Thomas came over to Griffin and whispered theatrically between hands cupped around his mouth, "Man."

"What?"

"She's a **man.** And a thief. She's always trying to take paperbacks, but I always see her doing it, so she always puts them back. She liked you."

"Guess it's my lucky night," Griffin said.

"I guess it is."

After twenty minutes, Griffin settled on the Marie Howe. He asked Thomas to gift-wrap it, then left the store and walked down the block to Borders. He wanted the anonymity he'd get there, because he wanted to look at self-help books. He hated them, but maybe he'd break down and take a look, what the hell. When his co-worker Tom Carmichael was trying to save his marriage, he'd sworn by one of the books he'd found in the self-help section—something he described as "learning to become more sensitive without having to cut your balls off."

The store was mostly empty—a few patrons sat

reading magazines. Griffin found the relationship section and was examining the titles when he saw the same man who'd spoken to him in Barbara's come down the aisle. "Well!" he said. "Buy me a drink, sailor?"

"No, thank you," Griffin said.

"What?"

"I said, 'no thank you.'"

"I didn't **offer** anything. That was just a joke. A kind of **greeting.**"

"Well. I apologize then."

"Accepted."

Griffin nodded, buttoned his coat, and turned to leave.

"I'm Nancy," the man said.

Griffin turned around. He had no idea what to say, settled on, "Ah."

The man rolled his eyes. "You are **pathetic.**"

Griffin bowed. "So it's been said."

# Chapter 9

· · · · · · · · · · · · · · · · · · ·

The house was dark when he came in. In the living room, he made out Ellen's dim form on the couch. Her back was to him. He tiptoed over to her, sat down beside her. Resting open on the floor was a small book: Marie Howe, **What the Living Do.** Great. Perfect. A gift from Mr. Oil Pan, no doubt.

Quietly, Griffin picked up the book, looked for an inscription. There was none. And tucked into the back was a charge slip, with Ellen's signature. She'd bought it at Anderson's in Naperville. When was she out there? Why? Is that where Stud lived?

He put the book back where it had been, started to get up, and Ellen turned over. She stared at him sleepily, blinked, then sat up. "Where have you **been?**"

"Out. What are **you** doing?"

"What do you mean?"

"What are you doing on the couch?"

"Sleeping."

He sighed. "This is ridiculous."

"What is?"

"You. On the couch. You can't be comfortable."

"Well, I just don't think we should sleep in the same bed, Griffin. In fact, I don't think we should be in the same house. As you know."

He took off his coat, went to the hall closet to hang it up. In the inside pocket was the book. Right. He thought, briefly, about showing it to her, then decided against it.

He came back to the sofa, turned on a table lamp. "I know all about what you think, Ellen."

She squinted at the sudden brightness, pulled the blanket around her shoulders. She was wearing a pair of Griffin's sweat socks and her favorite battered flannel pajamas, tiny purple flowers faded to a blur against a blue background. "So, can we make some decisions, Griffin?"

"Are those my socks?"

She looked down at her feet. "Yes."

"Give them back."

She pulled off the socks, handed them to him. "Here."

He stood silent for a moment, then held the socks out to her again. "Put them on, your feet will freeze."

"I don't want them."

"Put them on, Ellen. Obviously you **do** want them; you were **wearing** them."

"It was a mistake. They were in my drawer."

He sat down wearily beside her, leaned back, and rubbed his forehead. "Ellen. Put the fucking socks on, and then we'll talk. All right?"

Not looking at him, she took the socks and put them back on. Then she sat staring straight ahead, her hands folded in her lap. A woman in a waiting room, anticipating bad news.

Griffin got up and sat on the floor, began pulling off one of her socks.

Angrily, she pulled her foot away from him. "What are you **do**ing?"

He looked up at her. "It's on inside out." He took her foot in his hands again, gently, took the sock off, reversed it, and put it back on.

When he looked up again, she was crying. "It doesn't **matter,**" she said.

"Yes, it does. Now your socks are on right side out."

"Okay," she said, wiping her eyes; and then, in spite of herself, she began to laugh.

"That's right," Griffin said, apropos of nothing, really.

But then she drew herself up, looked seriously at him. "So. I guess we should talk about how to man-

age this. Oh, Griffin, I'm **sorry,** but I really think
you should start looking for a place."

He nodded, envisioning himself with the want
ads, calling this landlady and that. No. "When are
you going to understand this, Ellen? When are you
going to believe me? I'm not leaving. I'm not going
to suddenly change my mind. I'm not going to help
you out. This is your idea—**you** move."

"Right. And who will take care of Zoe when she
comes home from school? Who will make sure she
does her homework? Who will wash and iron her
clothes? Who will take her to her doctor's appointments? Who will make her dinner? I'm just trying
to do this right, Griffin. Someone has got to **be**
here for her!"

**"I'll** be here. I'll take time off from work until I
figure it all out. I've got a good six weeks of vacation time coming."

". . . You do?"

"Yes, I do."

She sat quietly. Then she said, "Well, why didn't
we ever—"

"Do you want to talk about my vacation time,
Ellen, or do you want to talk about Zoe? I want to talk
about Zoe. I'll take a vacation, and during that time,
I'll interview housekeepers. I'll find somebody to
come in after I go back to work. I've seen ads for people looking for that kind of work. I'll hire someone."

"I don't want some stranger taking care of Zoe!"

"That's too bad."

"But I thought—"

"You thought wrong."

"Griffin. Please. Let me take care of my daughter."

"You can. Every other weekend, and a couple of evenings a week."

"I can't leave her!"

"Neither can I."

Ellen sat still, stunned looking. He supposed this hadn't occurred to her. What the hell did these women think, that they could kick a man out and then keep everything? Ellen had no grounds for divorce, **he** did! Should she get rewarded for fucking some engine jockey? No. Not a chance.

"Griffin. What do you want me to do? What can I do to . . ." She looked up at him. "Would you be willing to meet him?"

"Who?"

"You know who."

"Yeah, I want you to say his name."

She opened her mouth, then closed it. Then, her voice tight and low, she asked, "What is this, Griffin?"

"I want you to say his **name.**"

"Peter. All right? **Peter. Peter. Peter.**"

"Dickhead. Homewrecker. Lying son of a bitch."

She turned away from him, nodded.

"No, I don't think I'm interested in meeting him, Ellen, thank you very much. Pass on my deepest regrets. I'm going to bed."

He started to walk away and Ellen grabbed his hand. "Griffin. There is a better way to do this. I wanted to keep Zoe's life as normal as possible. And I thought we could stay friends."

"Oh, Ellen, grow the fuck up."

"I thought we could **try** to stay **friends.** This isn't all my fault, Griffin! I know you think it is, but it isn't! You just won't ever admit that it's not right between us, and it never **has** been! Why won't you **admit** that?"

Griffin walked to the living room window, shoved his hands in his pants pockets, and looked out at the streetlight. It was beautiful, an old fixture that used to be a gas lamp. There were things in the world besides Ellen.

He heard her call his name, softly, and then she asked, "Do you have any idea how long I've been sad?"

He turned around impatiently. "Oh, for Christ's sake, Ellen. Yes, of course I knew you were sad, sometimes. But so what? So am I. So is Zoe!"

"It's not the same thing. It's . . . I just never felt right about marrying you. I mean, I loved you, but it was not the right kind of love. What I felt for you, it wasn't the same as what you felt for me. You can't force that kind of thing, even if you want to. It's there, or it isn't." She pushed the blanket off herself, rubbed at the side of her forehead. Ellen got severe migraines every now and then. Well, that was her problem, now—he wouldn't even ask.

"Did you know I called my mother the night before she was going to mail the invitations and asked her not to?"

He stiffened. "No."

"Well, I did. I knew we shouldn't go through with it. And my mother just said something like, 'Oh, honey, everybody feels that way before they get married. You're just nervous.' And then I thought of how you'd feel if I told you I didn't want to get married. And I just **liked** you so much, you were my **friend,** and I didn't think I'd ever . . ." She shrugged. "So. Here we are."

"Well, thank you for telling me, Ellen. I feel so much better, now."

"Don't, Griffin. This isn't easy for me, either. Do you think it's easy for me? So many times I sat at the kitchen table in the morning after you and Zoe left and I cried. Just . . . cried. I'd sit there for hours, sometimes. A lot of times I'd get dressed just before Zoe came home."

How could this be? He imagined himself at work: having meetings, swapping jokes with colleagues, sitting oblivious at his computer, while at home his wife wept into her cornflakes.

When had she stopped telling him things? Had he really been so unaware? He remembered a cartoon he'd seen as a child. A man was driving down the street, and when he turned to look casually behind him, he saw that half of his car was missing. Then he crashed. Only then. Griffin remembered what he'd thought, too, when he'd seen it: Why'd the guy look? Why didn't he just keep going?

"Once," Ellen said, "I went to a psychic for help."

"Oh, terrific." Griffin imagined the scene, his and Ellen's marriage being dissected by some heavy-accented woman wearing a kerchief knotted on her head and wondering how much she could get out of **this** sucker.

"I was desperate, I felt **desperate.** I'd sit with you at the dinner table every night and I'd be hating you, because I was so lonely and so . . . flat. And you didn't see it. You were so **satisfied,** and I was getting sadder and sadder and you just didn't **see** it! You'd chew and chew and ask Zoe how school went and tell me you were out of underwear and you did not even look at me, Griffin. And we never went **anywhere.** Every time I suggested something, you'd find some excuse not to go. All you ever wanted to do was go to work and watch television."

"We went places!"

She said nothing. The silence said, **Yeah, right.**

"So why didn't you **say** something?"

"Oh, God, Griffin, it just . . . It seemed redundant. I mean, it was like my arm was ragged and bleeding, right in front of you. Why, then, would I say, 'I'm hurt'?"

"That isn't fair. You didn't have any bleeding arm! I mean, I knew you were moody sometimes, you'd go through periods where you didn't really want to talk to me. But this happens, in a marriage! You just have to go through these things, sometimes!"

She put her hands on either side of her head, viselike. "Oh, you just make me want to scream! You knew I was having an **affair,** Griffin! Why didn't **you** say something?"

He stopped what he was about to say, that he didn't know why. Because he did know why. It was quite clear to him, in fact. "I was afraid if I said anything, you'd leave me, Ellen. That's why I didn't say anything."

She nodded. "Perfect."

"Are you going to move in with him?"

"No. I don't know what I'll do. I can't keep living here with you. It's too late for us to do anything about this. It's over. I just don't know what to do about Zoe."

"Zoe will be just fine."

"How can you say that!"

"Because it's true. I am every bit as capable of taking care of her as you are."

"But what will you do when your vacation time is up? You can't hire someone to take care of her!"

"I can and I will. You don't make all the decisions, Ellen. You're only one half of the team, here." Unbidden, the young waitress popped into his head, and he willed her image away. "You don't decide things unilaterally for Zoe, and you don't decide anything for me. We're just roommates, remember?"

She lay back down, pulled the blanket over herself.

"And I think I will meet Mr. Piston. Yes, I believe I will."

She said nothing, reached over to turn out the light.

"Did you hear me?"

"Yes, I heard you. Never mind. It wasn't a good idea."

"Well, it has to happen sometime. Let's get it over with. Hey, I've got an idea. Let's double date!"

"With whom? **Donna?**"

"Who's Donna?" He honestly didn't know.

"The woman who called here tonight when we were at school. Zoe took a message. Who is she?"

Ah. The Santa woman. But to Ellen, he said, "Someone I met." He'd leave it at that. "Good night."

Donna might like the book. He'd give it to her, next time he saw her, tell her he saw it and thought of her.

He turned on the bedroom light, sat wearily on the bed, loosened his tie. This day had lasted forever. Time was distorted now, undependable, a measure of nothing but levels of grief. He took off a shoe, held it high, and let it fall to the floor—Ellen was just below him. Then he heard Zoe calling him.

He found her sitting up in bed, her lamp on, holding something in her hand. "Look!"

"What is it?"

"My tooth!"

"Hey! Congratulations! Do you want to rinse your mouth out?"

"Yeah." She got out of bed, stumbling a little, and Griffin held her arm as they walked to the bathroom. After Zoe rinsed her mouth and the tooth, she held it up to the light. "Do teeth have guts? Like way inside, do they?"

"No. They have soft insides, called pulp, but not guts, really."

"Oh." She admired the tooth a bit longer, turning it this way and that. Then she turned to Griffin. "Where's Mommy?" Her cowlick, the same one he had, was at half mast. Griffin wanted to reach out and smooth it down, but he was afraid if he touched her, he'd gather her in his arms and start to cry, taking this bright moment of pleasure away from her, burying it under the pain of the people who were supposed to take care of her.

"Mommy's downstairs."

"How come?"

How come. He was about to say she'd gotten hungry, when Ellen appeared at the doorway. "What happened?"

"My tooth came out!"

"Oh, boy!" She hugged Zoe to her, smoothed her cowlick down. "And that was a big one, wasn't it?"

Zoe opened her hand, showed her mother. "Ahhh," Ellen said. "And you know the tooth fairy really, really likes those big ones."

**"Mom."**

"What?"

"There is no tooth fairy."

"Oh? Then who is it that leaves money for you under your pillow when you lose a tooth?"

**"You** do." And then, ". . . Right?"

Griffin waited for Ellen to argue with Zoe, to draw her once more into some harmless fantasy that her parents enjoyed as much if not more than she. But Ellen didn't do that. She took in a breath, looked at Zoe for a long moment, and then said, "-You're right. There is no tooth fairy."

Zoe's smile faded just slightly. Then, "I knew it!" she

said. "I knew it all along, anyway!" She looked down at the tooth. "But . . . What do I do with it, then?"

Silence. And then Griffin said, "I'd like to buy it. I'd really like to buy it. Will you sell it to me?"

Zoe handed him the tooth. "You can have it, Dad."

"Five bucks," Griffin said. "Would five bucks be all right?"

"I said you can **have** it." She looked at Ellen, then back at Griffin. "I'm going back to bed." She walked out, her back straight and so small.

Ellen rinsed the last traces of blood from the sink. Then she turned to look at Griffin. What was in her face, besides pain? Ambivalence? Pleading? Was she realizing what Griffin had, that the next time a tooth came out, only one of them would be there?

She smiled sadly. "I guess we might as well tell her the truth, huh?"

Griffin didn't answer. He left the bathroom and went into the bedroom, closed the door. He heard Ellen turn off the bathroom light, then go back down the stairs.

He undressed, put on his pajamas, and climbed into bed, lay there staring out the window. Then he got up and went into Zoe's room.

Her eyes were closed. "Zoe?" he whispered. He wanted to offer her some reassurance, tell her that he would take care of her tooth and everything else, don't worry, never worry. "Zoe?" Nothing. He knelt beside the bed, pulled the covers up higher, and lightly kissed her cheek. He would never leave her. Never.

Back in his bed, Griffin thought about Zoe's classroom, about Mrs. Pierce. He wondered if Zoe fell a little in love with her teachers, as Griffin used to. He always brought a present to his teacher on the last day of class, and once, in fourth grade, asked to be given money to pick something out by himself. He'd given Mrs. Vandalia a lacy, light blue half-slip. "Well!" she'd said. "Thank you very much, Frank!" Then she'd quickly stuffed it back into the box. Griffin had understood his error when the class burst out laughing. He'd been very glad it was the last day of school.

Griffin closed his eyes, folded his hands and rested them on top of his stomach, let out a long breath. The last day of school. The weather would be so warm, all the classroom windows open, the sound of lawnmowers and birds and distant airplanes calling like siren songs. Occasionally a bee would meander in through an open window, seduced by something like geraniums blooming boldly on the sill. It would fly slow and heavy for a while, buzz angrily and pick up speed when it became aware of being trapped, then die an ignoble death at the hands of some boy who ignored the impassioned, high-pitched pleading of the girls. The oversized geography books worked particularly well. Once, Griffin had been an accomplice, had lent Vince Larson his book because Vince always forgot his at home. But afterward, Griffin had felt terrible, and brought the dead bee home with him. He made a vain effort to revive it, offering it honey on a toothpick, blowing toward the bee's mouth in a crude attempt at mouth-to-mouth resuscitation. When it was clear that nothing was going to work, he'd put the bee in a single-serving cereal box padded with toilet paper and buried it in an apologetic backyard ceremony. He'd added blossoms from his neighbor's rose garden to the box and marked the grave with one of his better cat's-eyes.

Last days were always anticlimactic. You'd lost the regular feel of things—work hadn't been serious for weeks, not with spring as a relentless saboteur. You could never say exactly when things had started changing from middle to end. But when the last day came, and it was all over, you were ready for it, because of what had begun so quietly inside you without your even noticing.

From downstairs, he heard the irregular, muffled sounds of Ellen crying. He got out of bed, closed the door, opened the window, then lay down in the exact middle of the bed and fell asleep.

# Chapter 10

· · · · · · · · · · · · · · ·

In the morning, when Griffin came downstairs, Ellen was sitting at the kitchen table. He moved past her, saying nothing, and poured himself a cup of the coffee she'd made. When he started past her again, she said, "Griffin? Do you have a minute? I need to tell you something."

He sat down across from her, attempted a neutral smile. A **May I help you?** smile. The skin below her eyes was bruised-looking, translucent in the morning light. Her face sagged. "You look terrible," he said.

"Thank you."

"Didn't you sleep well?"

"Did you?"

"Actually, yes."

"Well, good for you. Listen. I've been thinking, Griffin. Maybe it's best if we really do live as roommates for a while. You do what you want and I . . . will, too."

He said nothing, stared off to one side of her, sipped his coffee.

"Do you think we can try that?" she asked.

"You may recall that it was my suggestion."

"Yes. So, since you went out last night, tonight will be my night. All right?"

"Yeah."

"I'll make dinner, I just wanted to tell you."

"Okay."

"And then, right after dinner, I'll go out. I'll remember to take my phone."

He got up, put his cup in the dishwasher. "Yeah, fine, Ellen."

She looked down at her hands. "I suppose there's no point in continually apologizing. I guess we just have to let this thing unfold in the way that it will." She waited. For what? For him to offer resistance? Encouragement? Reassurance? Well, he wouldn't. She could do whatever she wanted, so long as she understood one thing: He was done with her. He would make that clear to her tonight, after Zoe was in bed. She would not quite believe him. At first.

"I'll get Zoe up," he said, and headed back upstairs.

In her bedroom, he peeled back Zoe's bedclothes, then sat down beside her.

"No," she said.

"It's time to get up, Zoe."

She groaned.

"Want to go out with me after dinner and get a new video game?"

Now she was awake. She sat up excitedly. "What one?"

"Whatever one you want. You pick."

**"Any**thing?"

"That's what I said. I have to go to work a little early this morning—I won't be at breakfast. But you get up and get ready for school, and I'll see you tonight."

"Okay. **Any** game, right?"

"Right."

Griffin dressed carefully for work, selecting a shirt his mother had sent him, which Ellen had never liked. In front of the dresser mirror, he straightened his tie, then applied a little cologne to his cheeks, to his neck. Ellen had never liked this scent, either—he'd gotten it a few months ago from a buxom young sales clerk who'd asked him suggestively, "Now . . . do you **splash** or **spray?"** He had never worn it because when Ellen had smelled it she'd made a face, then said, "Well, wear it if you **want** to." He did want to, and now he would. He took the bottle over to the bed, sprinkled some cologne on the sheets. This was his bed, now. No more scent of Ellen permeating his subconscious.

He pulled up the window shade. The sun was

fully out; it shone hard through the bedroom window. It was going to be a beautiful day.

He came whistling down the stairs, got his coat out of the hall closet. What the hell, maybe this really would be better for everyone. Who wanted to be married to someone who'd never wanted to be with you in the first place? What was he worried about? He was prime quality, top choice: a pretty damn good-looking man who was kind, who had a good job and a great kid and a wife who was stupid enough to be leaving him. A million women would go for him.  A million and one. "Was she **nuts?**" they'd ask, and he'd say, yeah, she kind of was.

He left without saying goodbye, went out to the garage, got in the car, and started it. Good song on the radio. He'd sing along, something else Ellen never liked, owing to his inability to stay in tune. Or to remember the lyrics, big deal. But now he turned the radio up and sang along, more or less, at the top of his lungs. He put the car in reverse, backed out. From the street, he saw Ellen standing at the window and watching him. Arms crossed. Still as a mannequin. And as unreachable.

He called Donna from work. "Congratulations," she said. "You passed the background check. You're hired!"

"Just like that?"

"Well, we need you to come in for an orientation. A how-to-be-Santa class."

"The fine art of **ho-ho-ho**-ing, huh?"

"More like what to expect. Some information on the more difficult questions kids might ask, and what you might say back. How to handle little emergencies."

"What emergencies?"

"Well, to be honest, there was one where we had to call the police. A drunk rushed the set."

"No kidding. What did he want?"

"He wanted to beat up Santa."

Griffin frowned. "Really?"

"Yeah, he was pretty drunk."

"Did any kids see? Did anyone get hurt?"

"Not many kids were there, it was late. Maybe one or two. And . . . well, okay, Santa got his nose broken. But that was truly an exception! Most emergencies are **much** smaller in scale."

"Such as . . . ?"

"Oh, a kid pulls off your beard. Or wets on your lap. Or bites you."

". . . **How** much does this job pay?"

She laughed. "Nine dollars an hour, I thought I'd told you. But you'll like it, I can tell."

Griffin smiled. It was so nice to hear a woman laughing, to hear a woman speaking pleasantly to him. "Oh, yeah? How can you tell I'd like it?"

"I'm just really good at reading people. I can tell a lot about someone in the first few minutes. I was man advisor in my sorority—I gave instant personality analyses. I was really accurate, too—except when it came to myself. But that's another story.

"Anyway, the orientation is tomorrow night, seven to nine. Can you make it? "

He thought for a moment. Tonight was Ellen's night. And so tomorrow . . . "That would be fine," he said. And then, "Maybe we could have a drink afterward."

She said nothing.

"Or coffee." He felt a sudden plunge in his spirits. He knew nothing about her. Maybe she was a recovering alcoholic. Maybe she was a transsexual. It was horrible to have to start all over. **I grew up in . . . I voted for . . . I have a sister and two brothers . . . That scar is from . . . The first time I this, the last time I that . . .** It was exhausting to even think about.

But then when she said, "I'd love to," he felt instantly better. Her cashmere sweater, her pretty blond hair. Her open smile. His penis rose, settled, and he shifted in his seat. "I'll see you, then."

After he hung up, he sat staring out the window. This is how it went, he supposed. You suggested things, they happened. One thing led to the other, it must have been this way for Ellen, too. She smiled back, she met him somewhere, they talked, he leaned over slowly and kissed her that first time.

Yes. One thing led to the other, the dominos fell—they'd been up, and then they were down. You lost things you thought you couldn't be without, and you went on anyway. He remembered being Zoe's age and being given a silver dollar by his favorite uncle. He couldn't believe his good fortune. He was out in the street, flipping the coin, showing off for a friend, when he dropped it and it rolled down a sewer grate. He lay on top of the grate and saw the coin shining up at him from far away. He stared at it for a long time, wishing he could make time work backward. He wouldn't have flipped the thing. He would have put it in the cigar box he kept under his bed, maybe in its own leather pouch. He stared at the coin until his friend became impatient and told him to stop looking and come to the baseball field, where they were going to play catch. "It would be better if you couldn't see it," his friend said, as they walked away. But Griffin said no, this way he could still have it a little. But the next time he looked the coin was gone.

He picked up Ellen's picture, stared into her eyes, then put it in his drawer, facedown.

Ellen met Griffin at the door. She looked much better—pretty, in fact. She was wearing an apron over a long brown skirt and a loose-knit white sweater, pearl earrings. She was holding a wooden spoon, stained red. "Spaghetti and meatballs," she said.

"Uh huh." Griffin moved past her, hung up his coat. "Where's Zoe?"

He didn't want to look at Ellen anymore.

"Upstairs. Would you tell her dinner will be ready in two minutes?"

She couldn't wait to leave. Well, neither could he. "Yeah, I'll tell her. By the way, I need the car tonight."

She looked at him. "This is my night!"

"I know. But I'm taking Zoe out for some things she needs."

"What things?"

"Her pants are getting too short for her. And she could use a new coat."

Ellen hesitated, then said, "All right, fine. Take it. I'll get a ride." He heard her pick up the phone and start dialing as he went upstairs.

Zoe was sitting on the floor of her bedroom, star-ing into her lizard cage, which had never once held a lizard, but had been home to frogs, worms, grasshoppers, and a garter snake. Griffin sat on her bed, and she looked up at him briefly. "Hi, Dad."

"Got something in there?"

"Yeah. An ant. He was on my windowsill. See him? He's black. He looks like a booger."

"Zoe."

"Well, he does! Like two boogers stuck together." She moved some of the shavings aside, then looked up at Griffin. "There's nothing wrong with saying 'booger,' Dad. It is a natural thing that everyone has."

"Who told you that?"

"Grandma!"

"Which grandma?"

"Grandma Griffin!"

". . . Oh."

"And it's true! Plus I know something else, too."

"What's that?"

"If you don't fart when you have to, you can blow a hole in the side of your stomach."

"Who told you that? Grandma Griffin did **not** tell you that."

"No. Andrew Molner. But his **dad** told him."

"Well, that is not true, Zoe."

"But it is true about boogers. The only thing is, you shouldn't **eat** them, which that is **all** that Andrew **does.** One time he had to go to the principal." She shifted the shavings again. "Now, where did he go? Oh, there he is. See?"

Griffin got on the floor, peered into the cage. "Well, I see part of a cookie."

"Yeah, Mommy made chocolate chip."

"And I see a grape."

"Right. His dinner."

"But I don't see the ant."

"Well, he is shy with new people. But he's there, Dad, just **look.**"

Griffin looked once more. "Oh, yeah. I see him now."

"He's pretty, isn't he?"

"Very pretty. What's his name?"

She sat back, picked at the toe of one of her socks. "I think . . . Amos."

"Terrific name. Amos Ant."

She giggled. "Yeah, ubcept his last name is not **Ant,** Dad!"

"**Ex**cept."

"Huh?"

"**Ex**cept, not **ub**cept. So what is his last name?"

"**Griffin,** of course! He's in our **family.**"

"I see." Ah, Zoe.

"I've been teaching him to sit."

"Really."

"Yeah. Do you think you can teach an ant to sit?"

"What do you think?"

She sat back on her heels, sighed. "He's not **so** good yet."

"You might want to start with something easier."

"Like what?"

"Oh, I don't know. Eating from your hand, maybe."

"I tried. He won't. Hey, Dad, can I really get any game I want tonight?"

"Yes."

"The one I want costs fifty dollars. Frankie Anziletti just got it, and he thinks he's so hot."

"Fifty bucks!"

"Yeah, but you **said.**"

"You're right." Griffin stood up. "Time for dinner, sweetie. Go  wash your hands."

She looked at them. "Actually, I don't need to."

"You do need to. Wash, and then, after dinner, we'll go get that game. Did you do your home-work?"

"Yeah, stupid spelling sentences."

"What's stupid about that?"

"All homework is stupid."

"Why?"

Zoe picked up the cage, put it carefully beside her Tinkerbell perfume and lotion set, never opened since she'd gotten it on her last birthday, but she liked the bottles. **"Sit,"** she said, and prodded the ant. Then, to Griffin, "What did you say?"

"I asked why homework was stupid."

"Because kids need to play after school. Teachers always forget what it feels like to be a kid. They don't remember **anything.** Don't **ev**en get me **go**ing."

Griffin smiled. In the old days, he would have shared this with Ellen.

\*     \*     \*

Ellen was subdued at dinner, but friendly. "I hear you're going out for some clothes with Dad tonight," she told Zoe.

Zoe looked at Griffin. **"Clothes!"**

"And a game, too," Griffin added hastily.

"I don't need clothes!"

"A coat you need, Zoe. And maybe some pants."

"Okay, but don't make me try anything on."

"We'll see." The marinara was delicious. "This is good," he told Ellen. "Better than what you usually make."

"Yes, it's a new recipe." She wouldn't look at him, saying this. Ah. It had come from him. Lube Chef.

"I'll be going out tonight, too," Ellen told Zoe. "And I won't be here until after you go to bed. But you get to sleep on time, okay?"

Zoe popped a forkful of spaghetti into her mouth, talked around it. "Where are you going?"

"Don't talk with food in your mouth, Zoe."

She swallowed. "To your quilting class?"

Ellen nodded. "Yes."

He thought, for a moment, about saying, "Bullshit. Pass the cheese," but didn't. Instead, he sat still, staring at his plate.

"I'm done; can we go?" Zoe asked.

Before he could answer, she was halfway down the hall. "I'll get our coats."

"Did you get a ride?" Griffin asked Ellen quietly.

"Yes."

"When is he coming?"

"After you leave."

He stood, pushed his chair in. "This is very weird, Ellen."

"DAD!" Zoe called.

**"Coming!"**

He started for the hall, then turned back. "Don't you let him in here."

"I wouldn't."

"Don't even think about it."

"I said I **wouldn't!**"

" 'BYE, MOMMY!"

**"Goodbye, sweetheart!"** Smooth as silk.

The game was fifty-five dollars. In the car on the way home, Griffin said, "You know, I don't think I ever had a toy that cost more than ten dollars."

Zoe groaned. "Oh, no. Don't start telling me that."

"What?"

"About how hard it was when you were a kid and you got spanked with a belt and all that stuff." She yawned mightily.

"Are you sleepy?" He'd kept her out past her bedtime.

"No. Can I play one game before bed?"

"No."

"Please?"

"No."

Silence.

That was it? But then Zoe said, "Dad, that yawn was not because I'm tired. I'm not tired at all."

"No, Zoe."

There. Three usually did it.

After they got home and Zoe was tucked in, Griffin brought her a glass of water, then sat beside her. "Guess where I'm going tomorrow?" he said.

"Where?"

"To a class to learn how to be a Santa."

"Are you kidding?"

"Nope."

"What for?"

Griffin shrugged. "For fun!"

"Do you get any free toys?"

"No."

"Oh. Well, good night." She turned over.

Griffin sat still for a while, then said, "Zoe?"

"Yeah?"

"I thought you'd think it was pretty cool. Me being a Santa."

She turned over. "Actually, Dad, it's kind of embarrassing."

"Well, if any of your classmates come, I won't reveal myself as being your father."

"Huh. As if."

"What do you mean?"

"Nobody in my class still believes! Except for Sarah Kimball, who brings a **doll** to school every day!"

"Well. Maybe it will turn out to be fun for both of us. Somehow. But right now, you'd better start snoring. It's late."

"Okay." She closed her eyes, then opened them again. "Dad? When Mommy comes home, tell her to tuck me in, too."

"She will. She always does."

"I know. But tell her, too."

"Okay. I'll remind her."

He'd forgotten. Somewhere in the back of his mind, he'd been thinking that he'd go downstairs and Ellen would be there in the living room, curled up in an armchair, reading, her glasses perched on the end of her nose. Now, remembering, reoriented, he felt a dull ache in his stomach.

He went into the kitchen and poured himself a glass of milk, got two more cookies. He'd spent too much on that game. But he'd wanted to buy it for Zoe. Why? Was he trying to get her on his side? Well, so was Ellen. Chocolate chip cookies, indeed. Although she did do this often, bake things from scratch. Cakes, pies, apple strudel. She was a good mother, he didn't deny that. Whatever demons she suffered within herself, she put them aside to care for her daughter properly. They'd agreed before Zoe was born that a parent needed to be there for a child, and Ellen volunteered, having no real career plans, anyway, having worked listlessly at a bookstore before they were married. There were times staying home had been difficult for her—once, when Zoe was two, Ellen had sat on their bed weeping, saying she never read anything but the back of cereal boxes anymore. But she was committed to honoring her pledge. "I'll take the bad with the good," she'd said, later that night. "It's worth it."

Griffin went to the message pad by the telephone, and wrote,

**Ellen,**
**I'll always appreciate what a good mother you are. Not everything has to change.**
**Griffin**

He reread the note, thought for a moment about throwing it away, but left it there. Then he turned out all of the lights but a small one on the hall table, and went to bed.

# Chapter 11

· · · · · · · · · · · · · · · · · · ·

He dreamed he was walking alongside the ocean. Ellen was with him. They were holding hands; she was smiling. He picked up a luminescent purple shell and gave it to her. She admired it, turning it over and over to look at it from this angle and that. But then she dropped it, and it disappeared into the sand. She fell to her knees and dug for it, but couldn't find it. "Well, it can't just be **gone,**" she said. But it was. She looked for a long time, then put her hands to her face and burst into tears. "Hey, this is no big deal," Griffin said. "There's lots more—I'll find you another one." But she was shaking her head, saying, no, that was the only one. He knelt down to put his arms around her, to comfort her, to show her the shells that lay on the beach ahead of them. As he held her, he felt her grow smaller. He pulled away from her and, astonished, watched as she became the size of his thumb. "Don't drop **me**," she said. She was looking up at him, her sweater clutched tightly around her, her voice barely audible. Her face was full of fear.

He startled awake, opened his eyes to the empty space in the bed beside him—no matter how determinedly he started out in the middle, he always gravitated back to his old outside half. His mouth was dry; he was perspiring slightly.

In the old days, he'd have awakened Ellen to tell her about the dream. She was good at analyzing them, at making sense of things that seemed not to. She liked to be told dreams as soon as they happened; it didn't matter what time it was. She would always tell Griffin to say what he thought his dreams meant, first; she said that the dreamer knew best what his own dreams meant. But Griffin didn't think so. He thought Ellen knew best what his dreams meant, and he assigned that part of himself to her.

He closed his eyes to try to go to sleep again, but it was pointless: He was wide awake. He checked the clock: 2:14. He wondered if Ellen had come home yet. Well, what if she hadn't? It wasn't his business any longer.

Still.

He got up, put on his robe and slippers, and went downstairs. He would say that he'd forgotten to turn the heat down, which was true. No wonder he'd awakened perspiring.

She was asleep on the sofa, her purse gaping open on the floor beside her. Why? What had she been doing? Looking to see if there was enough in the checking account to pay for first and last month's rent for some apartment she and the Oil Pan King had looked at?

He went into the kitchen, turned on the night-light on the microwave. Milk might help him sleep. He poured a glassful, then stood at the sink, looking out the kitchen window as he drank it. He saw his reflection and, beyond that, the leafless branches of the maple tree. Maybe this weekend, he and Zoe would fix that floorboard—it was supposed to be unseasonably mild. And in the spring, he'd paint the tree house, maybe add the rope swing Zoe kept asking for, though he worried about doing that. Zoe was too daring, even for a tomboy. He worried that one of these days, she was going to hurt herself badly. It would be so much safer for her to be more . . . well, **girl**-like is what he'd say, though it was probably politically incorrect to do so. But why couldn't she play with girls once in a while, sit quietly in someone's pink bedroom playing Barbies instead of having demolition derby day with the "race car" she'd built with her roughneck friends from a discarded red wagon? The only Barbie Zoe owned lay ignored at the bottom of her closet. Once, he and Ellen had talked about whether or not Zoe was gay, and had decided not—**not that it mattered,** as they Seinfeld-ly agreed. Zoe seemed to have crushes on boys every now and then—Ben Picchiotti was someone she talked about lately. Ben was an older man, a sixth-grader and a superb base-ball player—legendary in Little League circles—whom Zoe seemed to admire for reasons beyond his athletic abilities. So why couldn't she giggle about Ben in the safety of some other girl's house rather than racing around outside all the time? Grace Woodward, one of the girls in her class, had called her to come over a couple of times, but Zoe always found a reason not to go. Maybe it was Griffin's fault. Maybe rather than asking her if she'd like to help hammer, he'd ask her to pick out curtains for the tree house. Wallpaper. If Ellen wasn't going to be around, he'd have to make more of an effort that way. Not that any of Ellen's love of the domestic and the feminine had rubbed off on Zoe yet.

He rinsed out his glass, put it in the sink, and started out of the kitchen. Near the phone, he saw a note, then remembered that he'd left one for Ellen. She hadn't even bothered to read it. He started to throw it away, then saw that it was not his note, but one from Ellen to him:

**Griffin—**
**Thank you for saying what you did in your note.**
**I saved it.**
**It's funny, what we keep.**

                                        **Ellen**

He read it three times, looking to see if there was something else he could find, something in the slant of her writing, the dotting of the **i**'s. But he couldn't find anything. Not what he wanted.

He went into the living room and stood over Ellen, watching her sleep. In her open purse, he saw his note, and the sight of it made for a small leap of happiness inside him.

He went back into the kitchen, got out a pencil, and on the notepad wrote:

**Ellen—**
**It's two-thirty A.M. I was dreaming of you. Remember once we set the alarm for two-thirty so we could walk around the neighborhood and see what it looked like? You wanted to go right up and look in the windows of the houses, but I was scared we'd get shot. We should have, anyway.**

He put Ellen's note in his robe pocket, then headed back upstairs. He would put it in the dresser drawer where they kept a huge pile of things from Zoe: notes to Santa and the Easter bunny, drawings from the time she could barely hold a pencil. Strange: At the same time Griffin was feeling a conciliatory warmth toward Ellen, he was also feeling that if she tried to take even one of those papers with her when she left, he'd kill her.

He lay back in bed, sighed. Of course he wouldn't kill her. But he would never give her a single one of Zoe's papers. They belonged here. In the family Griffin.

In the morning, Ellen awakened him, saying, "Do you know what time it is? Are you sick?"

He looked at the clock, bolted upright. It was 8:30, an hour and a half past the time he usually got up. Ellen was wearing the multicolored silk robe he and Zoe had picked out for her a few Mother's Days ago. She had thought about returning it at first, saying that it must have cost a fortune—which it had. But then, at Zoe's insistence, she'd decided to keep it. She didn't wear it except on special occasions—Christmas mornings, times when they had guests staying over—fearing that she'd stain it or damage it in some other way. Besides, she'd always liked wearing Griffin's flannel shirts as robes. He supposed she no longer wanted to do that.

"I didn't know whether to wake you or not," she said, her hands clasped tightly before her. He realized with some surprise that she was nervous.

"It's good you did. I just overslept. Thanks."

"You're welcome."

"Is Zoe up?"

Ellen frowned. "She's gone to **school.**" There was something in her tone Griffin didn't like. Some accusation, some disapproval: Did he not **know** this, he who insisted he'd be able to take care of their daughter just as well as she could?

"Look," he said. "I didn't set the alarm, okay? I was tired. I could have gotten Zoe up, but I didn't think you'd mind doing it."

"What are you talking about? Why would I mind? I do it all the time!"

"Not **all** the time. I do it sometimes, too. And if you hadn't been here, I would have gotten her up on time, believe me. **And** made her breakfast. **And** made sure she had what she needed for school, which **you** don't always do."

"Griffin. Jesus." She turned and left.

He sat at the edge of the bed for a while, trying to decide if he should be ashamed of himself or not. Then he got into the shower and stood with the hot water running full in his face, his eyes closed tightly, until it ran out. When he was dressed, he went downstairs and into the kitchen. Maybe he would apologize to Ellen—he'd been out of line.

She was sitting at the table with an empty coffee cup before her, reading the paper. He refilled her cup, set it down before her again. She did not thank him. She did not acknowledge him in any way.

He sat across her with his own cup of coffee, took a sip, then took another.

"Ellen."

Nothing.

**"Ellen."**

"What." She did not look up.

"I'm sorry."

A moment, and then, still glued to the paper, she said, "All right."

He leaned back in his chair, sighed. This . . . tightness. When was the last time it had been easy between them? He stared at Ellen, then substituted Donna for her. Donna in some blue robe, smiling, asking him about what he was going to do that day. Kissing him at the door when he left. When had it been that way with Ellen? Ever?

"I have to leave at six-thirty tonight," he said.

She raised an eyebrow, kept reading.

"Did you hear me?"

She looked up. "Yes, I heard you. Dinner will be at six. You can leave whenever you want to."

He noticed a smudge of mascara beneath her left eye. "What did you do last night, Ellen?"

She got up from the table, stood at the sink with her back to him. "I don't think we need to talk about that."

"You are still my wife."

"We are separated, insofar as we can be."

"You are still my wife."

She turned around. "I **really** don't think you would want to hear about it, Griffin."

He nodded. "I see." He picked up his briefcase and headed for the door.

"Are you really going to be a Santa Claus?"

He turned around. "Who told you that?"

"Zoe. Or is that your 'quilting class'?"

"I wouldn't do that, Ellen. I would never lie to her."

"Yeah. That's what I always thought, too. Well, I'll see you tonight."

Her voice was soft, nearly itself again. He remembered, suddenly, the notes they'd left for each other. **Had** they done that? Yes. Yes, they had. "Thanks for your note," he told her.

She looked away from him.

"Did you get my other one?"

"Yes." She moved past him, headed upstairs.

# Chapter 12

· · · · · · · · · · · · · · · · · · · · ·

Just before Griffin left work, Ellen called to say that Zoe had been invited over to a friend's house for dinner. Grace Woodward was having a spontaneous pizza party—all the girls in her class had been invited, and Ellen had persuaded Zoe to go. She could still make dinner for Griffin, if he wanted her to. . . .

"I'm fine," he said.

Louise, the waitress with whom Ellen was friendly, was working at the Cozy Corner. Griffin hadn't expected this—he thought she only worked the day shift. When she came to take his order, he wasn't sure how to act. Was he, in Louise's eyes, the wounder or the woundee?

"Hey, Griffin," she said, coming up to his booth, her order pad in hand. Nothing was in her face that told him she knew. She smiled at him—a disarming smile. She was an attractive older woman, always reminded Griffin of Peggy Lee—that nice beauty mark, that lazy sensuality.

"Hi, Louise. Just . . . having dinner, here."

"Good. The Greek chicken's good tonight."

He nodded. "Okay. I'll try it." He didn't want Greek chicken. He wanted meatloaf.

"Drink?" she asked, reaching up to tighten an earring that was coming loose. "Don't want to lose these," she said. "Your wife gave them to me."

"Did she."

"Yeah, she was in here on my birthday a few weeks ago. Next day she shows up with these pearl earrings, prettiest earrings **I'll** ever have. She's a nice woman, that wife of yours."

"Uh huh." He attempted a smile.

Louise looked at him. "Did I— Did you not know about this? I'm not going to get her in trouble, am I?"

"No, I'm glad she gave them to you, Louise. Happy birthday. What did your husband give you?"

"Him? Nothing!" But she laughed, saying this. "Let me put your order in, then I'll come and sit with you. It's slow tonight."

He watched her stand before the kitchen window and bellow the order in to the cooks. Then she poured a cup of coffee for each of them and came to sit opposite Griffin.

"So how is Ellen? I haven't seen her for a while."

"She's fine." He nodded, as if agreeing with himself. Then he said, "She wants a divorce."

Louise had raised her cup to take a drink; now, she put it down.

"Are you kidding?"

He shook his head. "No." He didn't want dinner anymore. He didn't want to be here anymore. "You know, Louise, I think I'm going to take off. I'm not really hungry. Let me pay you for what I ordered, though, I know—"

"You're not going anywhere. You look like hell. You need to eat." She turned back toward the kitchen, yelled, "Hurry it up back there with the chicken!" Then, to Griffin, "I forgot to ask you: green beans or carrots?"

"Green beans, I guess."

"GREEN BEANS!" she yelled. And then, "God, Griffin, I'm really sorry."

"Yeah. Thanks."

"When did this happen?"

"Just recently."

"Well, I'm sorry as hell. How's Zoe doing?"

"She doesn't know yet. We're having a kind of in-home separation."

Louise frowned. "What's **that** mean?"

"We're separated, but we're both living in the same house. For the time being."

"So you're looking for a place?"

"No. I'm not moving."

She stared at him.

"I'm staying in the house."

"So . . . **Ellen** is moving?"

"Yeah. If she wants to."

She leaned back in the booth, reached into her pocket for her pack of cigarettes. "Do you mind?"

"No."

"Want one?"

"No, thanks. Well, wait. Yeah, I'll take one."

Louise handed him a cigarette, put one in her mouth, then lit them both. She inhaled deeply, then blew a stream of smoke up toward the ceiling. Griffin tried doing the same, but began coughing— a little at first, then violently. "Sorry," he said. "I don't smoke cigarettes."

She smiled. "Put it out, Griffin."

Someone from the kitchen yelled, "Order!" Louise put her cigarette in the ashtray, and went to get Griffin's dinner. She put it in front of him, then sat down again. He looked at the plate and picked up a fork, tried a mouthful of potatoes. They were good, but he didn't want to eat. He put his fork down, smiled at Louise. "You know, I'm sorry—I'm just not hungry all of a sudden."

"You want something else?"

"No, I just lost my appetite. I really don't want anything."

Louise pulled his plate over to her, put out her cigarette, and began to eat. "Hope you don't mind."

"No, enjoy it."

**"I'm** starving!"

"Well."

She sliced a piece of meat off the chicken breast, then looked up at Griffin. "What's happening between you and Ellen is none of my business. But I'm going to tell you something."

"What's that."

"That woman needs you. She's . . . Well, that's it. She needs you." She put the chicken in her mouth, said around it, "This is really very good."

"I don't think so, Louise. I mean, what you said about Ellen, I don't think that's true."

"It is. And I'll tell you something else. I think she loves you, Griffin, and she doesn't even know it. Okay? That's what I think."

He felt his face growing warm, looked down at the table.

"We talk about things, sometimes," Louise said. Her voice was kind.

He looked up, and she said, "I can't tell you everything. But I know she's a complicated woman, full of . . . I don't know. She's shy. Real sensitive kind of person. And she . . . Well, I hope it doesn't hurt your feelings for me to say this, Griffin. But she really needs to grow up."

"Doesn't hurt **my** feelings. I agree."

"Well, here's a surprise for you, Griffin. She agrees, too."

"That's hard to believe."

"It's true. She's pretty down on herself, and that's one of the reasons why. Now, that's all I'm saying. Don't want to break the girlfriend rules, probably shouldn't even have told you this much. But there, I did."

"Well, thanks." He looked at his watch. A little over half an hour to get to the mall, and parking could be bad. "I've got to go, Louise. Let me pay you."

"Are you kidding? No charge."

He put a five-dollar bill on the table. "A tip, at least."

She handed him back the money. "Get lost. And let me give you some coffee for the road, you want some coffee, at least?"

"Sure."

He waited at the door for his coffee. When Louise handed him the Styrofoam cup, she said quietly, "Don't feel bad, sweetheart. Things will work out all right, one way or another."

He nodded his thanks, walked out into the dark. The wind had picked up, and he shivered. The coffee would be good to have.

He drove to the mall, thinking about what

Louise had told him. The bad news was that Ellen had confided so much in someone other than him. But he supposed that was the good news, too—at least she had a friend. The really good news, though, was that if there were sides in this, Louise was on his.

The orientation class was being held in a small room behind the hardware department at Sears. There were several folding chairs set up, and a metal desk stationed at the front of the room. An ancient wreath hung on the front of the desk, its formerly red bow faded to a weary pink. Griffin was the first to arrive, but shortly thereafter an older man came in and sat beside him. His weight alone qualified him for the job, Griffin thought. And his incredible white hair. The man held out his hand and Griffin shook it, saying, "Frank Griffin, how are you doing?"

"Ernie Powell. You new?"

"Yes, I've never done anything like this."

"Nothing to it. I've been doing it for years. Wouldn't miss it. I'll tell you, seeing these little kids? That's the only part of Christmas I like any-more. Before I came back here, I was just out walk-ing around the stores. Did you see the decorations out in the hall?"

Griffin nodded.

"Did you know they started putting them up in October? I swear to God." He pulled a cigar out of his pocket, started chewing on it. "Trying to quit," he told Griffin. "But I like the feel of it." He reached for another cigar, handed it to Griffin. "Here you go. It's a Cuban. You might as well enjoy it."

Griffin put the cigar in his pocket, nodded his thanks.

From out in the hall, he heard a woman's voice, and then Donna walked in. She looked terrific— her blond hair curled softly on her shoulders, and she was wearing a red knit dress and gold hoop earrings. She smiled at the men, then turned her back to lay out some papers on the desk.

"That tamale right there?" Ernie said quietly, pointing toward Donna with his cigar. "She's the photographer."

"Right," Griffin said. "She's why I'm here."

"I don't blame you."

"No, I mean, she's the one who told me about the job. She was taking applications the other day. She kind of talked me into it."

"You won't be sorry."

Two more men entered, then another three. "Them two guys are the Luigi brothers," Ernie said, pointing to the two swarthy-complexioned men who had entered together. "They're friends of mine. Be right back."

When Ernie left to go and visit with the brothers, who looked to be twins, Donna came over to Griffin's chair. "So. You **are** Frank Griffin, aren't you?"

"I guess we didn't have so much time together the other day, huh?"

"We'll make up for it tonight." She smiled. One dimple, left side. Nice.

Another small group of men came in and took their places. Donna looked around the room. "I'd better go, it looks like everyone's here."

As Donna moved behind the desk, one more person, a large, masculine-looking woman, burst through the door. "Hey. I'm L.D.," she said. "I called?"

Donna stared at her.

"I **did** call, they said to come tonight. I'm transferring from Wisconsin."

"Oh, okay. Well, welcome. Sit anywhere."

L.D. chose the chair on the other side of Griffin, took off her hat, smoothed down her short hair, and glared at him. "What are you looking at?"

"Nothing." Griffin faced forward.

Donna cleared her throat. "Okay! May I have your attention, please?"

"You can have whatever you want," Ernie muttered, and beside him, Griffin heard L.D. chuckle.

"First of all," Donna said, "I'd like to welcome all

of you, especially those of you who are new. The more-experienced people here can tell you how rewarding it is, I'm sure. But what I want to focus on, so to speak, is the photography."

Griffin listened to Donna explain that it was essential to remember that although it may be your one hundredth shot of the night, it was the child's first. That the best thing to do was to look off to the side, to avoid flash fatigue. She told them that the way to hold the child was angled toward the camera, not so tight as to frighten them, but not so loose as to drop them. Then she introduced the man in charge of the company that had hired them, Henry Marshall.

Henry was tall and rail thin. He nodded hello, then pointed toward three large boxes lined up against the wall. "These are your costumes. We've got new beards this year—they shouldn't irritate your faces like the old ones did." Then he sat on the desk and gave what he called his Santa spiel, apologies to some of the people who had heard most of it before.

There was a four-hour limit for any one shift—that was as much as anyone could take. Remember to keep ice water in your "cocoa" mug—it got hot in that uniform. They would have fans blowing, but if you needed a break to cool off at any time, just say the word, they'd put up the "Gone to feed the reindeer" sign. He said it was important to be natural, to try to relax. If a kid pulled your beard off, you should simply put it back on with some measure of dignity, and say something like "Old Santa's whiskers aren't what they used to be!" If they asked where the reindeer were, you were to say they had been brought to a barn off the premises to rest. Last year, when one Santa had said they were on the roof of the mall, a group of kids had tried to climb up there, so no more of that. Use lipstick to redden your nose and your cheeks, a water-based white paint to whiten your brows. And **never** say, "Ho, ho, ho!"—use a genuine laugh, instead.

If you were found to be ignorant of a toy a child asked for, you were to say there were so many toys that you sometimes got mixed up, that was why you had elves to help. If they cried, you gave them back to their caretakers promptly. "Now, some of what I'm telling you are just suggestions—we want you to feel you can relax, enter into the role, have some fun with it. And it **is** fun—just ask old Ernie, here. You've been going at it for . . . how long now, Ernie?"

"Sixteen years," Ernie said, proudly. He patted his belly. "What the hell. Gives me a good reason to keep this around. The wife gives me any heat, I say, 'Hey, what do you want to do, spoil some kid's Christmas?' Not that she's any featherweight, herself."

Henry handed out papers with the names and addresses of all the Santas, in case they needed to call one another to trade shifts. Then he asked for questions.

A short, older man sitting in the back raised his hand. "What do you do if a kid wants to know Mrs. Claus's first name? I was asked that last year and I didn't know what to say, because I thought someone else would say something different. So I just said our time was up, and we'd talk more next time."

"Well," Henry said. "I know one fellow who says, 'Oh, Santa's been married to Mrs. Claus for over one hundred years, and all this time I've called her Mrs. Claus. I've **forgotten** her name!'" The class chuckled, and Henry shrugged. "What can I say? It works!"

L.D. raised her hand and reminded the men that oftentimes a child would ask for a dead person to be brought back to life, and that an effective answer was, "Even though he would really like to, Santa can't do everything. But that person will always be alive in your memory."

"Good point," Henry said. "Same thing with divorce—kids will ask that their parents be brought back together. You can respond in much the same way, remind them that though a parent may not be there all the time, the love is."

Griffin rubbed his eyes, looked at his watch. Right.

"If there are no more questions," Henry said, "let's get these costumes handed out. Please try them on, make sure they fit—we've got plenty of sizes this year in boots, so I don't want to hear about any more Santas showing up in sneakers. Trim the beards, if you have to, so your mouth shows. Remember, you're responsible for keeping these costumes in good shape—get them cleaned if you need to, and **definitely** before you return them. After you have your costume, confirm your hours with Donna—then you're free to go. Thank you!"

Griffin found a medium-sized costume and pulled it out of the box. Then he pulled a foam rubber belly out of another box, a beard and a wig out of yet another. The other men were trying their costumes on over their clothes, so Griffin did, too. When he had finished, he looked around. There were Santas everywhere. Ernie was Santa, the Luigi bothers were Santa, L.D. was Santa, and he was, too. He felt different, as though the costume had truly transformed him, had empowered him. He caught sight of himself in the window and gave himself a quick wave. White gloves. He'd never worn white gloves before. He wished Zoe could see this. He'd try on the costume for her tomorrow. He walked around for a while, making sure the boots fit and the belly didn't fall, and talked for a while with another man who was new this year. "You're sure I look right?" the man kept asking. Finally Griffin took his costume off, packed it in the bag he'd been provided, and waited at the end of the line to see Donna.

When it was his turn to step up to her table, she smiled and pointed at his chin. He'd forgotten to remove the beard. Her teeth were so white, her lipstick such a creamy red. He pulled off his beard, embarrassed, and stuffed it into the bag. Looking at Donna's mouth reminded him that it had been a long time since he'd kissed a woman. And many years since he'd kissed anyone other than Ellen.

"Let's see," Donna said. "You're doing the six-to-ten slot, right?"

He nodded. She studied a complicated-looking schedule full of penciled-in names. "Could you do Monday and Thursday?"

"How about Monday and Wednesday?" he asked. "Or Monday and Friday?"

She pursed her lips, tapped her pencil lightly against the schedule, then began making entries. He could smell her perfume, a light, spicy scent. Pretty. Sexy.

He wished, suddenly, that he'd never suggested coffee. He wasn't nearly ready for this kind of thing. What the hell would they have to talk about? He was a married man, still in love with his wife. He was the father of a daughter who would be horrified if she knew the kinds of things he'd been thinking about this woman. In spite of himself, he saw himself pressing his mouth to Donna's, running his hands through that thick blond hair. It appeared to be natural. Of course, there was only one way to tell. Horrified, he felt himself responding, and he shifted his bag to hold in front of himself.

"Okay, Monday and Friday," Donna said. She wrote in his name, then closed the calendar and clasped her hands in front of her. They were beautiful hands, well-manicured, not like Ellen's. Everything about her was different, and while it excited him, it also made him deeply sad.

He was a man who loved the calm normalcy of a long-term relationship. Romance was all right, but what really appealed to him was comfort. He liked the simple safety of marriage, the relief in it, the ease with which you could flop down on the sofa, exhausted after a hard day's work, and know that you had company that required nothing of you. You could say you wanted to stay home and watch the stupidest thing you could find on television and have someone join you, maybe make popcorn before she sat down beside you. You could ask questions you'd never ask anyone else, express fears without fear. Griffin had always hated dating, and, until recently, had been so satisfied being married. And now here he was, thirty-eight years old and starting all over. He didn't want to start all over. He wanted to go home and press his head into Ellen's stomach and say, "Please. One more chance." And if that wasn't possible, he wanted to go home and be with Zoe, and walk around in his pajamas, drinking a beer. He wanted to go to sleep early, he was tired. He would apologize, say he just couldn't do this. Maybe some other time, he'd say. He definitely could not go out with her tonight. Out of the question.

Donna picked up her coat and purse. "Ready?"

"Absolutely."

As they walked out together, Griffin thought of an ad he'd seen on the Internet showing a page from a yearbook and declaring, "Your classmates are all here!" No, they're not, Griffin thought. Some are dead. All are changed. Nothing stays.

# Chapter 13

· · · · · · · · · · · · · · · · · · ·

Donna picked a restaurant in Forest Park. It was quiet, she said, and the kind of place that didn't mind if you came in and ordered just a cup of coffee. "Although actually, what I'd really like is a beer."

"Me, too," Griffin said.

He followed her to a brown-shingled single-story building on Madison Street where he'd never been. It looked more like a house than a restaurant. A sign outside identified it as ESTELLE'S, and a smaller sign read, WE SPECIALIZE IN BREAKFAST, LUNCH, AND DINNER.

Griffin got out of his car and walked up to Donna, who was exiting hers. "I like it already!"

"The best part is that there really is an Estelle. One of a kind. She'll come out of the kitchen to yell at you a little, but it makes you feel great. I eat here a lot."

"You live in Forest Park?" Griffin asked.

"No, River Forest." She opened the door of the restaurant. "But I like the antiques stores in Forest Park—I'm over here a lot."

Inside the restaurant, a thin graying waitress, midfifties, Griffin guessed, greeted them. She had an extra-short hairdo and deep wrinkles on her still-handsome face. She stood up from a booth where she'd been sitting reading the paper and smiled, then headed toward them. She was wearing a low-cut red blouse with several layers of ruffles, tight black pants, and white sneakers. A gold necklace spelled MARIE in flowery script; a pearl dotted the **i.** She stared uninhibitedly at Griffin until Donna said, "This is my friend, Frank Griffin. Frank, I'd like you to meet Marie Costa."

"How are you, hon?" She pumped his hand enthusiastically, winked at Donna. Then she gestured toward the empty room. "Sit anywhere youse want."

They chose a booth alongside a wall. Duct tape covered long tears in the red leatherette. They ordered beers, and Marie set down two overfilled mugs with a flourish. "Anything else?"

"No, thanks, Marie," Donna said, and Marie disappeared into the kitchen. "She's gone to get Estelle. Get ready."

Within moments, a huge woman with an exaggerated brown bouffant appeared. She lumbered over to the table and glowered at Donna. "Where the hell you been?" She was wearing a tentlike red dress covered with a white apron. She wiped her hands across her belly, then put them on her hips, waiting.

"Hey, Estelle, how are you? This is my friend, Frank Griffin."

Estelle ignored him. "I asked you where you been."

"I actually made my own dinner the last few nights."

Estelle frowned. "I made them pork chops you like the other night, and you didn't even come for any."

"Well, I'll be here tomorrow for dinner. What are you making?"

"Chili and corn bread. Lucas will be here to help."

"So it'll be the hot stuff."

"That's right." She pointed at Griffin. **"Who's** this trash?"

"Frank Griffin," Griffin said, holding out his hand, and she regarded him balefully. Then she stomped off toward the kitchen.

"She likes you," Donna said.

"Really. What does she do if she **doesn't** like you?"

"Throws you out." Donna held up her mug. "Cheers."

He clinked mugs with her. This wasn't so bad. "How did you ever find this place?"

"My ex-husband brought me here. He defended Lucas in a murder case. He was innocent," she added quickly, "it was a case of mistaken identity. But Lucas offered him a free dinner—him and 'the missus.' We came here on a Friday night, and the next morning, Michael told me he wanted a divorce. He moved out that night. We've been divorced now for two years."

Griffin didn't know what to say. The apparent disregard with which she told him this, the practiced nonchalance. It had to still hurt her. He'd forgotten that things like this happened to other people.

"I'm sorry," he said.

She shrugged. "It's okay. It gets better. You'll see."

"What do you mean?"

"You're newly divorced. Or getting a divorce, right?"

"Getting. Right. How did you know?"

She took a long swallow of beer, then said, "I told you. I can read people really well. Another beer?"

He smiled, almost shyly rubbed the top of his head. "I think so, yes."

*       *       *

Within two hours, Griffin had told Donna much about himself, including the fact that he once whimsically asked a drugstore "love computer" about Ellen and him. He'd been thinking he'd bring the analysis home and give it to her, a little joke. "I put in our birth dates and our names," he told Donna, "and it gave back a printout of personality characteristics that was supposed to indicate how compatible we were."

"So what did it say?" Donna asked. "That you were a match made in heaven, right?"

He looked down, skated his mug around in a small circle on the wet tabletop. "Well, no, actually. It said we could be good friends, but that to try to have a serious relationship would be dangerous. It said my idea of fun was to go shopping for filing cabinets, and hers was to go on a spur-of-the-moment safari." He smiled. "It said my 'compatibility partner' was a fashion model."

She smiled back at him. "And who was Ellen's?"

"A movie star."

She burst out laughing.

He supposed it was ridiculous. And yet he'd saved that printout, carried it around in his wallet for months, reading it so often he memorized it. It had described Ellen as **reluctant to lose control** and **independent plus,** as being **able to easily walk away from situations,** as **in demand for**

**every dinner party.** One night he'd showed the thing to Ellen. She'd read it, then looked up at him. "Where'd you get this?"

"At the drugstore. What do you think about what it says?"

"I don't get invited to any dinner parties." She read it again, then asked, "Did you want this?"

"No, just wanted to show you."

"Why?"

"No reason. Just thought it was interesting. You can throw it away."

There was a reason, he realized now. Even then, all those years ago, he'd been looking for something, and had found nothing.

Now he told Donna, "It's funny, though, how accurate those things can be."

"What, you really are thrilled by shopping for filing cabinets?"

He feigned surprise. "You aren't?"

"Well, how big is the markdown?"

He sat back in the booth, smiled. "I am less . . . adventurous than my wife. We really **aren't** very compatible."

She shrugged. "But what difference does it make? God above could come down and tell some people they were wildly incompatible with their spouses, and they'd still want to be with them. It's like artists sacrificing so much for their art. For some people, their relationship is their art, and they'll give up everything for it. That's how it is for you, Griffin. Right?"

"Don't be so sure. I'm changing quickly."

"I don't think so." She touched his arm. "But I still like you. And if you're . . . dating, I'd like to see you."

Estelle stuck her head out of the kitchen and yelled, "CLOSING TIME!"

Donna raised her mug. "And to all a good night."

He walked her to her car. It was cold after the beer-and-grease warmth of the restaurant; the wind blew up his coat sleeves and down his neck. He could smell snow coming. "So!" He hugged her— quickly, awkwardly. "Good night."

"Do you like to ski?" she asked, suddenly.

"I tried it once. I wasn't very good at it. In the winter, I hold heat in very high regard."

"How about dinner at my house next week, then? I have really good heat."

When he hesitated, she said, "Look. I don't have any illusions about your . . . availability. I just like you. Think it over. Call me."

"I will."

She slammed her car door, started her engine, waved goodbye. He stood shivering, watching her go, then started for his own car. A beautiful, blue-eyed blonde, whom others admired, liked him. He heard a door slam behind him, and then Estelle said, "What are you doing standing around out here? Getting ready to rob me? Well, forget it. I could lay you out flat as a shadow, boy, and tend my business at the same time. I cook turkeys that weigh more than you."

"Ah, **Estelle.** I was just saying good night to Donna."

She glared at him. "Ain't a man on the face of the earth deserves that one. And not you, neither."

He smiled; she scowled harder, and began walking away. She carried two overstuffed shopping bags that bumped into her legs with every step.

"Want me to give you a hand?" he called after her.

"Do I look like I'm helpless?" She didn't turn around, saying this. He couldn't wait to make her like him. Next time he came to her restaurant, he'd bring her a beautiful bouquet. He knew women like this. Women like this, he understood.

It was 12:30 when he pulled into the driveway. He was tired; he'd be slow at work tomorrow. He was trying to remember his schedule for the next day when he noticed a small red car parked at the curb. He looked toward the house; no lights on. Who was here?

In the hallway, he turned on a light to hang up

his coat. Ellen came out from the kitchen, holding a glass of water. "Oh. Hello."

"Hi. Do you—" He stared. "Ellen? What did you do to your hair?" It was dyed black, the color it used to be, only different. A flat, false color, not the shiny darkness it once was. He'd once told her her hair reminded him of a lake at night, and she'd smiled.

"I just wanted to try it."

"Oh, Ellen, why?"

"I never liked the gray, you know that."

He said nothing.

"It's **my** hair."

"Did Zoe see it?"

"Yes, Zoe saw it."

"What did she say?"

"She didn't like it." Ellen walked toward the living room. "Okay? Are you happy now?" She took a drink from her glass, set it on the floor beside her, then lay on the sofa, covered herself with the blanket with elaborate care. Then she looked at Griffin, still standing there. **"What?!"**

"You look . . . I don't know. You look different."

"Well. That was the idea, don't you think?" She turned out the light. "Good night."

"Ellen?"

"What?"

He came over to stand beside her. "Pretty soon

we're going to have to tell Zoe about your sleeping down here. I don't want her to—"

"I already told her."

"You . . . **When?**"

"Tonight. I told her my back was bothering me, and I was going to be sleeping here until—"

"When were you going to tell me?"

"Tell you what?"

"What you told **Zoe,** Ellen. Jesus."

"I **was** going to tell you."

"When?"

**"Tonight.** But then you got going on my hair, and I . . . I'm sorry, I was going to tell you. But now you know. She was all right with it, she—"

"Enough."

He went upstairs and into Zoe's room, pulled her covers up higher over her. When would this elemental pleasure ever feel normal again?

He went into his bedroom, undressed before his mirror. Did he have any gray hair? Not yet. If he did, would he ever consider dying it? Of course not. Not even if he were a woman. For God's sake.

He turned back the covers, then remembered the car parked outside. He turned on the hall light and went back downstairs. "Ellen?"

She turned over. "Yes?"

"Do you know whose car is out front?"

"It's mine."

"What do you mean? You bought a car?"

"No. Peter gave it to me."

"He **gave** you a **car?**"

"Yes. He got a good deal on it."

"I thought we agreed that we'd only have one car in this family."

"This is two families, now."

He stood silent for a moment. Then he said, "I really hate your hair."

"Thank you."

"It looks ridiculous."

She turned over again, away from him.

He awakened suddenly, and in the dimness, he made out the top of Ellen's head. She was sitting on the floor beside the bed. He raised himself up on one elbow. "Ellen?"

"What."

"What are you doing here?"

"It's . . ." She sighed. "I had a nightmare."

He lay still for a moment. It occurred to him to tell her to go and call Engine Block, but here she was, Ellen in the darkness, wearing her crummy flannel pajamas, afraid. And here was he, no less frightened than she, really. He would take this mid-Atlantic brushing of elbows for whatever temporary comfort it might offer either of them.

"What was the dream about?" he asked.

"I don't know. There was this man who kept calling me on the phone, saying really obscene things. Then I walked outside—it was afternoon, real bright outside—and there he was and he started stabbing me all over the place. And I could feel it, it **stung,** you know, like big paper cuts. And I—" She stopped, began to weep. "Griffin, do you think I might have a brain tumor?"

He wanted to laugh. Instead, he sat up, turned on the nightstand light, and patted the bed. "Come here."

She sat down beside him, though far enough away so as to not have her intentions misunderstood. "I think I might have a brain tumor or something."

"Ellen, what the hell are you talking about?" Her, pale-faced against a hospital pillow, **Can we let bygones be bygones?**

She looked at him, then away. "A lot of times, at night, I wake up totally disoriented. It's not just that I'm not in my bed, either. I feel disoriented about **everything.** I feel really crazy, and I wish I'd never started anything. I think how you're my **friend,** and I **like** you so much, and I **know** so much about you and things like . . . I know just how big your wrist is, from holding it when we used to sleep spoons, remember?" She was crying steadily but unmindfully, as though her tears had nothing to do with her.

"I remember," he said. "It wasn't that long ago."

"Yes. I know. But anyway, I get this feeling of . . . **Oh, God, what have I done?"**

Now his sympathy converted to anger. "Well, for Christ's sake, Ellen, I thought you'd found this great **love."**

"I know! But I wake up and I wish none of it had ever happened! I wish I'd never met him! And then the next morning, everything's . . . Everything's different the next morning. And Griffin, I've been getting terrible headaches. I think maybe I've got a brain tumor."

"Ellen."

"Yes?" She stopped crying, sat waiting for him to help her, as Zoe might.

He sighed. "You're under a lot of stress, that's all. So am I. That's what happens when people decide to split. What did you expect? People going through a divorce get crazy. Everybody knows that."

"I guess." She looked down, picked at a cuticle. Her hands were so different from Donna's. As though reading his mind, she said, "Did you have a good time tonight?"

He laughed a little, shook his head.

"Did you?"

"Yes. Yes, I did."

"What did you do?"

"Why should I tell you?"

She thought about this, then said, "I don't know."

"I have to go to sleep now, Ellen."

She stood. "Okay. I'm sorry I woke you up."

"It's all right."

She started to leave and he said, "Ellen? I had a few beers with this woman, Donna. That's all. She knows I'm still married."

"Oh."

"All right?"

"Yes. Okay." Her voice. Its sleepy softness. Its utter familiarity. But he needed to remember the other side of her. He lay down, closed his eyes, said nothing more.

In the morning, as he was leaving, he asked Ellen, "Any more bad dreams?"

"No." And then, "Griffin? Zoe's spending the night with Grace on Friday night, did she tell you?"

"No. No kidding."

"Yes, she's going home from school with her. So I guess we can both . . . I guess neither of us has to stay home that night."

"Uh huh."

"I'll be leaving pretty early. And so if you want to—"

"I'm fully capable of making my own plans, Ellen."

He closed the door, walked outside. There was the red car. Piece of shit.

He called Donna from work. So nice to hear from him! She'd love to make him dinner on Friday! Did he like pot roast? Why yes, he said! He certainly did!

# Chapter 14

· · · · · · · · · · · · · · · · · · · · · · ·

After work on Friday, Griffin stopped by the men's room. He stood before the mirror, trying to see himself as Donna might see him. He looked pretty good, damn it. He was an attractive enough man. He straightened his tie, leaned in closer to the mirror. "How are you?" he practiced. No. More casual. "Hey, how **are** you?" He'd kiss her cheek when he said that, lightly but warmly.

He ran his hand over the side of his face. A little rough. Maybe he should stop by home and shave. He looked at his watch—not enough time. He looked himself over once more, then undid his pants so he could retuck his shirt. He was wearing new underwear, blue and white striped. Just in case.

Donna had given him clear directions to her house, but Griffin wondered if he'd made an error when he pulled up in the driveway. The place was huge, a Tudor surrounded by a high, iron fence. He walked up to the front door and rang the bell, full of a jangly nervousness that bordered on mild irritation. He felt like he used to when he went around the neighborhood selling raffle tickets for his elementary school. Taking a deep breath in, he leaned against the door, then turned around quickly when he felt it opening.

"You found it," she said, smiling, and he nodded, then brushed past her as she held the door open for him. She was wearing blue jeans and a black V-neck sweater. Her hair was held up with a silver barrette, and stray strands curled loosely at the base of her neck.

"You look nice," he said, and it came out wooden rather than rich. "Something smells terrific," he added, and it came out lame. He sounded like Homer Simpson when he wanted to sound like James Bond.

"That's our dinner," she said, and then, smiling at his obvious discomfort, she said, "Oh, come on. I'll pour you a glass of wine."

He followed her into the enormous kitchen. It had a center island with copper pots and utensils hanging from a wrought iron holder. There were three different sinks, a massive refrigerator, and the six-burner cast iron stove Ellen had always fantasized about having. "Your kitchen looks like a page out of a magazine," he said. "I mean that as a compliment. But I guess you know that."

"Thanks." She handed him wine in an elegant, thin crystal glass. He remembered with some unwillingness the last time he'd drunk wine with Ellen. They'd used juice glasses decorated with smiling oranges. They'd been watching a television movie, and Griffin had fallen asleep almost right away. Ellen had gotten angry and shook him awake, saying it was no fun watching a movie alone. He'd straightened up, tried to pay attention, but then fell asleep again. He'd awakened when she snapped the TV off. "You missed everything," she said. "And it was really good."

"Was it?" he'd asked, following her to bed.

"Yes. It was the best thing I've ever seen on television." She switched off the light, turned angrily onto her side. He lay awake for a while, staring at the ceiling. He didn't understand her reaction—it was all out of proportion. What was the big deal? He thought about talking to her about it, but she was so damn crabby. He'd gotten out of bed to make a sandwich, sat at the kitchen table reading the editorials in the newspaper, then a magazine; then he had come back to bed, willing to talk it out. But she had fallen asleep. Why wake her up and get her going again? Better to let it pass.

Now he held his glass up to Donna. "Cheers."

She clinked her glass to his, and he took a long swallow. Better.

Donna took a pan from the oven, and lifted meat and vegetables onto a platter. He loved watching this, he had always loved the ritualistic and cleanly simple demonstrations of domestic life. He liked the satisfaction in routines, in chores completed; he liked the concrete nature of those things in a world grown increasingly abstract. Man. Woman. Food. Drink. It was good.

"I hope you like it when everything is overcooked," she said. "I like pot roast so that it's falling apart."

"Me, too," Griffin said. He was hungry. His mouth watered at the sight of the rich brown gravy she poured over the platter.

They ate in a large dining room at a black lacquered table. "This is very good," Griffin said. And then, later, after another glass of wine, "Is this . . . **your** house?"

She looked around the room as though she too were seeing it for the first time. "Not in spirit. To tell the truth, I never liked it—this is all Michael's taste. I didn't want the house, but he insisted I take it as part of the settlement—guilt, you know. I need someplace smaller. But I just haven't gotten motivated enough to move." She pushed the remaining food around on her plate, then looked up. "Can I get you some more?"

"No, thanks. Let me help you clean up."

"Not quite yet," she said. "You just stay there." She took their dinner plates into the kitchen, then came back to the table carrying a wildly lopsided pie. She set it down in front of him.

"Well!" he said.

She began laughing. "I think it **tastes** good, though."

And it did. It was cherry, Griffin's favorite, and together they ate nearly half of it. When they had finished, Donna leaned back in her chair and groaned. "I never eat this much. It's fun to eat with you!"

"It is?"

"Yes, you're . . . Well, you're very appreciative." She looked at his empty plate, from which he'd scraped every last bit of pie.

He laughed. "I've never been a problem eater. I was a chubby kid—my father used to call me 'Whale Belly.' "

"Ohhhh," Donna said. "Did it hurt your feelings?"

"I don't know."

She stood up, began stacking dishes. "How can you not know? It must have! I got called 'Lard-Butt' by one of my cousins—just once—and I've never forgotten it."

He followed her into the kitchen, insisted on being the one to at least load the dishwasher. "You were never fat, though," he said.

"I was." She leaned against the counter, swirled the wine she had left in her glass. They'd finished the bottle, begun another. "Yup, I surely was."

"I don't believe it." He closed the dishwasher and looked up, found his face very close to hers. "I mean, you're . . . Well, you must know this, Donna. You're a very attractive woman. Very sexy."

She smiled, looked into his eyes for a long moment, and then leaned forward to kiss him. She was so warm, so good tasting. He pulled her closer. When they broke, he stepped back from her, not sure of what he was meant to do next. She put her glass on the counter, then asked, "Would you like to see the rest of the house?"

He didn't look at her. "Yes. Sure."

She showed him around downstairs, taking him into the study, the living room, the library. Then she led him upstairs, to a large bedroom at the end of a long hall. "And this, of course, is . . . this." She took his hand, led him to her bed, pulled him gently down to lie beside her and kissed him again. Her skin was so softly, wonderfully perfumed, and her hair, unpinned now and loose about her face, was as silky as he'd imagined it might be. But he felt nothing that he wanted to. He was limp, unaroused. His palms were wet. Zoe's face suddenly appeared before him. **"Dad!"** she would say.

Griffin pulled away, cleared his throat. "I'm sorry.

I think I'm . . . I guess I'm a little nervous." He sat up on the edge of the bed.

"I'm not expecting—"

"Oh, I know!"

"I just thought—"

"Right! I'm just . . . It's just been a long time since . . ." He looked at her, smiled helplessly.

She sat up beside him, repinned her hair, straightened her sweater. "I'm sorry. I guess I had a bit too much wine—I didn't really mean to do this. But you're the first person I've met that I've felt any attraction to since . . ."

"I have to tell you something. I have a really hard time understanding why you're attracted to me."

"Really?"

"Yeah. I mean, I don't see myself as someone a woman like you would be interested in."

"But you're so . . ." She touched the side of his face. "You know what I think? I think you've been living too long with someone who hasn't the slightest idea of how wonderful you are." He started to protest and she said, "No. I can tell, believe me. You think you're not attractive because your wife has been telling you that, one way or another, for years. But you're so open, so caring. And you're quite attractive, yourself—you have a **very** charming cowlick."

Reflexively, he reached up and she stopped him.

"I like it! And you know what I like best about you? That you waved at yourself in your Santa suit."

"Oh, terrific. You saw that?"

"I see a lot about you," she said. "Now. What do you say we get out of here and go somewhere? Want to go to a late movie?"

He stood up, grateful. "Anything you want to see?"

"Let's go to the Music Box. Even if we don't like the movie, it's always fun to go there."

He'd heard of the unique movie theater, but had never gone there. Ellen had mentioned it a couple of months ago after reading an article about it in the paper, and she had suggested that they go that night. But they had not. She was carrying on about how there were twinkling **stars** and moving **clouds** on the ceiling, and he, frankly, was thinking about how difficult it would be to park in that part of town; he hated dealing with lousy parking.

But now he put on his coat uncomplainingly and headed with another woman to the place he'd denied his wife. It nagged at him, but only a little. Surely Ellen was doing favors for Mr. Flywheel, and had been for some time.

Before he started the engine, he looked over at Donna. "I want you to know, I . . . I mean, I hope this doesn't spoil our chances of—"

"We've got lots of time, Griffin. Let's go to the movies."

As Griffin turned to back out of the driveway, he caught a glimpse of Donna. All these years of having Ellen on the seat beside him, and now here was a relative stranger, whom he had just gotten off a bed with. Life was so arbitrary. What if it had been Donna's profile he'd grown used to? He could have been married to someone like her, lived in a house that differed radically from his own. It was Ellen who had always dictated the style of the places they'd lived. She preferred a warm and somewhat cluttered look; "eclectic," she'd called it, though Griffin called it sloppy. You could see Ellen in every room—in the books she left lying open on the armrests of chairs, in casual arrangements of the rocks and shells she collected, in the changing displays of things she brought in from outside: forsythia and lilacs in the spring, blue delphinium from her garden in the summer, bowls full of red and gold leaves in the fall, holly berry draped on the mantel in the winter. You could see Ellen in the wear of the furniture, the familiar sloping of the cushions in the chairs she favored.

She started sewing projects and left them on the dining room table; she drank half her coffee and left the mug on the hall radiator. It always annoyed him. And yet Donna's house, with all its elegance, was cold and uncomfortable—no place he'd want to hang around. When he got to know Donna better, he'd help her sell it and find another place that suited her better.

They found a parking place nearly directly in front of the theater. "I don't believe this!" Griffin said, and Donna laughed, saying she always had good luck with parking. "Stick with me, kid," she said, and though he smiled at her, another part of himself grew cold and said, **Don't.**

They agreed to buy tickets for whatever movie the people ahead of them were going to; neither of them knew anything about what was playing. Donna had said that she would buy the tickets, and Griffin had just said no, he would pay, when he saw Ellen. She was standing in the crowded lobby beside a young man Griffin had assumed was there with someone else until he put his arm around Ellen, then looked down at her smiling face and kissed her quickly. He thought, for one red instant, about attacking the guy, then quickly got his emotions under control. He shoved his hands in his pockets, stared at the man. For God's sake, he had a **pony**tail! And he was wearing a white turtleneck sweater with his blue jeans. Ellen hated turtleneck sweaters. For that matter, she hated ponytails, too, hadn't she once told him that? Or was it that she'd said she hated businessmen wearing ponytails. Yes, that was it.

Griffin continued to stand immobilized until he noticed Donna moving up to the ticket window and requesting two tickets. He stepped up beside her, apologized for his inattentiveness, saying he'd just seen someone he knew, and paid for the tickets. Then he put his arm around Donna and led her into the lobby. He was halfway across when Ellen saw him. Her face froze, and Griffin could tell she was considering moving away. But she didn't. She glanced briefly at Donna, said something to Peter, then stood straight, waiting.

"Hello, Ellen," Griffin said, his voice remarkably smooth and even. Beside him, he felt Donna stiffen, then move slightly away, out from under his arm. Griffin thrust his hand forward, toward Peter. "I'm Frank Griffin."

"Peter Galloway." He was calm, guardedly friendly. For an adolescent, his confidence level was pretty high, Griffin thought. Peter nodded at Donna, then, and Griffin said, "Ellen, Peter, this is Donna." He realized with horror that he'd forgotten her last name. But she smoothly extended her hand toward Peter, then Ellen, and greeted them warmly, supplying her last name of "Parsons." **Remember!** Griffin told himself. **Like the actress.**

"What are you seeing?" Ellen asked. There was a

look on her face now of weary reserve, a look completely different from the one Griffin had seen her giving Peter. That look had been relaxed, full of joy.

Griffin told her what movie they'd selected, and Ellen nodded. She and Peter would be seeing it, too. The line began to move into the theater, and Ellen said, "Enjoy it," then pushed forward.

Donna hung back. "We don't have to go. This must be terrible for you."

"Not at all." He moved forward, staring straight ahead. He wanted to keep track of Ellen and Peter, he wanted to see where they sat. He wanted to sit behind them. They were holding hands now, he saw, and sharing some confidence, undoubtedly about him. Griffin had an impulse to grab Peter by the ponytail and alert him to the fact that Ellen would come with very little money, did he know that?

Griffin chose seats several rows behind Ellen. "Griffin," Donna said.

"What? These are good seats. They're just good seats. Do you want to move?"

She sat down, and Griffin, making a point of looking only at Donna, made sure nonetheless that he had a good view of Ellen. He could see her looking discreetly left and right, trying to locate him, and enjoyed the fact that she did not find him. When the movie started, he reached over for

Donna's hand. Then, though he pretended to watch the movie, he watched Ellen and Peter instead.

Twice, he kissed her. Once on the cheek, and once on the top of her head. On the top of her head, like he was her goddamn father! When the lights came up, Griffin rose rapidly. He wanted out of there, he didn't want to see them anymore.

The ride home with Donna was silent, awkward. He walked her to the door and started to follow her in. But she stopped him, saying, "What are you doing?"

He smiled. "I thought I'd just come in and maybe we could take up where we left off."

She nodded. "I see. Well, I'm not interested in being your means for revenge. I like you very much, Griffin, but I haven't been with you tonight since we saw your wife. I don't blame you; I understand. But don't come in my house and use me to hurt her."

He stood quietly for a moment. "It wouldn't be that."

"Maybe not all. But mostly."

He nodded. "I'm sorry." He took her hand, kissed it. "Next time, let's rent a movie."

She laughed. "Okay."

"I'm really sorry."

"Forget it. I'll see you another time."

*       *       *

He drove home, overwhelmed with conflicting feelings. Primary among these was his anger with Ellen. Peter was so young! That had to be why Ellen had dyed her hair. She was having a full-blown midlife crisis, and everyone around her was having to pay the price.

He walked into the darkened house, switched on the kitchen light, and saw Ellen sitting at the kitchen table. They were both surprised. "What are you doing here?" he asked.

"I was just going to ask you that."

"I live here."

"Well, so do I."

"Why are you sitting in the dark like a crazy person?"

"I'm thinking."

"I'll bet you are." He got a spoon, then went to the freezer and pulled out a half gallon of chocolate chip ice cream. Then he sat at the table with Ellen and began to eat it. "Why aren't you spending the night with Lancelot? Or isn't he toilet trained yet?"

"Very funny."

"Jesus, Ellen. It's really weird. You're old enough to be his mother."

"Not quite, Griffin."

He spoke around a mouthful of ice cream. "Give me a break. What is he, twenty-one?"

"Twenty-seven."

He rolled his eyes, took another huge mouthful of ice cream. Ellen got up for a glass, then poured herself a good-sized serving of wine. "It is not unusual for a younger man to be attracted to an older woman." She sat down, took a sip of her wine. Then, quickly, another.

"And vice versa. Right, Ellen?"

"Yes. We find each other very attractive. That's right."

"So why aren't you with him now?"

She looked into her glass. "We had a disagreement."

"Really!"

She looked up, challenging him. "Yes. Really."

He pointed to her glass. "Give me a sip, would you?"

She sat immobile, and he reached over and helped himself, then set the glass back in front of her, moving it with exaggerated care very slightly to the left so that it would be exactly where it was.

"I didn't say you could have any of my wine," she said.

"Didn't say I couldn't, either."

She pulled his ice cream toward her, took a gigantic bite of it. Griffin rose, went to the cupboard and returned with a tablespoon for her. "Help yourself. **I** don't mind sharing."

"The hell you don't."

He stopped his spoon midbite. "What's that supposed to mean?"

"Nothing."

"No, you—"

**"Nothing.** I just said it. I just felt like saying it, okay? I felt like being mean." She looked away from him and ran her hand through her hair, that old gesture. It was as close as she could come to an apology; he knew that.

They sat quietly for a while, eating ice cream, drinking wine. And then Griffin said, "Well, what did you fight about?"

"You, actually." Ellen's eyes had the bleary look they got whenever she drank. Griffin was feeling a quarter past mellow, himself. He was feeling . . . generous, in fact. He would listen to all she had to say about Lug Nuts and not get upset at all.

"He thought I was . . . preoccupied with you."

"Did he."

"Yes."

"Were you?"

**"No!** I mean, I was a little . . . It **was** bizarre, seeing you there. With that Donna." She took another swallow of her wine, finishing her glass. "You know, I hate that name. It's such a **non** name. I mean, no offense, she was very pretty. And seemed very nice. Very nice."

He scraped the bottom of the carton for more ice cream—it was almost gone. "Yeah, she is very pretty." He held the carton out to Ellen. "Want the last of it?"

"No. I'm stuffed."

"Hey, no pain, no gain."

She smiled, then laughed out loud. He watched her, his teeth hurting from so much ice cream, then laughed with her. Then he said, "Let's go out."

She stopped laughing. "What do you mean?"

"I don't know. Want to go to Halsted Street and hear some blues?"

"We've never gone there!"

"I'm asking you if you want to go." He brought his dishes over to the sink and washed them.

"Why do you always do that?" Ellen asked.

"What?"

"Why do you always have to immediately clean up every dish you use?"

"Well, what should I do with dirty dishes, Ellen? Decorate the house with them, as you do?"

"Yes! Yes, you should! Every once in a while, you should just let something lie there! You're so . . . You need to just loosen up a little, Griffin."

He stared at her, wondered if he were weaving a bit. Then he took her glass from her and brought it into the living room. "What do you think?" he called. "The mantel?"

She came into the living room, giggling a little. "The lamp," she said. "Put it on the lamp."

When he laid it carefully on the top of the shade, she applauded. "Good!"

The phone rang then, and Ellen's face turned serious. "Something's happened to Zoe." She walked quickly into the kitchen, picked up the receiver, and said hello. And then she said, "Oh," and turned her back to Griffin.

"No, I did not," she said.

She was quiet for a while, listening. Then she said, "Well, I should think so. At least." Her tone was soft, flirtatious.

"I can't now," she said, taking a quick look at Griffin, who sat near her at the kitchen table. "No, I can't. Let's just—"

She listened, laughed. "Oh, all **right.**"

She hung up and turned around. "I'm . . . going out."

He sat motionless while she got her coat and her purse. Then he called out for her to wait a minute.

He came into the hall, where she had her hand on the doorknob. "Hold on, Ellen; I want to ask your opinion about something."

He picked up the glass he'd laid on top of the lamp and hurled it at the fireplace. The sound of the glass breaking was high and bright and satisfyingly loud, an epithet in silica and silicates, a splendid piece of nonverbal communication, he thought. Quite economical, too—so much contained in so little. Wonderfully specific. "How's that?" he asked. But by the time he turned around, she was gone.

# Chapter 15

**·················**

Griffin awakened to the sound of Ellen's voice. It was low, musical. She was talking to Zoe—he heard his daughter's high, excited responses. Apparently Zoe was back from her sleepover and wanted to go outside and play with the neighborhood boys. Ellen was negotiating with her to put the things in her overnight bag away first. "Put your dirty clothes in the hamper, put your toothbrush back in its holder, and put your duffel bag back in your closet. That's all you have to do. That's not so much, Zoe."

Griffin heard the muffled thump of Zoe's falling onto the stairs, her position of choice for protest. She would be assuming the whine-and-sigh position, becoming the boneless mass of flesh she transformed herself into when she didn't want to do something. It was a miracle, really; her weight actually seemed to increase—Griffin knew from the times he'd tried to pick her up when she was like this. "Come on, Zoe, let's get going," he'd say, and Zoe would hang lifeless from the circle of Griffin's arms, nearly breaking them.

"Can't **you** do it, Mom?"

"I told you to, Zoe."

"Why do **I** have to do it?"

"Well. Whose things are they?"

"Yeah, but you're the **mother.**"

"Yes, I am. So?"

A pause, and then Zoe said, "So it's your **job!**"

"My job," Ellen said, "is to teach you to take care of yourself someday. Now, do what I asked you to do, or you will not go outside."

"They're **waiting.**"

"Well, the sooner you do it, the less time they'll have to wait."

**"Okay!"** Zoe stomped up the stairs, slammed the door to her room.

Griffin got out of bed and went to knock at her door. "I'm **doing** it!" she yelled.

He opened the door, and Zoe said, "Oh." She was sitting on her bed, the contents of her duffel bag spread out around her.

"What seems to be the problem?"

"Mommy. She's in a bad **mood.**"

"Is that right."

"Yes."

"What makes you say so?"

"Because she is so **crabby.**"

Griffin sat beside her. "And why is it that Mommy's so crabby?"

Zoe shrugged, ran her toothbrush absentmindedly through her hair. **"I** don't know." She got up to throw her empty duffel bag into her closet. "She makes me do **everything.**"

"Like put your things away."

"Yeah."

"That's why she's in a bad mood."

**"Yeah."**

"I see."

Zoe picked up her dirty clothes. "Will you put these in the hamper?"

"I think you can do that, Zoe."

"I got **other** stuff to do, Dad!"

**"I've** got other **things** to do."

"Fine. **I've.**"

"Well, you'd better do what you have to, so that you can do what you want."

Zoe sighed, then gathered her clothes together and went down the hall to the hamper. Then Griffin heard her clattering down the stairs, saying, "Mom! I'm done!"

"You did everything?"

**"Yes!"**

"All right. Be home at noon for lunch. We'll have pizza."

"Okay. Oh—Mom, will you feed my ant?" A pause, and then, "All right, I know, **You can do it, Zoe.**"

"That's right," Ellen said. And then, "What's the matter with you today, Zoe? Are you tired?"

"No! I just feel like taking the day off!"

"Ah. Well, another day, perhaps."

The door slammed. Griffin went back to the bedroom and got his robe, his slippers. He was reluctant to go downstairs after what had happened last night; he was embarrassed about his behavior. After Ellen pulled away from the curb, he'd cleaned up the glass and taken it out to the trash. He'd stood outside for a while, looking up at the stars and shivering. Then he'd come inside and finished the bottle of wine he and Ellen had been drinking and gone to bed. He'd lain there, imagining the things Ellen would report to her sympathetic boyfriend, emphasis on **boy.** "And then he threw a wineglass across the room," Ellen would say, and Peter would say, "What? **What?**"

"Yes," she would say, nestled against his chest.

"If he ever hurts you, I'll kill him," Motor Man would say. And then, in an act of supreme consolation, he would make love to her, so tenderly. Well, so what? What difference would one more time make? They'd been at it for a long time, now.

Griffin stood at the mirror, raked through his hair with his fingers. His mouth was dry, his head hurt, his eyeballs felt heavy in his skull. Hangover.

He came into the kitchen, where Ellen was. He nodded at her, then sat at the kitchen table.

"Coffee?" she asked, her back to him.

"No thanks. Zoe's tired, huh?"

Ellen came to sit across from him. "I guess so."

"You know, maybe we shouldn't let her—"

"I'm moving out, Griffin." Her voice was impossibly flat.

He stared at her, could not speak. Finally, he said, "Look, I'm sorry about the glass, okay? I don't know why that happened. You know I never do things like that. I'm sorry."

"It's not because of that, Griffin. I understood that. Actually, I was kind of glad to see you react to something. To me."

He would never understand her. She liked him throwing glasses. Maybe she did have a brain tumor. "What are you talking about, Ellen? I didn't **react** to you before? What are you **talking** about?"

"Oh, Griffin. You know, this whole thing is so . . . It's so hard to talk about. But one of the reasons I want to leave is . . . Well, it's **true!** You don't ever react to me as **me.** I mean, you live your own, neat, circumscribed life. You have what you want; you see what you want to see. You are so impenetrably self-satisfied. I feel like this package you carry around and never open. You—"

He held up his hand. "Stop. I get the point. Just . . . stop. Stop telling me how I failed with you. Stop calling me a failure."

"I'm **not!** I'm **not** calling you a failure! I'm just trying to tell you why we don't **work** together, as far as **I'm** concerned." He stared at her moving mouth, thought about how up and down their block people were having normal conversations, making plans for what to do that night. He heard the shouts of children, the barking of dogs. Birds gathered at feeders, clouds moved across the blue sky. And here he sat, disintegrating.

Ellen started to get up, then sat down again. "You know, **you** can have an opinion about us! You can tell me whatever you want! I'll listen! What **do** you think, Griffin? I mean, **truly.**"

He was so amazingly tired. His headache had worsened. He stared at the tabletop. Then he said, "Didn't we . . . sort of . . . **have** something last night, Ellen? Weren't we having fun? Wasn't it really comfortable, being together like that? Doesn't it **mean** something, to have that kind of comfort?"

"Yes." Her voice was quiet now.

"I mean, there we were, laughing and talking, and then you get this phone call from Opie and you just . . . **leave.**"

"Griffin. You and I get along, sometimes. We get along almost all the time. But that's not enough."

"So what does he do, Ellen? What is better with him? What does he give you that I can't?" He asked this question, but he was thinking, **Don't tell me. Don't tell me. Don't say it.**

She leaned back in her chair. "You know, I don't think I even know, Griffin. It's just that I . . . open up with him."

"So to speak," he said, bitterly.

"Yes. I do open up with him sexually. But also, I open up to him intellectually. He cares about what I think, about how I **think,** what I **am."**

He stood up. It was crazy for him to sit here and ask such questions. The answers killed him, a piece at a time. He felt like vomiting. And his **head.** He moved to the window, looked out, asked, "When are you leaving?"

"Today."

He turned around. "You're kidding."

"No. I think it's better to do it on the weekend to give Zoe time to recover a little."

"But you don't have anywhere to go! I thought you said you weren't going to move in with him!"

"I'm not."

"Well, you can't have found a place already."

"I looked at a place a few weeks ago. I called this morning and it's still available."

**When** had she called? How could she do this, walk around full of such secrets? What kind of person did such a thing? Somewhere inside him, a vital seam threatened, then gave. He clenched a fist, made himself go blank.

"How much is this going to cost?" he asked.

"I have money."

"From where?" Oh, God, please, not from him.

"Birthday money from my parents, things like that. I've been saving for a while."

"You've been saving for a while."

"Yes."

She might as well have been telling him about the sixteen people she'd murdered and buried under the front porch.

He walked across the kitchen, then turned and stood at the threshold. "We're going to tell Zoe today."

"Yes. Good, I'm glad you agree we should tell her together."

"We are going to tell Zoe, and then, immediately afterward, I want you the **fuck** out of here, Ellen."

Her mouth tightened and she looked away from him, muttered something he did not hear and did not ask her to repeat.

He sat on the edge of the bed for a while, thinking. He shouldn't have been in his pajamas when she told him. He should have been power-dressed—he should have at least been dressed. Everything he did lately was wrong.

So. This was the last morning he'd wake up to the sound of Ellen and Zoe's voices. When Zoe was a baby and would awaken in the middle of the night, Griffin would lie in bed and listen to Ellen talking to her. He'd hear the creak of the rocker moving back and forth, he'd hear the little stories she would tell Zoe as she nursed her. She would make up tales about friendly giants who had weaknesses for chocolate cake, about cats who talked on the phone to other cats, about fairies who lived behind the walls of houses, in houses of their own. She would tell Zoe the names of all her relatives (and Aunt Lottie in Nebraska? She makes the most **wonderful** sugar cookies, Zoe, bigger than your whole **head**). She would tell Zoe the names of the flowers in the garden, of the trees that lined the block. She would sing nonsense songs that comforted with their words and melody, in the same way that a few simple notes, played on a piano in a certain way, could move you.

What Griffin liked best, though, was when Ellen told Zoe what they would do the next morning, all about Zoe's bath and breakfast, her apricots and her yellow towel; how afterward they would take their usual morning walk to the grocery store, and maybe they would see Bennie the dog lying on McPherson's porch, and how they would buy things for dinner—for **Zo**e and for **Mom**my and for **Dad**dy. Always, it was that last detail that, however exhausted he might be, he stayed awake for, because it told him he belonged. And it told him he wasn't dreaming, that the plain beauty of his wife talking to his baby daughter about the life they all lived together was something he really had, and could keep.

He never told Ellen he could hear her. He was afraid if he did, she would stop doing it.

He was sitting at the edge of the bed, had just finished tying his sneakers, when Ellen came into the bedroom. She avoided looking at him. Instead, she went straight to her closet and took out a suitcase, then laid it on the bed Griffin had just made. She began filling it with clothes. He watched her for a while in silence, but when she picked up some sweaters, then decided against them and put them back in the drawer, he said, "Take them. I don't want anything of yours in my dresser."

She turned around and he saw with some surprise that she was crying. "I can't take everything now, Griffin. Obviously I can't take everything now. I'll get it eventually. For now, I can only take a few things."

She added underwear to the suitcase, a couple pairs of jeans. Then she zipped the bag and sat on the bed beside Griffin. She did not appear to be breathing.

"Don't you need pajamas?" he asked.

"Oh! Yes." She got up and took a pair from the drawer, added them to the suitcase. Then she sat down again, her hands folded in her lap, staring straight ahead. She cried quietly, steadily, occasionally reaching up to wipe the tears from her face.

Griffin sighed. "You need your toothbrush, Ellen, and you need . . . I don't know, don't you need your hair things? Your brush and barrettes, and those things you use for ponytails, for when you wear a ponytail? And you need your makeup, sometimes you like to wear makeup." And then he was crying, and she was holding on to him saying over and over that she was sorry, she was so sorry. He stroked her hair, spoke softly. "It's okay, Ellen. We'll work everything out. Don't cry." But she did not stop, nor did he, for a long time.

Finally, he got up and crossed the room, leaned against the dresser and asked her if she would like to talk about how to tell Zoe.

She nodded, sniffling. A long, shuddering sigh. And then, straightening, "Yes. Let me just wash my face, and then, yes, I would like to."

"You should be the one to tell her," Griffin said,

when Ellen came back to the bedroom. "You must have been thinking about this for a while. You must have something in mind. I want you to tell her, but I'll be there."

She nodded. "I thought I would just say that I needed some time alone to think about some things. I know she's going to ask if we're getting divorced and I'm going to just say no for now, Griffin, all right?"

"I don't know. Is that smart? Maybe we should just be honest and get the whole thing over with."

"I think we should take it one step at a time. Let her get used to us being apart and see that it's not so terrible, before we tell her it's going to be permanent."

"All right."

She swallowed, started to speak, then stopped. And then she said, "Does your stomach hurt?"

"Yes."

"Yeah. Mine, too."

He had no idea what to say, settled on "Right."

"So I'll be here every day after school, until you come home, and on your nights out. Can you get her off to school?"

"Yes." He thought about Zoe and him having breakfast alone. It might not be so bad—Ellen had never been a model of morning cheerfulness. He and Zoe liked certain things that Ellen didn't:

sausage, pineapple-orange juice, eggs scrambled dry and not wet, as Ellen preferred. He'd take Zoe to the grocery store today, and they'd pick out things together. They'd have a good time; Griffin would make it a good time.

The door slammed, and they both stiffened and looked at the clock. Eleven. They walked downstairs together. There was Zoe at the foot of the stairs, looking up at them, and Griffin had a thought to take Ellen by the elbow, bring her back upstairs, and say, "I can't."

But he did not. Instead, he watched Ellen kiss Zoe's forehead, then say, "You're home early. Are you hungry?" Her voice had a quality of distracted control, as though she were speaking while carrying an overly full water glass across a room.

Zoe took off her jacket, hung it on the low hook Griffin had put up for her inside the closet. "No. I'm not so hungry."

"Just felt like coming home?" Ellen asked.

**"Nooooo."**

Ellen looked quickly at Griffin, then said, "What's going on?"

Zoe walked into the kitchen, slumped into a chair. "I **hate** Eliot Bensen!"

"What happened?" Griffin asked, coming quickly into the room.

Zoe ran her hand along the edge of the table, her

chin trembling. Griffin saw a Band-Aid on her thumb and thought, **Enough. No more today.**

Ellen sat beside Zoe. "What did he do?"

"He called me Dumbo. Because of my ears."

Ellen sighed. "He's at it again, huh?"

"What do you mean?" Griffin asked. "He's done it **before?**" He knew where Eliot lived. He could go over there. He'd be happy to go over there.

**"Dad,"** Zoe said.

"It's just when they fight," Ellen said. "When they get into a fight, Eliot does this."

"It's **not** just that," Zoe said. "He says they all decided I can't play with them anymore. He says I have to play with **girls."**

". . . Oh," Ellen said.

Zoe looked quickly at her, then away.

"So . . . how do you feel about that?" Ellen asked.

Zoe stood up, pushed her chair in. "I'm going to my room." She sped upstairs, and they heard her door softly close.

"Ellen," Griffin said, "we can't—"

"I know what you're going to say, Griffin. But this is nothing unusual. It comes up all the time. Then it blows over and she's right out there with them again. It usually happens when she beats Eliot at something, which is often. She'll be back out with them this afternoon. Believe me."

She began to assemble ingredients to make pita

bread pizzas, one of Zoe's favorites. "Want one?" Ellen asked, her back to him. And he said no, and he could tell she was glad. It would weigh too much, her making lunch for him, too.

He went outside to see if he could catch sight of the group of boys Zoe played with. No kids around but the three little girls who lived across the street, bundled up in their snowsuits and chasing each other across their front lawn.

He came back inside and went upstairs, knocked on the door to Zoe's room. "Zoe?"

Nothing.

He started to push the door open and she yelled, "No!"

"Zoe? Can I come in?"

A pause, and then, "Okay."

He came in and saw her lying stretched out on her bed. In the corner was her panda, apparently flung there just before she told Griffin to come in.

He sat on the bed beside her, pushed her hair back behind her ear. Quickly, she reached up and pulled the hair back over it. "Don't."

"You know what, Zoe?"

"What?"

"Sometimes when people are angry, they say things they don't really mean."

Zoe rolled her eyes. "He means it, Dad. My ears are big."

"They're not so big."

"Yes, they are! They stick out for about five hundred miles! Everybody says so!"

"I don't think they stick out so far. I think they are lovely ears, and I think they just might need some earrings."

She wouldn't look at him, but one eyebrow raised.

"Yes, I think some nice little birthstone studs would be nice. Don't you?"

She looked at him. "You said I can't pierce my ears until I'm a hundred years old."

"I don't think I said one **hundred.**"

"Yes, you did, one time. But usually you only say, 'Not until you're six**teen.'**"

"Move over," he said, and then lay down beside her. "Tell me something, Ms. Griffin. Do you believe that people have the right to change their minds?"

"Yes. I guess so."

"Well, I have changed my mind about you getting your ears pierced."

**"Really?"**

"Yes."

Her face clouded. "But Mommy won't let me."

"Oh, I think she might. I think she might have changed her mind, too."

"No, she hasn't."

"I think she has."

"Why?"

He shrugged. "I just do. Let's go tell her."

"Can I get my tongue pierced, too?"

"No. And Zoe?"

"Yeah?"

"Don't lie on your bed with shoes on."

She looked down at her red high-tops, wiggled her feet. "You mean these? These aren't shoes, Dad. They are expeditors."

"I see. Well, keep them off the bed, and come down to lunch."

In the kitchen, Ellen had set a place for Zoe, and the pizzas were on a cookie sheet on the table, covered with sauce and vegetables. "You want to grate the cheese, Zoe?" Ellen asked.

"You said I can't anymore!"

"It's time to try again. But I want you to be careful. Remember what happened to your knuckles last time. You have to go slowly."

She handed Zoe a block of mozzarella, laid some waxed paper on the table, and Zoe began grating furiously. **"Slow**ly," Ellen said, and Zoe began grating in extreme slow motion until Ellen said, "Not **that** slow," whereupon she happily sped up again.

Griffin watched silently, as did Ellen. When Zoe had finished, Ellen put the pizzas in the oven, then said, "Zoe, I'd like to talk to you about something."

Ah. Here it was. Griffin crossed his arms, leaned back against the kitchen wall.

Zoe scooped up some of the cheese left over on the waxed paper, dropped it into her mouth. "I am an **excellent** cook!" One little girl, sitting on her knees on a kitchen chair, happy. One little girl, held up high between the fingers of her parents, about to be dropped.

"Sweetie?" Ellen moved her chair to be closer to Zoe. "Listen. I have something to tell you. It's about something I want to try for a while, something different from the way we live now. I will see you every single day, but I'm going to be moving to a different place, to a little apartment very near here."

Zoe stopped chewing. "What?"

"I'm going to be moving today to a place very close by. An apartment. I'll be here every day after school, just like always, but Daddy will get you ready for school in the mornings."

She frowned. "What do you **mean?**"

"Well, I'm going to live in another place for a while so I can think about some things."

"What things? What did I do?"

"Oh, Zoe, nothing. You didn't do anything. I just . . ." She looked up at Griffin, who quickly shook his head. **Uh-uh. You do it.**

"See, sometimes when people are really thinking hard about their life, they need to—"

"You're getting a divorce. Are you getting a divorce?"

"Did I say that?"

". . . No." She looked at Griffin. "Are you, Dad?"

He picked her up, sat her on his lap, and she pushed off him and stood before him, her hands on her hips. "Tell me! I'm not a stupid baby!"

"Mommy did tell you," he said. "She wants to go and think about some things. That's all." The buzzer for the pizzas sounded, ridiculously. "I'm not hungry," Zoe said. "I **told** you I wasn't hungry!"

"All right," Ellen said. "That's fine. You can eat later." She took the pizzas out of the oven, put them on the counter. Then she came back to the table, sat down.

"I need to go away for a while to be by myself. You know how sometimes Daddy goes on a business trip? Well, it's like that. Only now I'm the one who's going."

"Can I come?"

"Well . . . No. I will bring you there to visit very soon, but you will live here."

"Why can't you decide things here?"

Ellen nodded, as though agreeing with an answer that had not yet been given. Then she said, "Because sometimes a person just needs a lot of quiet in which to think."

"I'll be quiet."

"Oh, it's not that, honey. It's not that kind of quiet. It's not that kind of quiet on the inside. It's deep on the inside, like a holy place that is just in you. Do you know what I mean?"

To Griffin's surprise, Zoe said, quite calmly, "Yes." And then, "But you will come back."

"Well, I . . . Yes, I'll come back."

"When?"

Ellen hesitated, then said, "I'm not exactly sure, but I think it will be . . . around Christmas. Okay?" She looked quickly at Griffin and he saw the message she was sending him: **A step at a time, remember?**

Zoe shrugged. "Okay." She looked over at the pizzas. "I guess I'll eat." And then, as Ellen placed her food in front of her, "Guess what, Mommy? Dad said I can get my ears pierced!" She looked fiercely at Griffin. **"No backsies."**

"Is that something you really want?" Ellen asked. And when Zoe said yes, Ellen said all right.

After lunch, the group of boys with whom Zoe played came to get her—minus Eliot. Ellen told Zoe goodbye, that she would call her that night, and Zoe kissed her, then quickly put on her jacket and went outside.

"I guess she's all right," Ellen told Griffin, watching Zoe run down the street.

"I guess."

"I didn't do such a great job, telling her."

"There is no good way. You might as well go now, Ellen. I don't think it will help for you to hang around any longer."

She nodded, went upstairs for her suitcase. When she came down, she was all business. "My address is written at the front of the phone book. I'll call you with my number as soon as I get it; it's supposed to be Monday. And I'll have my cell, and—"

"We'll be fine."

"I wish I—"

"We'll be **fine.** Are you sure you have everything you need?"

"I guess so." She smiled. "You know, I used to run away all the time as a little girl. I don't think I ever told you about that. But I could never figure out what to bring then, either."

"It doesn't surprise me."

"Okay, so . . ." She shrugged, pulled the door shut behind her.

He stood still for a long moment, then went upstairs to find the aspirin. Time to take care of himself. The Diana Krall CD that Ellen had never liked. That Cuban cigar Ernie gave him. Tomato juice and vodka, hair of the dog. And next time he was at the drugstore, condoms.

*       *       *

At five in the afternoon, Griffin stood outside Zoe's bedroom door, listening. She was singing in a soft, high voice. He leaned closer, hoping to hear the mood in the music, trying to make sure she was all right. But then the singing stopped abruptly, and Zoe yanked open the door. "Aha!" she said. "Spying!"

Griffin said nothing. Instead, he stood nearly openmouthed, taking in Zoe's outfit. Her usual high-tops. A baseball cap, also usual. A leather lanyard around her wrist, a red-checked flannel shirt. But beneath the flannel shirt, she wore a white formal dress, one she'd been sent by Ellen's Aunt Mary, a remarkable seamstress who believed little girls should be little **girls.** The dress was beautiful, a light, filmy thing that seemed alive, the way it moved. Griffin had seen it on Zoe only once before. It was last Christmas Day, when Ellen had beseeched her to at least try it **on,** after all the work Mary had gone to, my goodness, the seed pearls **alone.** Zoe had tried it on reluctantly, then stood scowling until the exact moment before Ellen took the Polaroid that would be sent to her aunt. "Why don't you tell her I **don't like** this?" Zoe had said. "If you make me smile in the picture, she'll think I **like** it. And then she'll send **more!**"

"You may learn to like it," Ellen had said.

The dress had lived in the bottom of Zoe's closet, until now. Griffin stared until Zoe finally said, **"What,** Dad?"

"Well, it's . . . I'm just surprised to see you wearing that dress, that's all."

Zoe looked down, pulled at the waist. "It's gotten too small."

"Uh huh."

"But it's nice. I like it."

"Yes, me too. Nice piece of work, there. Old Aunt Mary."

"Grace Woodward has a fancy white dress. It's her First Communion dress. It has pearls, too. She **loves** it. She's always putting it on. Plus then she puts on lipstick, too. **Only** a pink color."

"Do you think you'd like to wear lipstick?"

**"I** don't know. Like, what is it for, anyway?"

Griffin thought for a moment. Sexual attraction, he supposed, but he wasn't going to tell her that. "I guess women think a little color on their face makes them look better."

"Mommy looks weird when she puts on makeup."

Griffin came in, sat on the edge of Zoe's bed, picked up the baseball book she'd been reading. **Veeck as in Wreck.** "Where'd you get this?" he asked.

"The librarian. Not at school. The Oak Park library. She has better ideas."

He nodded, paged through the book. Then he stood, clapped his hands together. "How about we go to the Cozy Corner and get a little dinner? Then we'll go to Jewel and get some of your favorite things for breakfast."

"Okay. But wait! Maybe Mommy will call me!"

"Why don't you call her? Tell her we're going out, and you didn't want to miss her."

"Okay. I just have to do something, first." She stood still, waiting.

". . . What?" Griffin asked.

"Can you get out?"

"Oh! . . . Yeah! Sure!" She had never asked him that before. He thought, in a sudden, blind panic, about breasts, bras, her first period.

But then she said, "I have to call Grace."

He smiled, got up, and headed for the door. "Okay."

**Girl talk. Okay.**

"Can I call Mommy from the car?" Zoe loved talking on the cell phone in the car. She said the phone worked better there, but Griffin had an idea that it had more to do with the sort of image Zoe thought she might be projecting.

"Yes," he said. "You can call Mommy from the car."

Something must have shown in his face, then, because Zoe said, "Dad? Do you feel bad?"

"Oh . . . I don't know. A little, I guess. How about you?"

She nodded. "Some, expecially at first. But now it's okay. Because one thing about Mommy, is you have to know something. You have to be careful. She is very gentle."

Griffin stood still for a moment, trying to think what she might mean, keeping himself from correcting her **expecially.** Finally, he said, "Do you mean, she's very **fragile?**"

Zoe pursed her lips, thinking. Then she said. "Yes. But also she is very gentle, too."

". . . Right," he said, and started to close the door. He stopped when he heard Zoe call him.

"Why do girls play dolls?"

"Why? Well, because they like it. It's kind of for them what baseball is to you. And also, I guess it's practicing, for when they have babies."

"How do **they** know they'll have babies?"

"Well, they don't. But they . . . assume they will."

**"I'm** not."

"All right."

"But . . . Dad?" She scratched at her neck, sighed. "Could we play one game of doll tonight?"

"Yes. Yes, we can. As soon as we get home." He would not think of telling her he had no idea how. For the next several weeks, he would know how to do everything. That would be his job, to show her that.

*          *          *

"So now what?" Zoe asked. The Barbie doll had been dug out from under a mountain of toys in Zoe's closet, and she had been dressed in a shimmering apricot-colored evening gown.

"So now . . . she goes out," Griffin said.

"Where?"

He leaned back against the side of Zoe's bed. It was hard to sit cross-legged on the floor anymore; he was getting old. "To a nightclub."

"What for?"

"Well, to dance with Ken."

"I don't have Ken."

"Do you want to ask for him for Christmas?"

She thought for a while, her chin resting on her knee. She smelled of soap and shampoo, was dressed in her pajamas, though the hour was early, only seven. She'd wanted to get ready for bed before they watched **A League of Their Own**— again—but first she'd wanted to 'play doll.'"

"If I get Ken, does it take away something else?"

"What do you mean?"

"Like do I get him instead of something else?"

"No. I think you would get him in addition to other things."

"Oh."

"Should I put him on your Christmas list?"

She lay on her back, sighed. "No. He's boring."

She held the Barbie doll high over her head. "I can see up her skirt."

"Well."

"Want to see?"

"No thanks. What do you say we watch the movie?"

"Okay." There was some regret in her voice.

"If you want to keep playing doll, I will."

"No. It's nothing to it."

"There's nothing to it."

She stood, stashed the doll in her top dresser drawer. "That's what I said." And then, "Uh oh."

"What?"

"I think Amos is dead."

Griffin got up and came over to the cage. "Where is he?"

"I don't know. But before, you could find him, because he'd be moving all around. I think he's dead."

Griffin pushed gently at the shavings, looked carefully. "I don't see him. I think he escaped."

"No," Zoe said. "He didn't." She put the cage on the floor, knelt beside it, and poked around. Then, "Yeah, there he is. He's dead." She put the cage back on the dresser, turned around and burst into tears. "I fed him, and he wouldn't eat!"

"I know you did, Zoe. You took really good care of him."

"He's so **stupid!**"

"Come here, Zoe."

"No."

"Come here." She came to him and put her arms around his neck, sobbed against his shoulder.

"It's okay," Griffin whispered. He rubbed Zoe's back, gently outlined her shoulder blades, her small vertebrae. He closed his eyes, rocked her.

"I miss Mommy."

And now in his own eyes, the prickle of tears. "I know you do, sweetheart."

"Why did she go?"

"Well, I think she tried to tell us both today. What did she say when you talked to her tonight?"

"That she would see me tomorrow. She's coming to get me tomorrow and we're going somewhere special, that's all she said."

"Do you know where?"

"No."

"Well, tomorrow is pretty soon, isn't it?"

She rubbed at her eyes. ". . . Yes."

"Only a few hours away, right?"

"Yes."

He leaned in, spoke to her nose to nose. "Soooooo . . ." He kissed her forehead. "So should we watch the movie and eat some beef jerky?"

"I gotta bury Amos."

"I think the ground's a bit hard, Zoe."

"So what should I do?"

"Well . . ."

"We could flush him. He'd dead, I guess he won't care."

"True."

She got the cage and brought it into the bathroom, Griffin close behind her. Then she dropped the still form of the ant into the toilet. "Rest in peace, amen," she said, and flushed the toilet. She stood silent for a while, then turned around.

"I guess I won't find any more ants for a while."

"I'm surprised you found this one."

"He was in the house. In my room. Mommy really hated him. Dad? Can we get a puppy?"

"Maybe sometime. But not just yet."

"You **always** say that."

"I suppose."

"Dad?" Her face serious now. "Do you think Amos starved to death?"

"No. I think he died of old age. I don't think you had anything to do with his death. I think he ate when you weren't looking. I think he liked living with you very much, and that he died of old age."

"Yeah," Zoe said. "He did like me. I know that."

They put the cage back in Zoe's closet, and then he took her by the hand to lead her somewhere else.

# Chapter 16

Sunday evening, they were eating dinner when Ellen called. Griffin had told Zoe she could have anything she wanted. The menu was buttered noodles, sweet pickles, and ice cream sundaes for dessert with whipped cream from the can— **no restrictions** on the amount used, Zoe added firmly, and made Griffin promise. She was in a hurry to finish the noodles so that she could get to the ice cream, was putting them down at an alarming rate, and Griffin had just said "Slow down so you don't choke!" when the phone rang. Zoe answered it, talked briefly to Ellen, then handed the phone to Griffin.

"How's she doing?" Ellen asked.

"Pretty good." He watched Zoe reload her fork and finish off the noodles.

"She sounded a little sad."

"No. I don't think so. We're getting ready to make ice cream sundaes—we just finished dinner."

"Oh, yeah? What did you have?"

Griffin hesitated. Maybe he should make up a basic-four-food-groups menu. But what the hell. "Noodles and pickles," he said. "Sweet pickles."

Silence.

"Hello?" he said.

"That's all?"

"Yeah. Zoe got to pick what she wanted."

"Maybe you should make a little salad. She likes the raspberry vinaigrette in the fridge. And maybe a little cheese."

Griffin said nothing, nodded yes to Zoe about getting out the ice cream.

"Griffin?"

"Yeah?"

"Can you make her a salad or something?"

"She had pickles," Griffin said, and then, "Listen, we're pretty busy around here. Going to see how much whipped cream will fit on a bowl of ice cream."

"On a **sundae,**" Zoe said, loudly. "We're going to have ice cream **sundaes.** Why? Because it's Sunday!"

"She sounds good," Ellen said, and there was some wistfulness in it. No. He would not tell her to come over.

"Gotta go," he said, and hung up.

He took two bowls from the cupboard. Was Ellen alone? "Ready to make your masterpiece?" he asked Zoe. Probably she was in her apartment, curled up on some secondhand piece of furniture, smiling up at Struts. "You want hot fudge?" he asked Zoe, and she nodded with her whole upper torso. "And two other toppings, too, Dad, I want three!"

"All right, let's see if we have that many." **Want to go out for dinner? Ellen would say. And he would say, Let's order in.**

"We do have that many!" Zoe said. "Remember? We just got them at Jewel when we went! We got strawberry and caramel and hot fudge!" She went to the refrigerator and pulled the jars out, dropping one in the process. "It's okay," she said, quickly picking it up. "It's not broken."

Griffin handed Zoe the ice cream and a serving spoon. "Knock yourself out," he told her.

"Really? Like I can do **anything** and you won't say anything?"

"That's what I promised." It was someone else whom Ellen would wake up to, someone else who would see her tousled hair in the morning. Someone else would comfort her if she had a nightmare, someone else—

**"Dad!"**

"Yeah?"

"Watch!" Zoe loaded her bowl with ice cream, then poured the first of three toppings over it.

"Hold on a minute," Griffin said.

"No fair! You said!"

"I just want to put a plate under that," he said. "It's going to drip all over the place.

Griffin watched Zoe put on more topping, then nuts, then a six-inch pile of whipped cream. And then, as the ice cream tower began falling over, he grabbed the mixing bowl. When the sundae had been safely transferred into the larger vessel, he watched as Zoe put a cherry delicately on top. It was like putting a half-inch bow on a hippo's head.

"Do we have any film?" Zoe asked.

He hesitated, asked gently, "You want to show Mommy?"

"No. I want it for my room, by my bed. And to bring to school!"

Griffin got the camera, took a close-up of Zoe's creation, already melting, and then watched as she knelt on her chair and began eating it. "They have contests with these things, " she said. "There's an ice cream parlor that makes big ones like this and if you eat it all, you get a prize. Can I get a prize if I eat all this?"

"I think maybe this **is** the prize," Griffin said.

"Please? Just, like, one dollar?"

"All right."

**"Yes!"** She shoveled huge mouthfuls of ice cream into her mouth.

"Zoe."

She looked up.

"Not so fast."

She swallowed. "It's a contest, Dad! You have to eat fast!"

"There's no one you're racing."

"Uh huh!" She took another huge mouthful. "The clock!"

He sat at the kitchen table with her, reading the sports page, until she said, "Finished, Dad."

The bowl was empty. He looked at her, amazed.

"I don't feel too good." She undid her pants button. "I think I ate too much."

"Well, I guess so."

"My stomach hurts."

"Zoe, you should have stopped. You must have eaten half a gallon of ice cream!"

"It was a contest! I had to— Wait. I think I have to throw up."

Griffin stood, alarmed. "Do you have to? Do you think you're going to?"

Zoe held up her hand. "Take it easy, Dad. I'm not going to do it here." She sat back in her chair, uttered a very soft **oh,** and vomited all over herself and the floor.

She looked up at Griffin. "Sorry."

Griffin sighed, headed for the mop and bucket. "Get out of those clothes. Just leave them here. Go wash up and put on your pajamas."

"It was a accident!" Zoe said.

**"An** accident," Griffin said wearily.

**"Yes!"**

"Go and change." It always made him feel a little sick, too, when he had to clean up after someone this way. When he was in elementary school, where someone seemed always to be getting sick, he used to feel sympathetic waves of nausea. Once, he had thrown up on the classroom floor moments after another child had, sending the second-grade teacher into a tizzy and thrilling the rest of his classmates. Soon afterward, he and Cynthia Mayfield, the pretty little blond girl whom Griffin told everyone he loved, were lying side by side on cots in the nurse's office, waiting for their mothers to come and take them home.

"You're not even **sick,**" Cynthia had said. "You just want to go home."

It was true. Griffin liked it when he was ill and his mother let him lie in her bed. It had a wide expanse, compared to Griffin's twin-sized mattress. It had four pillows and a comforting smell to the linens that was a blend of his mother and his father. There was a comforter with a silky blue cover, and Griffin used to punch it down to make valleys in which he hid his plastic soldiers from the enemy. His mother would make chicken soup and bring it to Griffin on a tray. She would play Chinese checkers and hangman with him, and she felt his forehead frequently, which he loved: he could smell her perfume and hear the jingle of the charm bracelet she never removed. His father would call to check up on him, and his mother would talk in a low, concerned voice, and Griffin would strain to hear all the **he, he, he's.** He compared notes with Ellen once; all she would say was that her parents were "not that way."

After Griffin cleaned up, he went into Zoe's room and found her lying on her bed in her underwear, reading, the bill of her baseball cap pulled low over her forehead. "I thought I told you to get ready for bed," he said.

She pointed to a pair of pajamas, lying on the floor.

"You might think about putting them on."

"I will." She kept reading.

Griffin pulled the book from her hands. **"Now."**

"Jeez! **Crabby!** I can't help it if I got sick!"

"Zoe, I am not angry at you for getting sick. I just want you to get ready for bed. You have school tomorrow."

"I know it! I'm the one who goes, not you!"

The phone rang, and Griffin said, "I'll be right

back, and when I do, you'd better be ready." Ellen again.

"Okay! You don't have to **yell.**"

"I'm not yelling."

"Are too."

"THIS IS YELLING! YOU SEE THE DIFFER-ENCE?"

She stared at him, and Griffin, embarrassed, left her room and went to answer the phone. He'd tell Ellen to stop her damn calling; she was making everything worse.

But it was not Ellen on the phone; it was Donna, asking if he was ready to start work tomorrow.

"Oh, God," he said, flopping down on the bed. "Is it tomorrow?"

"You forgot?"

"No, I . . ." He got up to close the door, then sat at the edge of the bed. "It's just . . . Ellen moved out today, so it's a little chaotic around here."

"Oh, Griffin, I'm so sorry. I'll get someone else."

"You don't have to. I'll do it. I **want** to; I just for-got for the moment. Listen, can I call you back?"

"Of course. Take your time; I'll be up late."

Griffin went back to Zoe's room. She was in bed, the lights out. He sat down on the bed beside her. "Zoe, I'm sorry I yelled at you. I really am."

Silence.

"Did you brush your teeth?"

"Yes, way before, because my mouth tasted gross."

"Okay, so you're all set then? Ready to go to sleep?"

"I guess." Her voice was so small.

"You okay, Zoe?"

She was quiet for a long time. Griffin watched her bending her panda's ear back and forth. Finally, "I kind of miss Mommy a little. What is she doing right now?"

"Well, I'll bet she's missing you, too."

"Is she sad?"

"I think . . . a little, maybe, because when you miss someone, you feel sad, right? But I also think she's kind of happy."

Zoe looked at him. "Why?"

"Because she's going to see you tomorrow."

"Dad? But **we're** staying here, right?"

"We are."

"One thing is, I do not want to move."

"We will not."

"Okay. Can I have a drink?"

When Griffin came back, Zoe's eyes were closed. He set the water on her nightstand without a sound. Of course she wasn't really asleep yet. But he, too, needed to pretend she was.

Back in his own bedroom, Griffin pulled a pillow over his face. The absolute darkness was comforting, even the slight suffocation. He pulled the pillow closer to his face, then closer, then flung it off. He picked up the phone to call Donna, but then put the receiver back in the cradle. Maybe he should tell her to find someone else. Maybe he shouldn't be doing something that would take him away from the house so often. But then what would he do every night? Sit around the house, pretending not to care that she was gone? No. He liked kids; he needed the diversion; he had said that he would do it.

He dialed Donna's number, and she answered on the first ring.

"Hi," he said. "It's Santa. Are you being good?"

"Oh, Griffin, how are you?"

"I'm all right. It's probably better this way. It was getting too tense, us both being here."

"I know what that's like. But listen, if you do need some time, and you want me—"

"No. Thank you. I'm fine, really." He looked out the window, at the branches moving in the wind that had just picked up dramatically. Did Ellen have a good blanket over there?

"How's your daughter doing?"

"She's fine, she seems to be just fine. Ellen told her she was just going away to think about some things, and that she'd be back."

"Hmmmm."

"What do you think about that?"

"You really want to know?"

"Yes." And now snow was starting. She definitely didn't have a shovel.

"I think it might be easier to be honest."

"That's what I thought, too."

"Well, I'm sure Ellen had her reasons. The good thing is that your daughter—what's her name?"

He wanted, for some reason, not to tell her. As though doing so would make everything too real, or make Zoe more vulnerable than she already was. But he did tell her, and Donna said that she had always loved the name Zoe, that if she had had a daughter she would have named her that, as well.

"Uh huh," Griffin said, and then, "So. Tomorrow night."

"Do you want to bring Zoe?"

"No." He answered too quickly. It was almost rude. "She'll be fine, she'll be with her mother." **Don't suggest that we go out after,** he thought, but then, when Donna said nothing about it, when she said only that the orientation room where they'd met before was now the dressing room, he was disappointed. Did she not want to see him again? Maybe he should ask her if she'd like to go for drinks.

**Let it be,** he thought, and told Donna simply that he would see her tomorrow.

He stood, stretched, and tiptoed back into Zoe's

room. The flakes were falling faster now, furiously. **Oh, Ellen.** He pulled the blanket up over Zoe's shoulder; she was asleep for real now, her mouth partway open, her bear pulled close to her and resting beneath her chin. He envied her her easy escape.

He went downstairs and stood at the window for a while. He'd call the weather line, see how bad it was going to be. He'd find something on television. He would not give in to this mounting pain he felt at the center of himself.

He brought a bag of potato chips, a few slices of cheese, a jar of pepperoncini, a beer, and a pepperoni stick out into the living room, and turned on a movie channel. **The Trip to Bountiful,** one of Ellen's favorites. Not a bad movie, but nothing to get as worked up about as **she** did when she watched it—she would cry every time. Hard to explain, then, the reaction he was having. The way he was crying. For Christ's sake. He wiped his face, changed the channel.

# Chapter 17

• • • • • • • • • • • • • • • • • •

The beard was all wrong, and he had only two minutes before he had to be out there. Griffin stared into the mirror mounted on the wall of the dressing room and yanked again on the side that kept rising up, giving his Santa's face a lop-sided, almost drunken appearance.

The door to the room opened and Ernie walked in. His beard was perfect. "You're up, Griffin." He pulled off his hat, then his wig. His thinning hair was matted flat against his head; the bald parts of his scalp gleamed. "Whew! Hotter than hell out there."

"I can't get this beard right," he told Ernie. "It was fine the other night—I don't know what happened."

Ernie undid his belt, unbuttoned his jacket. Then he came up close to Griffin and inspected his beard. He reeked of Old Spice—it was all Griffin could do not to hold his nose. "Sometimes it's just the strap. Let me have it for a minute." Griffin handed his beard to him, and Ernie made a minor adjustment to the elastic. "Here. Try that."

The beard lay perfectly straight. Griffin put on his hat at a jaunty angle, checked to see that both eyebrows had been whitened evenly, that the lipstick he'd reddened his nose and cheeks with hadn't smeared. And then realized how nervous he was.

Ernie could tell. "Don't worry," he said. "First kid sits on your lap and, I don't know, something happens. You'll see. Most of the kids are just great. Only thing that's really hard are those teenage girls that show up in a group and take turns sitting on your lap, all of them showing off for each other. They can drive you nuts. But I didn't see any of them roving around tonight."

"All right. Well . . . . thanks."

"Good luck!"

Griffin started down the mall, trying to walk quickly, but finding it difficult to do so with his rubber boots. People he passed smiled and sometimes waved. He waved back self-consciously, worried that his belly might slip if he raised his hand too high, but no; it was secure.

When he saw the Santa display, he slowed down—no line yet, not a kid in sight. They were right about how hot this costume was; he could feel a fine line of sweat on his forehead already.

The place in which he would sit was a tiny white house, complete with picket fence in front and a woodpile behind. Voluptuous drifts of artificial snow lay along the bottom of the fence, and three snow-men wearing hats and mufflers stood behind it like benevolent guards. Deep yellow light from inside the house poured out through diamond-shaped panes onto sparkling snow that lined the windowsills. The children were to pass through a gate and onto a path that would lead them past Donna, her camera, and a cash register, to an "elf" assistant named Gini. Griffin was to sit in the tiny living room of the house, which was wallpapered in a homey yellow print. His thronelike chair was next to a Christmas tree, beneath which were dozens of presents, all gaily wrapped. All empty boxes, Griffin supposed, but it was nice to imagine they were not, that instead they held exactly what you wanted. Against another wall was a miniature fireplace where stockings were hung. "White Christmas" played softly in the background.

Donna, spotting Griffin, stood up and smiled at him. She wore a green velvet dress, red lipstick, and tiny gold bell earrings. The elf, Gini, wore a short red velvet skirt, a white blouse and a green vest, and green satin shoes that curled up at the end. Her hair was tied back with a large red ribbon.

"Sorry I'm late," Griffin said, climbing into the chair. He'd never sat in such a large chair before. He liked it. It was comfortable, and it gave him a view of the entire length of the mall, where the decorations made the place gloriously changed.

"You haven't missed a thing," Donna said. "For the last half hour it's been really slow."

"I had some trouble with my beard. Is it straight now?" He reached up, felt it gingerly.

"It's fine," Donna said. "Don't adjust it out here!" Then, seeing someone approaching from behind Griffin, she said quietly, "Get ready; here comes your first customer."

A little girl, around five years old, Griffin thought, came through the gate with her mother. The mother, harried-looking, checked her watch repeatedly and told the little girl she had to **hurry.** He saw Donna offer to take a picture, saw the mother's adamant refusal. Then, while the mother stood off to the side, arms crossed, Gini brought the girl forward. "You can sit on Santa's lap," Gini said, but the girl shook her head, stood firmly in place before Griffin. She was dark-headed, some hair held back from her face by yellow plastic barrettes, the rest escaping to partially cover her eyes. She wore a pink sweat outfit, the top decorated with a faded kitten playing with a ball of yarn. Her coat hung stolelike off her shoulders.

"Hello," Griffin said, gently. And then, to Gini, "This is my friend who likes to stand."

The girl regarded him silently and Griffin stared back, unsure as to what he should do.

Finally, the girl asked, "Where are your reindeer?"

Ah. He knew this one. "In a barn, not too far from here," he said.

"Oh." She inched closer. "Can I go and see them?"

"Well, they're eating right now. And then they'll have to take their naps."

"Oh," she said again, and looked over at the box of antlers and candy canes at Griffin's side.

"Would you like one?" Griffin asked.

She nodded, stepped close enough to reach out and take a candy cane, refused the antlers. Then, her blue marker–stained hand on Griffin's knee, she whispered, "I would like that Barbie mansion."

"Uh huh. Anything else?"

"No, thank you." She started to leave, then turned back to say, "I have been very good except that one time that was not my fault."

"I know you're a good girl."

"Yes." She stared a while longer, then said, "I thought you had blue eyes."

"Well, they change."

"Oh. Okay. 'Bye."

She turned, walked a few steps away, then suddenly turned back. "Oh! And could I ask for one more thing?"

"Of course." He leaned forward listening carefully.

"Sparkly Band-Aids. Just my **own box** that is not for **anyone else.**"

"Got you."

She walked closer. "Really, I don't care what you bring me as long as it's nice and I can always treasure it."

He smiled. "Okay."

"Because I wouldn't get mad at you, no matter what, because you and your elves are too nice. And also you can bring my baby brother a toy, okay, he can't talk."

"I'll do my best to bring something he'll like."

She sighed, pushed her hands in her pockets. "All I mostly want for Christmas is a happy Christmas."

"I know just what you mean," Griffin said.

"One thing. Can you write back to me?"

Now what? "I can try," he said. "But even if I don't write, you know I'll be thinking of you. I'll leave you signs."

"Okay."

Griffin waved at her. "Merry Christmas!"

He watched as the girl and her mother hurried off.

The mother was complaining about her daughter not sitting on Griffin's lap. "Why didn't you want to?" she asked. "You're **supposed** to sit on his **lap.**"

Donna came up to Griffin's chair. "Well? How did it go?"

He leaned back in his chair. "Fine."

"We probably won't get too many more tonight. It's getting late, and anyway, most people like to wait until Thanksgiving is over."

Thanksgiving. Three days away! He'd forgotten about it. What would happen this year? Surely Ellen planned on spending the holiday with him and Zoe. Surely she would make the food she always did, and though the atmosphere at dinner might be somewhat strained, it would also be what it should be. But he supposed he should prepare himself for anything. Such as her spending Thanksgiving with Auto King. And what if she wanted Zoe there as well? Should he forbid it? Which would be more hurtful to Zoe, to make her stay with him or to let her go with her mother? All these decisions with no good answers, suddenly thrust upon them.

Although things had been all right, thus far. Zoe had awakened that morning in a good mood, eaten a huge breakfast, made her bed without being asked, and had slammed the door in her usual way when she left for school. Ellen had made dinner for the three of them that evening and seemed perfectly content to stay in the house until Griffin returned that night. They'd had a relaxed enough dinner, the only awkward moment coming when Ellen told Zoe she'd fixed up her apartment a little now, and Zoe was welcome to come over any time.

But "I don't think so," Zoe had said.

"Why?" Ellen asked. "You said just yesterday you wanted to see it."

"I know." She looked down into her plate, pushed her potatoes around with her fork.

"Well," Ellen had said, "whenever you're ready. Any time you want."

"Here comes somebody else," he heard Donna saying, and she moved off to take her place at the camera. This mother did want a picture. She took off her son's coat, straightened his plaid shirt, zipped up completely his corduroy pants, wet her fingers in her mouth to smooth down his hair. Then she stepped back, nodded, and busied herself filling out the form while her son strode confidently forward and climbed onto Griffin's lap.

"It's kind of early, isn't it?" the boy said.

Griffin smiled. "I guess it is."

"I just wanted to beat the rush, that's all."

"That's a very good idea."

**"Max."** Griffin heard the mother whispering loudly, but the boy paid no attention.

"I guess you want to know what I want, huh? Well, here goes!"

**"Max!"**

Again, he ignored her. "I am **desperate** for a new Super Mario Brothers Game Boy game. And I would like some hockey pants. And a real crystal unicorn, rearing up? You get the idea. And—"

**"MAX!"**

The boy sighed, then turned to look at his mother. **"What?** What do you want from me?"

"The **picture!"**

"Hold on a minute, Santa," Max said, and turning to look at the camera, smiled widely. After the flash, he said, "All right?"

"All right," his mother said.

"So anyway," Max said to Griffin. "Basically, I would like anything you think is right for me. I think you have good judgment."

"Well, thank you."

"I have to go now, but I enjoyed meeting you."

"Likewise."

Max hopped off his lap, then dug in his pocket for coupons. "I have these, in case you need them. For the Game Boy games."

Griffin leaned over, took the coupons. "Thank you very much."

"I would really love to lend you a hand."

"That would be nice, but I'm all set for this year."

"Okay, so . . ." The boy smiled, waved, and started away, then turned around. "Oh! One more thing! Crackers and cheese or milk and cookies?" He was holding up one finger, looking every inch the miniature host.

"Crackers and cheese would be nice."

"Hey, Mom!" the boy yelled. "I told you! Cheese and crackers!"

**"Mazel tov,"** she said. "Let's go."

# Chapter 18

· · · · · · · · · · · · · · · · · ·

When Griffin let himself in the door, he saw Ellen lying on the sofa, her eyes closed. He'd kept his Santa suit on and carried his clothes home in a paper bag, which he tried now not to rustle. He set the bag down at the foot of the stairs, then tiptoed over to her. She was sleeping, her breathing deep and regular, her hands folded loosely across her stomach. He checked his watch. Ten-thirty. This was late for Ellen; she was never one to stay up at night—said she was "resting during the commercials" when they watched the ten o'clock news, but he'd always had to wake her up to go to bed.

She stirred slightly, then opened her eyes and stared at him. Blinked. **"Griffin?"**

"Yeah?"

"Is that you?"

"Yeah!"

She sat up. "Oh, my God, I was sleeping, you know, and I woke up and . . . there was **Santa!** Too bad this never happened when I was a kid." She leaned back, took him in from head to toe. "That is a great costume. Wow. Even your eyebrows."

"Check out the boots," Griffin said, pushing one foot forward. Always, she would be the one he needed to tell.

She leaned over to look at the boots, touched the furry trim at the bottom of his pant leg, then rubbed her fingers gently over his calf, saying, "Ummm, velvet." The moment was, however vaguely, sexual, and Griffin felt himself not so vaguely responding. Always she would be the one to so easily elicit these feelings in him. He stepped back, away from her. "I've been thinking about wearing it to work. Do you think a tie would be too much with it?"

"You **should** wear it to work," she said. "It would put people in good moods."

She stood up, yawned, folded the afghan she'd thrown over herself. "I guess I'd better go."

He didn't want her to. "How about a cup of tea with old Santa, first?"

She smiled. "Now there's an offer I've never had."

"Come on," he said, walking into the kitchen. "I bought some herbal tea the other day—Zoe liked the packaging."

She followed him, sat at the kitchen table. "I've

got to go soon, though—I have to get up really early tomorrow."

He filled the kettle, set it on the stove over a high flame. "Why?"

She hesitated, then said, "I'm applying for a job."

He turned around, surprised. Well, irritated, if the truth be told. "I thought we agreed that you wouldn't work until Zoe was all right alone after school."

"I'd be finished by two, plenty of time to come back here before she gets out of school."

He came to the table, sat across from her. "So what's the job?"

"Why don't I see if I get it, first?"

"What's the big secret? I mean, it's not exactly the CIA, is it?"

She looked away from him, and he immediately regretted what he'd said. He reached his hand partway across the table, toward her. The fur trim around his wrist looked ridiculous, now. "I'm sorry. I didn't mean that the way it sounded."

She shrugged. Then, looking at him, "Speaking of jobs, how was yours? I mean, was it fun? Were there a lot of kids?"

"No. I guess there won't be until after Thanksgiving."

"Oh . . . You know, we need to talk about that. Thanksgiving."

He would like, right now, to enact a law prohibiting the phrase "We need to talk." Here came another one.

"I'd like to spend Thanksgiving with Peter, and I'd like Zoe to be there."

"Uh huh."

"So . . . what do you think?"

"I don't know, Ellen. You've told her you want some time alone to think. What's she going to think when some guy shows up?"

"I can handle it, Griffin. I'll introduce him as a friend."

"You must think she's an idiot."

"I said I can handle it."

The teakettle whistled, and Griffin got up to prepare the tea. The good thing about Ellen taking Zoe for Thanksgiving was that he could have her for Christmas. But he wouldn't say that now.

He brought the mugs back to the table, took a cautious sip.

"Griffin?"

"Yeah."

"You're getting your beard all wet."

He'd actually not noticed, had forgotten entirely that he had the costume on. Now he felt around the area of his mouth; the beard was indeed wet. He pulled his hat off, then the beard, put it on the table beside him.

Ellen put her hand over her mouth. "Oh, it's so weird! Even when you know someone's not Santa, it's still so strange to see him come apart."

"Good thing you didn't see this when you were a kid."

She smiled. "Although I never really believed in Santa. I wanted to, but I didn't. You know that."

He looked up, surprised. "You didn't?"

"I told you that, a long time ago."

No memory. "Oh, yeah," he said.

She smiled, thinking of something. "What?" Griffin said.

"Isn't it funny how Zoe has started playing dolls?"

"Well, for what it's worth."

"I don't know how any daughter of mine can not love dolls. I was so crazy about them. Especially the ballerina doll. Although that . . ." She shook her head. "Ah, well."

"What ballerina doll?"

Ellen waved her hand. "Oh, it was a doll I got for Christmas one year, and I was so excited. She had blue hair and I thought it was just extraordinary, so absolutely beautiful. I wanted to bring her to school and show off a little—I wasn't exactly the most popular kid around. I used to sit on the steps at recess and read. All the other kids were playing four-square and hopscotch and braiding each other's hair and I'd be sitting there with my nose in a book. I just couldn't find a reason to go **over** there. I thought if I brought this doll, all the girls would just naturally gravitate toward me." She looked at her watch, stood up. "I should go."

"So what happened?"

"You don't really want to hear about it."

"I do."

She looked at him, evidently judged his expression sincere, and sat back down. She said nothing until Griffin said, "So, what? They still ignored you?"

She shook her head, stared into a middle space that was years ago. "No, they didn't ignore me. What happened was, I brought the doll to school in a paper bag—big surprise, you know. I put her in the cloak room, and I must have checked on her a hundred times. At recess, I took the bag outside, sat at my usual station and pulled the doll out. I remember I was so excited, breathing kind of fast, even, and my stomach hurt a little. But it was a good hurt, excitement. She had a crown on her head, and the rhinestones sparkled so hard in the sunlight. I just kept looking at her, waiting for others to notice. She had silvery nylons, and silver ribbons on her ballet slippers that crisscrossed so delicately over her ankles—I was worried about how I'd ever fix them if they got messed up. She had a blue tutu, with pearls and sequins all over the bodice, and she wore pearl earrings, too—little studs. Very tasteful." She smiled at Griffin. "Can you imagine such a thing? I don't know what the equivalent for a boy would be, but this doll just thrilled me. Sometimes now I wonder if she could possibly have been as wonderful as all that; I wonder if I just made her up."

"You mean you don't still have her?" Griffin asked. "That seems like the kind of thing you would have kept. You kept your baby doll, and she looked like hell."

"No, I didn't keep that ballerina doll. What happened is, the other girls saw it and came over and started making fun of it. They didn't think she was beautiful; they thought she was ridiculous. **'Blue hair!'** they kept saying. And then they took her from me for a little game of keep-away. By the time I got her back, I didn't want her anymore.

"When I walked home from school that day, I threw her away, in some garbage can I passed. I remember it was in front of a white house with green shutters, and there was a cat on the windowsill. There was a banana peel and some coffee grounds on top of the garbage, and I put the doll facedown, right in it. The coffee got all over the crown, and I remember trying to knock a little off, but then I just left her there. And you know, I've never seen anything like her again. I asked my mother once where she'd gotten her and she couldn't remember, just had no idea. So, she is . . . gone." Her eyes filled and she laughed, defensively.

"I'm sorry," Griffin said.

"Oh, it's . . . It was a long time ago. But thanks for listening, Griffin."

"You don't have to thank me for listening to you, Ellen."

"It feels like I do, though. Because before, you never would have. . . . This is **very** different, okay?"

Now he was irritated. "What do you mean?"

"Well, like . . . Do you remember when we had that parakeet, Huey?"

He stared at her. "Yeah?"

"Remember that time I worked with him almost all day, to teach him how to sit on my finger?"

"I guess so."

"Well, I asked you to try it. I told you how wonderful it felt, how his feet were so scratchy and his weight was . . . well, it was kind of **thrilling,** this tiny little force on your finger! I asked you to try it, to just put your finger in there and let the bird sit on it. And you got all pissed off. You said, 'Just let me do things by **myself.** I don't need you to **show** me things all the time!'"

"I said that?"

"Yes."

"Really?"

"Yes!"

"Well, Jesus, Ellen, hold a grudge, why don't you? You're angry over something that happened over ten years ago! Maybe I was just having a bad day or something!"

She shook her head, impatient. "No, it's not that I'm still angry about that. Or maybe I **am** still mad, I don't even know. The point is, you were always so unwilling to **share** in anything with me. Even Zoe. I love her; I know you love her, too, but where did we **meet** about her? Where was the **we** in us as parents?

"You just . . . you always kept so much of yourself to yourself. You never seemed particularly interested in me. You wanted me around, but you didn't want to have to do any **work** to forge any kind of . . . You just seemed to want to keep things on a very superficial level. But when you listened to me, just now, it was like you were really there. **Working.** Do you know that?"

"What I know is that you just said everything in the past tense. As though there's no chance that . . ." He took in a breath, looked at her. "Ellen. Don't you think we could try again? Can't we just start over, in a way, and—"

She stood. "No. It's too late. Too much has happened."

She went to the closet, took out her coat and slid it on. "I'm sorry." She closed the door softly behind her.

He sat at the table until he heard her car drive away. Then he went upstairs, checked on the soundly sleeping Zoe, and prepared for bed. That parakeet had been green, with tiny streaks of yellow here and there. He'd liked classical and rock music equally, had chirped along happily with them. He'd liked potato chips, and he'd liked toast—unbuttered, preferably. Yes, he remembered that bird. Griffin had had his own relationship with him that was in no way inferior to the one Ellen had. It was just different. Did she ever think of that, that things experienced in ways different from hers were equally valuable? That the way that he chose to love her was, in fact, **loving** her, that the face of love depended on the person giving it? Couldn't she see that the difficulty came not from Griffin withholding, but from her unwillingness to receive? But he would not confront her with this. Even as he tried to convince himself that it was true, he was aware of his own self-deception. He admitted, now, if only to himself, his catalogue of intentional slights, his moments of soft cruelty, his awareness of complicity in creating a relationship that could not work.

He lay on the bed, pulled the covers up over himself and closed his eyes, forced himself to move toward the undemanding island of sleep, the much more comfortable state of unawareness.

# Chapter 19

······················

Griffin dreamed he was in a bank, waiting in a long line. Soft music played in the background, an anemic version of "Penny Lane." The carpet beneath his feet was thick, a lush blue-green color; the wall sconces glowed; the sounds of conversation were muted and friendly. The man in front of him suddenly brandished a gun and ordered the tellers to put their money on the counter before them. He was wearing all black, including a skullcap over a long, blond ponytail. Griffin realized it was Peter at the same time that the bank alarm began ringing. "Help me get the money!" he told Griffin, and Griffin did—walked slow-motion up to the tellers and collected neat stacks of bills to put into Peter's paper bag. The alarm was deafeningly loud, but apparently useless; no one came to help. Peter ran to the door, turned, and threw his gun to Griffin. Then he was gone. Griffin stood still, open-mouthed, the gun heavy in his hands. Everyone in the bank turned toward him and slowly raised their hands.

Griffin awakened, reached over to turn off the alarm. He always set the thing, but rarely needed it. Today, though, he felt dizzy with fatigue. He lay still for a moment, reconstructing the dream, details of which were already fading. Peter as robber, though; that detail was clear. Not too much work required there for interpretation. Although Ellen might tell him the dream wasn't about Peter at all.

He put on his robe, went downstairs to make coffee and to turn up the heat. The sky was blue, the sun coming out strong, but there was frost etched delicately along the edges of all the windows. It would melt soon. He'd wake Zoe a couple of minutes early, bring her down to show her how pretty it looked.

Her room was dark and when Griffin raised the shade, she moaned, "Dad! **Don't!**"

He moved to stand beside her. Her eyes were closed tightly, the blankets pulled up to under her nose. She smelled of childsleep: a combination of hair and salty flesh and cotton. "It's time to get up, Zoe. Come downstairs; I want to show you something."

She opened her eyes. "What?"

Griffin pulled back her covers. "Come on, I'll show you."

Angrily, she pulled the blankets back up. "Don't! It's freezing! And anyway, I don't want to see **anything.**"

He sat on the bed, put his hand to her shoulder. "Hey. What's up? What are you so mad about?"

She closed her eyes again, lay still. It came to him that, given the circumstances, this was a stupid question to ask. She had a million things to be angry about.

"Zoe?"

**"What?"**

Griffin sighed. "Get dressed and come down for breakfast. You don't want to be late for school."

"I don't care if I am."

"I care. Now come on, get dressed."

When Zoe appeared at the breakfast table, her spirits had not improved. She scowled into her bowl of cereal, ate a few bites, then pushed it all away. "What did you want to show me?"

"Nothing."

Now she was interested. "What was it, though?"

"Nothing—really, Zoe. There was frost at the windows this morning. It was really pretty. I just wanted to show you."

"You wanted to show me frost?"

"Yeah."

"I've seen frost before, Dad."

"I know that. It was just very pretty."

"I don't think it's pretty."

"Well, you are entitled to your opinion. As am I."

"I think it's stupid."

He stood up, cleared away her dishes, began rinsing them for the dishwasher. "Did you brush your teeth? Make your bed?"

Nothing.

He turned around. "Zoe?"

"I'll do it! God, Dad, you treat me like a baby! You always have to ask me did I do this, did I do that!"

Griffin looked at the clock. "Well, here's what I'll ask you now, Zoe. Are you prepared to go to school late? Because unless you are out the door in five minutes, you will be. And you will not go out the door until your bed is made and your teeth are brushed."

She stood, shoved her chair under the table. "In my house, there will be no beds, and no toothbrushes."

"Fine."

"You're crabby and mean," she muttered.

"What was that?"

Nothing.

"You're the one who's crabby," he said.

She started upstairs, then called down, "Nobody cares about frost! It just **melts,** anyway!"

On the way to work, he passed a parking place directly across from the Cozy Corner. This was too rare to pass up—he'd stop in for some breakfast of his own. He hadn't eaten anything at home owing to the extreme unpleasantness of his tablemate.

He found a booth in Louise's section and ordered two over easy, hash browns, bacon. After Louise delivered it, she sat down across from Griffin. "How are you doing?"

He smiled, shrugged.

"Your wife's not much better, either, huh?"

"Oh?"

"I'm not spilling any beans, but . . ."

He loaded up his hash browns with catsup, waited expectantly.

"How's the kid doing?"

"She was crabby as hell this morning."

"Yeah. It takes a toll."

"I guess." He took a swallow of coffee, asked casually, "So, Ellen's been talking to you about things?"

"Yeah." She stood up, put his bill on the table, facedown. "I hope things work out all right, Griffin."

"Did she—"

"I gotta go."

\*        \*        \*

When he arrived, late, to work, Evelyn handed him a piece of paper saying, "Mrs. Griffin called. She said to give you this. It's her new number." Her face was carefully empty of expression.

He took the piece of paper from her, nodded, then asked, "Could you come into my office, please?"

"Yes, sir." Now her forehead was wrinkled with concern. She followed him into the office, stood quietly while he closed the door.

"Sit down, please," he told her, and she sat at the edge of one of the chairs before his desk. He sat opposite her. "Evelyn, Mrs. Griffin and I have . . . Well, we're separated."

"Yes, sir."

"Did she tell you that?"

"Yes, sir."

"Just today?"

"Yes, when she called with the number. I'm so sorry."

"Did she tell you anything else?"

She shook her head. "No, sir. No, she did not."

"Just gave you the number and that was it, huh?"

"Yes, sir. Well, she did ask me how I was."

"Uh huh. And how are you, Evelyn?"

"I'm just fine, sir, thank you."

"Evelyn?"

"Yes, sir?"

"I would really appreciate it if you wouldn't call me 'sir.'"

"Yes, sir. Oh—sorry. It's just a habit. The one before you, Mr. Crenshaw, he insisted upon it."

"Who, Arthur?"

"Yes, sir. Yes."

"Well. He was an ass. I just really don't like being called 'sir,' okay?"

"Okay."

"So." He turned and looked out the window. More snow, the lazy, drifting variety, melting almost as soon as it landed; the weather was warming to an unseasonable high today. "Mrs. Griffin and I have separated."

"Yes. As you said."

He looked at her. "Evelyn, I have to tell you, I'm pretty fucked up."

She flushed, looked down into her lap.

"I'm sorry," he said. "Just slipped out."

"It's all right."

"I'm sorry, though."

"It's fine. I imagine this must be very difficult. I've noticed you haven't been yourself for a while. And I would like to say how truly sorry I am. I like you both very much."

"You like Ellen?"

"Yes, I do."

"No kidding."

She laughed, a soft sound. "Is that so surprising?"

"No, it's just . . . Not many people know her, really. She's kind of shy."

"She is. But over the years, we've . . . We talk a little sometimes—recipes, books. She didn't say much today. She did ask how **you** are, though. How you seem to be doing. I said you seemed just fine." Her fingers flew up to the bow at her neck. "I hope that was all right!"

"It was perfectly fine. I'm glad that's what you said. Even though it's not true."

"Well, you do look a little tired. . . ."

"A few details slipping."

"Nothing that hasn't been taken care of, Mr. Griffin."

"Ah, you're a good woman, Evelyn. Tell me, were you ever married?"

She all but pointed to herself. "Me? Oh, no. No."

"Why not?" His phone rang. He ignored it. They both did.

"I lost him."

"Lost who?"

"The man I loved. He was killed in an automobile accident, on the way to pick me up. We were going to have a picnic by the river. I'd packed deviled ham, and I was so nervous he wouldn't like it. And I'd made my first apple pie—it came out just right. But of course he never saw it." She shook her head sadly. "My goodness, so many years ago—we were just nineteen."

Griffin had a sudden image of Evelyn at nineteen: a short-sleeved white blouse and a belted full skirt, nylons and black flats, swaying to Fats Domino on the radio as she did her weekly ironing. She would have been plain, but invested with the stubborn beauty of youth. Bangs might have curled high on her forehead. She might have worn scarves tied around her neck, charm bracelets on her wrists, and, with the discovery of love, perhaps a new red lipstick.

"Were you engaged?" Griffin asked. The boy: earnest and hard-working. Polite. Shy, but less so than Evelyn. Focused on a three-bedroom rambler, a dependable station wagon.

"Oh, no. Didn't have time for that. We had only a few dates before he . . . But I knew that if he'd lived, we would have stayed together. We fit. He was the one for me. When he died, that was that."

"You mean, there were no more men after him?"

"No."

"But you were nineteen!"

She shrugged. "He was the one."

"Oh, Evelyn. There's always more than one."

Gently, she said, "No, Mr. Griffin. For some of us, there really is only one."

She was remarkably self-assured saying this. Still, he asked, "But . . . don't you regret not at least trying to find someone else? So that you could have had a husband to share your life with, maybe some children?"

Her face grew serious. "I suppose we all think about other roads, Mr. Griffin. But . . . I don't know, maybe I can't really explain this so that you can understand. But the love I had for that young man was enough, somehow. I knew right after he died that I would never feel that way again. I knew it. And I never did. So I wasn't surprised by that; I was never bitter. It was just . . . my life, what was given to me. I accepted it. I cherished it."

"I have to ask you, though—don't you get lonely?"

"Oh, well." She laughed a little. "There is more in the world than a marriage and children, Mr. Griffin. More than a love relationship. I have friends. I sing in the choir at church. I travel, I read, I go to plays and concerts. I have a little gray cat that sleeps at the foot of my bed. I buy outrageously expensive cheeses and I eat them all. And you know, I still love that boy. Not a day goes by that I don't think of him. He lives on in my heart. And in that way, I have love in my life, too." She leaned forward, spoke earnestly. "You see? I feel lucky to have found such a love. So many people don't." She smiled. "You shouldn't feel sorry for me!"

"It's true that I used to."

"Yes, a lot of people do."

"I'm sorry."

"It's all right."

He stood, straightened his tie. "You know, I'm really glad you told me all this, Evelyn."

"I am, too." She hesitated, then asked, "Was there anything else?"

"No. But . . . Evelyn? I just want to say that I think you're pretty wonderful."

"Thank you."

"I really mean it."

"I know you do. You're a kind and honest man, Mr. Griffin. I've known it since the day I first met you."

"Is that what you think?"

"That's what I know. And here's something else I know. Right now you need to get to a marketing meeting that started ten minutes ago."

Ellen made beef stew. He smelled it before he opened the door. When he came into the kitchen, he found her at the table, drawing pictures with Zoe. He rubbed Zoe's head. "Hello, you."

"We're drawing."

"I see that." It was landscapes they were focusing on: Zoe had drawn a mountain, the peaks craggy and imposing; Ellen had drawn a green field full of flowers. "Smells good," he told Ellen.

"It seemed like a good day for it, even if it is so much warmer," Ellen said, and there was a kindness in her voice he'd not heard in a long time.

"How long until we eat?" Zoe asked, and when Ellen told her twenty-five minutes, she said, "If I finish my homework before then, will you give me a dollar?"

"No," Ellen said.

"Anything?"

"My admiration."

"Okay." She ran up to her room.

There was the sound of the stew beginning to boil, and Ellen went over to turn down the flame. He watched her hold back her hair, blow carefully on the spoon, then taste. "Mmmm. It's good."

"I saw Louise this morning," Griffin said.

Her back stiffened. "Oh?" She did not turn around.

"Yeah. Stopped for breakfast, just for a change. She's a very nice woman."

Ellen went to the sink for a sponge, wiped down the counter. "Yes, she is."

"She's a friend of yours, huh?"

She turned to look at him. "What do you mean?"

"Just that. Jesus, just **that,** Ellen."

"Oh. Well, yes. She is. Listen, how was Zoe with you this morning? A little cranky?"

"A lot cranky."

"Yeah, with me, too. I think it's because last night I told her we wouldn't be having Thanksgiving dinner together. But I guess we need to remember she used to have these days before, too."

"I guess."

"I got the job I was telling you about, Griffin. I start tomorrow."

"Good. Now I can hear what it is."

"Don't make fun of it."

"I wouldn't do that."

"Well, don't."

"I said I wouldn't!" Stuffing envelopes? Delivering newspapers?

"It's just . . . as a waitress. At the pancake house on North Avenue. Louise told me you can make pretty good tips there."

"The one next to the optician's?" She nodded, and it was all he could do to keep quiet. The place was run-down, tacky looking. Oftentimes, there was a line of motorcycles outside, a group of beefy Hells Angels inside. He and Ellen had taken Zoe there once, Zoe having heard they made great chocolate chip pancakes. The waitresses were mainly teenagers; they wore brown dresses with puffy sleeves, orange ruffled aprons. And they had to wear silly little hats—puffs of transparent white, with orange and brown ribbons hanging down the back. On the day they went, their sullen waitress

had lost her hat in the middle of Ellen's blueberry short stack.

He looked at her, unsure of what to say. Finally, he nodded, in what he hoped was a noncommittal way. "Ah."

"You said you wouldn't make fun of me!"

"I'm **not!** But . . ." He sighed. "Is that really the best you could do, Ellen?"

She took off her apron, hung it on its hook. "I'm going."

He moved beside her, put his hand on her arm. "Ellen. Wait a minute."

She went to the closet for her coat and purse. "You don't need to say anything, Griffin. I shouldn't have told you. I knew you'd do this."

"Do what? What did I do? I just think this job is beneath you, Ellen. Is that so bad? You're too good to do it."

"It is a job that will let me earn some money and still take care of my daughter."

"**Our** daughter."

"I don't know how to work in an office, nor do I want to. This place will take me with no experience, and it's better than McDonald's. The answer to your question is yes, I did the best I could."

Their life was a minefield. It probably always had been. He could not say anything to her without it turning into something else.

She opened the door, turned back. "This is why, Griffin. This, too." She took in a deep breath. She was very close to tears. "I'll pick up Zoe at school tomorrow and bring her home with me. I'll bring her back Saturday. You work Friday night, right?"

"Right."

"At **your** job as a Santa."

He hung his head, and she shut the door softly behind her. What would he say when Zoe came down to dinner? Mommy had to go? Why not the truth? Why not, **Dad hurt Mommy's feelings, Dad is always doing that.**

The phone rang and, miserable, he picked it up.

"Hi!" It was Donna.

"Hey. How are you."

"Uh oh. Bad time, huh?"

"No. I'm all right. What's up?"

"I'm just calling to see what your plans are for Thanksgiving. If you're not busy, would you like to have dinner with me at Estelle's?"

He said nothing.

"Hello?"

"I'm sorry. Uh . . . Yes."

"Yes, what?"

"Yes, I'd really like to have dinner with you. We need to talk."

*     *     *

It was as he was tucking Zoe in that night that she began to cry. She turned away from Griffin, pulled the covers up over her face.

"Zoe."

She would not look at him.

He wrapped his arms around her. "I know."

"No, you don't!" Her voice was muffled, angry.

"Well, I just want you know I'm sorry you feel bad. I know how it is to feel bad. Are you thinking about Mommy?"

She said nothing, turned over and looked at him. "Why did she go?"

This question was too hard for him. The truth was too hard; lies were too hard. But he said, "She went because she needed to find something out, Zoe. It is something that she has to do all by herself. And even though she loves you very much, she had to leave you for a while to do it. I'm so sorry for how hard it is. I wonder if you could tell me some things to do that might help."

She sniffed, wiped at her eyes. She had stopped crying already. "I want to see some pictures of her."

"Okay."

"Will you go get some?"

"Yes, I will."

He went into the family room, grabbed an album, and brought it up to her bedside. "Want to look with me?" she said, and he said of course he did, though he did not. He was afraid to look.

But there, she had opened to the first page. "Here's where we went to Washington, D.C.," she said. "I was six."

"Yes," he said. "We were feeding the ducks at that pond, you and I. Look at how pretty the cherry blossoms are."

"But where's Mommy?"

"She was taking the picture."

"Oh." She turned the page. "There's one of Mommy."

It was last summer. Ellen stood in the backyard at the picnic table. She was handing Zoe a plateful of food, and had turned to the camera as he had called her name. She was wearing an old T-shirt and some cutoffs, and her hair was pulled back into a loose ponytail. She was smiling, her face flushed with pleasure. A daisy was tucked behind her ear. He remembered, suddenly, something Ellen had told him that night, long after Zoe had gone to bed. They'd been sitting on the porch steps sharing a beer, Ellen leaning back on her elbows. "I am living in the wrong time," she'd said, suddenly. And when he asked her what she meant, she said, "I am fulfilled by the making of hamburger patties, by the care of my child. I like the smell of laundry detergent. I like listening to

what Zoe says more than reading the newspaper. I
don't want to be a photographer or run for office.
I don't want to make a million dollars. I want to
read poetry and novels and raise my daughter and
make chocolate chip cookies." And when he said
there was nothing wrong with that, she told him
he was the only one who thought so, and she
wasn't so sure he really thought that, either. He
asked her why she would ever say such a thing
and she said, "Well, you just don't seem very . . .
proud of me." He started to say that he was, but
she interrupted him, saying, "Don't. It's like my
saying you never say you love me, and your saying
it then. It doesn't matter, then. It doesn't count."
It was so clear, this memory. Every word. The
smell of the grass that night, newly cut that afternoon. The way the heaviness in the air had lifted,
after it had been so muggy all that week. And the
nagging irritation that came from what she said,
the way he'd felt, **Oh, Christ, now what?**
Because it had been just a nice summer night, and
then she'd had to start something. Was that
wrong of him? Was it?

Zoe ran her finger down the side of Ellen's face.
"Let's put this picture on my nightstand. Can I take
it out?"

"Of course."

She took the photo out from behind the plastic

and leaned it against her lamp. "Okay," she said. "You can go now."

He smiled, kissed the top of her head. "Call me if you need anything."

**"Anything?"**

"You know what I mean."

"Okay. Dad?"

"Yes?"

"Am I feminine?"

He had no idea what to say. But, finally, "Yes, you are," he said.

"Okay. Good night."

"Zoe?"

"Yeah?"

"Why do you ask?"

"I don't know," she said. But he felt she did. It was just that she was beginning to keep things to herself. Well, her mother's daughter.

He closed her door, began walking toward the stairs. Her mother's daughter, unless she were her father's. Was it him? Was there something about him that told females that he would not be receptive?

He went back to Zoe's room, opened her door. "Hey, Zoe?"

"Yeah?" Already her voice was sleepy.

"You know you can tell me anything, right?"

Silence. And then, ". . . Yeah."

"Well, I just wanted to remind you of that. You can tell me everything."

"Okay. 'Cept I don't **want** to, Dad."

"Well, that's . . . all right. I just wanted to tell you that you can."

"Okay. Good night, Dad."

# Chapter 20

· · · · · · · · · · · · · · · · · · · ·

The Wednesday before Thanksgiving, Ellen called Griffin at work. "I can't pick up Zoe at school," she said. "My car is . . . I don't know, there's something wrong with it."

And? If Peter was a mechanic, why didn't he fix it? "Well, what is it? Some big deal, expensive thing?"

"I don't know, yet. I'll take care of it. But the thing is, you'll need to bring Zoe over here. Can you do that?"

"I could."

"And . . . I'm at work. Would you mind picking me up and giving me a lift home as well?"

"You're at work now?"

A beat of silence. He felt her embarrassment come over the phone like a scent you walk into. He started to say that he didn't mean anything by asking, he was just making conversation, but then she said briskly, "Yes, I'm at work. Can you just do what I asked you to do?"

"I said, yes."

"No, you didn't. You said you could."

"Well, I will. Is that clear enough for you?"

She hung up. He sighed, went out to Evelyn's desk to tell her he'd need to be leaving early today. "You could go right now," she told him. "There's nothing pressing this afternoon."

He stood there, frowning slightly. Then, "Maybe I will," he said. He went into his office for his coat and briefcase. On the way out, he said, "Don't eat too much turkey, Evelyn."

"Oh, I never do. I hate turkey. I always eat prime rib."

He stopped, turned around. **"Do** you?"

She shrugged. The phone rang, and she waved him away, saying to the caller, "I'm sorry; he's left for the day."

When he stepped outside, he took a deep breath of the cold air. The sky was getting clouded over. An excuse to hurry.

Zoe disagreed with Griffin over what she should pack. She claimed she needed only one set of clothes. "But you'll be there for three days!" Griffin said.

"So?"

"So you need at least two outfits."

"Why?"

"Because you can't wear the same thing every day!"

"Why not?"

Griffin sighed. "Because it might get dirty."

"Then Mommy can wash it."

He stared into her clear eyes, so like Ellen's. Then he said, "Fine. But you have to bring clean underwear for all three days."

"I **know.** And you don't need to be here. I can pack by myself."

As they pulled out of the driveway, Zoe asked, "What does it look like, where Mommy lives?"

"Don't know. I haven't been there, yet. But we're going to pick her up at work, first."

"We are?"

"Yes. You knew she had a job, right?"

"Yeah. At the pancake house." She was looking out the window, her knee bouncing rapidly.

"What do you think about that?" Griffin asked.

She turned toward him, stopped her knee. "About what?"

"About Mommy's job."

She shrugged. "I don't know. She gets to eat for free. She gets tips every day."

"Uh huh."

"I guess it's good." The knee again. "Is it?"

"Oh, sure, it is." He turned on the radio, and Zoe immediately tuned it to another station.

"Hey!" Griffin said. "Why did you do that?"

"It's old-mannish, your music."

"It's **what?**"

"Old-mannish!"

"I see. Tell me, Zoe, are you a little nervous?"

"Why would I be **nervous?**"

"No reason. Never mind."

"It's just **Mommy!** Jeez! Why would I be **nervous?**"

All right, question answered.

When they arrived at the restaurant, Griffin turned into the parking lot, checked his watch. A few minutes early. He cut the engine, looked out the windshield at the darkening sky. "Looks like rain."

"Snow," Zoe said.

"How do you know?"

"My teacher said. She knows the weather all the time. She calls it on the telephone."

They sat quietly for a while, and then Griffin said, "Let's go in and get her."

"Can I wait here?" Zoe asked. "With the radio on?"

What had happened? Had she become a teenager in her sleep? "Don't you want to go in?"

"I want to listen to the radio. Even Mommy lets me wait in the car alone."

"She does?"

"Yeah. When she's coming right back and she can see me and if the doors are locked."

"Well, I will be coming right back. Okay."

When Griffin pushed open the door to the restaurant, he saw Ellen right away, standing directly across the room. Her back was to him. She was totaling up a bill—she tore it off her pad, and laid it facedown on the table where two grossly overweight men sat. One of them looked at it, then called her back as she was starting to walk away. "This isn't right," Griffin heard him say.

Ellen took the bill, looked at it again. The man waited, then said, "Check your addition, honey." He adjusted the toothpick in his mouth, winked at his tablemate.

Ellen added again, and he could see the faint blush on the back of her neck. Then, "Sorry," she said, and handed the bill back to the man. He shook his head. **"Here's** the mistake," he said, and gave the bill back to her again. "Christ's sake," he muttered.

Two tables away, a young woman wearing multiple bangle bracelets waved her hand in the air. "Excuse me! Do you think I could get more coffee today?" Ellen started toward her and the man with the incorrect check grabbed her arm, saying, "Hey! What about **this?**"

Griffin started toward her, then went back out-side, instead. He wouldn't let her know he had seen this. When he got in the car, Zoe turned the music she'd been blasting down to a normal level. "Where's Mommy? Isn't she coming?"

"She's on her way." He turned the radio back up, bobbed his head in time to the music, and Zoe rolled her eyes, turned to look out the window, and began to sing softly along.

He saw Ellen come out the door, tooted the horn, and she began walking quickly toward them. She was wearing new waitress shoes, and when she slid into the car next to Zoe, he could see the perfect circle of catsup stain on one of them. "Have you been waiting long?" she asked.

"Just got here, really."

"How are you guys?" She hugged Zoe, smiled at Griffin. Her face was weary and beautiful. He wanted to kiss her full on the mouth.

"How are **you?**" Griffin asked, starting the car.

"I'm okay." Too quick, Griffin thought.

"My place is about ten blocks away," she said. "Left out of the lot and then straight."

"How much tips did you get?" Zoe asked.

Ellen reached inside her purse, pulled out a

Baggie full of coins. "Would you like to count it when we get home?"

"Wow, you got a lot!"

"Yeah, folding money, too, but that's in my wallet."

Griffin stole a look over at them, their two heads together over the nickels, dimes, and quarters. He saw some pennies, too, but in his mind he made them Ellen's before she started her shift. He didn't want anyone putting down such an insignificant amount to say what they thought of his wife.

The door to Ellen's apartment was at the back of a large white house. After she unlocked it, they stepped into a tiny living room furnished with a green tweed sofa, a pole lamp, and a battered coffee table. A kitchenette was off to the right, separated from the living room by a long, off-white Formica counter. In the center of the counter were picnic-sized containers of salt and pepper and a small pile of paper napkins. Two bar stools sat before the counter, covered by tufted black plastic. There was a percolator coffeepot on the stove and a new white wall phone looking, by comparison, elegant. And that was all. There were no flowering plants, no soft pillows, no framed pictures, none of the things he knew Ellen believed were essential. He ached for the emptiness he saw here, but Zoe was excited.

"This is it?" she asked, climbing up on one of the bar stools. "This is the whole thing? Cool, it's like a clubhouse!"

"Well, there's a little bedroom and a bathroom," Ellen said. "But this is an apartment, Zoe; it's not big, like a whole house."

"Where's the bathroom?"

"You want to see?"

"Yeah!" Zoe hopped off the stool and followed Ellen to a closed door. It opened onto a huge bathroom, considering the size of the rest of the place. There was a claw-footed bathtub and a pedestal sink. Griffin stood at the doorway, watching Zoe examine the feet of the tub. "It's so deep! Is it really a bathtub?"

"I take baths in it every night," Ellen said. Griffin saw the razor in the soap dish, a bar of pink soap. There was the shampoo she used, and there was a flowered bottle of bubble bath. Ah yes, Ellen had a lover. And the tub was big enough for two.

He remembered the first time he'd bathed with Ellen. He'd sat behind her, wrapped his arms around her as she lowered herself gingerly down in front of him. Her back was to him; her long black hair hung nearly to her waist in those days. He'd watched her hair blossom outward in the water, then cling to her when she rose up higher in the water. "Don't feel my fat," Ellen had said, pushing his arms away from her stomach. "You're not fat," he'd told her, and had kissed the back of her neck gently until she had relaxed against him. They'd soaped each other—lazily, at first, and then with extreme intention.

"Can I take a bath?" Zoe asked.

Ellen laughed. "Now?"

"Yeah! Can I?"

"Sure. Let me put the plug in for you—it's tricky."

"Hey, it has a chain!" Zoe was peeling off her clothes, watching wide-eyed as Ellen turned on the faucets. What the hell was she so happy about? Griffin wondered.

After Zoe was in the bathtub, Ellen and Griffin went into the living room together. Ellen sat at one end of the sofa and Griffin at the other, the distance between them measured and sharp. "She didn't bring anything but underwear and one outfit," Griffin said. "She insisted on it."

"That's okay," Ellen said. "I'm glad she seems so . . . excited to be here!"

Griffin looked around the room. "I hadn't imagined it like this."

"Not exactly **House Beautiful,** huh? But things cost a lot."

"I'll help you, you know," Griffin said.

She stood up, went into the kitchen. "I know. Thank you. But I need . . . it's important that for once in my life, I take care of myself." She reached up into the cupboard. "Want some tea?"

"No, thanks." He came into the kitchen, walked up close to her. A piece of hair had come loose from her ponytail, and he moved it gently, tucking it behind her ear.

"I'm a mess," she said. "I should change clothes."

He wondered if he were allowed to see this anymore, then realized immediately that he was not. She was telling him to go.

"I'll just say goodbye to Zoe," he said, and she nodded quickly.

Zoe was leaning back in the tub, her arms behind her head. The water level was up to her chin. When she saw Griffin, she sat up excitedly. "You can go **swimming** in here. Want to see?"

"Well, actually, Zoe, I have to get going. But you have a good time, okay?"

Zoe's face changed and she stood up quickly, dripping and shivering. She wrapped her arms around herself. "I want to come out."

"You don't have to come out."

"I want to."

"Well, let me just get you a towel first, okay?"

"Okay." Her teeth were chattering.

"Sit down!"

"No."

When Griffin came out of the bathroom, he

found Ellen bending over a cupboard in the kitchen. "I'll get her," she said. "I've got the towels right here."

"Ellen, I want to tell you something."

She stood, wary.

He cleared his throat. "It's just that . . . I'm proud of you. Okay?"

"You are?"

"Yes."

"Well . . . for what?"

"For being you. For . . . I just am."

She smiled. "Thanks, Griffin."

"Ellen? One more thing."

She looked at the closed bathroom door. "Is it quick?"

He swallowed, spoke softly. "Yes. It is." He walked over to her, looked down into her face and kissed her gently. "I love you. I want you back. I will always want you back."

She moved away from him, put her hand to her hair in confusion.

"That's all I wanted to say. You don't have to say anything back."

Outside, he sat in the car for a long time, thinking. Then he drove away, through the sleet that had begun falling. He hated weather like this, this unsettling mix of something that was neither here nor there.

# Chapter 21

· · · · · · · · · · · · · · · · · ·

Griffin was at a stoplight when he realized something had been different about Ellen. It was her hair: It had been itself again, lightly streaked with gray. He felt a small rush of happiness, a kind of pride, as though her coming back to her natural color were something for which he could take credit.

The light changed and he started forward, thinking about her upturned face when he'd kissed her. Her mascara had been slightly smudged. He smiled, thinking about how, despite her attempts to apply makeup perfectly, Ellen almost always suffered this imperfection, but his reverie was abruptly interrupted by the thought of Peter seeing that same smudge and having the permission Griffin now lacked to do something about it, to tenderly rub under her lid, saying, "Here. Let me fix this." Ellen would hold still, childlike, trusting him. When he was finished, he would kiss her lightly and say, "There you go," and the simple exchange would be charged with sexuality. He knew that. He remembered.

Tomorrow, Zoe would meet Peter. What would she think? What if she liked him, found his youth and his job exciting, a welcome change from the dull familiarity of her father? Some weeks would pass, and then it might happen that Zoe would say that Mommy was going to marry Peter and wasn't that cool? And oh, by the way, could she live with them? Because she and Peter were fixing up a car together and this way they'd have more time. Peter let her help all she wanted and he did not yell at her when she goofed up. He treated her like a partner.

Griffin's stomach began hurting, a vague, dull ache. His daughter was going to meet his wife's boyfriend, and he was going home to an empty house. He couldn't recall the last time this had happened. Since Ellen, someone had always been there for him to come home to.

He let himself into the house, and went to sit in the darkened living room with his coat on. What should he do? Call Donna? Go to a movie? A sports bar? He didn't recognize this life he was living; he didn't know how to negotiate it.

In the kitchen, he flipped on the light. Slinky appeared, meowing, and rubbed against his leg. He reached down to pick her up, but she wanted no part of it—she leaped immediately from his arms. "Okay, okay," he said, and went to the cupboard where her food was kept. "This is what you want, right?" She sat still, watching him. He took out a package of food, rattled it. She stood, her back arched in pleasure, then padded to her bowl and sat down. He put the food in her dish, then got a Heineken out of the refrigerator and sat beside her while she ate. "So," he said, after a long swig of beer. "How was your day?"

The cat ate noiselessly, her tail wrapped neatly around her feet.

"See any mice? See any other cats?"

One flick of one ear.

"Want to go out with me tonight?" He stroked the cat's back, scratched behind her ears. "Want to stay in? Want to order an anchovy pizza and listen to **Cats?**" She finished what was in her bowl, got up, and walked away. "Hey!" Griffin said. "Where are **you** going?" She looked back, briefly, then continued on her way.

Why did they even have a cat? What good were cats? What they needed was a dog. A huge slobbering dog whose eyes glazed over with love every time he looked at you. Maybe he'd go out tonight and buy a puppy, tell Zoe it was an early Christmas present. A Newfoundland. A Saint Bernard. A Great Dane. All three.

But there was no one to take care of a dog anymore. Or of him.

He opened the refrigerator and stared. Then he opened the phone book. He'd get an extra-large pizza, extra sausage, extra cheese. He'd eat, and then he'd get the hell out of here.

He called and ordered dinner, then went into the basement in search of the paper-bag turkey Zoe had made in school when she was a first-grader. They always put it out for Thanksgiving, and he certainly wasn't going to stop now.

In the furnace room, where holiday decorations were stored, he found a large cardboard box marked THANKSGIVING/XMAS. Inside, at the top, was a wreath made of eucalyptus leaves and curling grapevine that Ellen had bought last year. Not that Griffin had wanted her to. When she'd shown it to him, he'd said it was too expensive, meaning he didn't like it. Uncharacteristically, she had bought it anyway, had marched resolutely up to the cash register and pulled out her checkbook.

Normally, Ellen asked him about buying nearly everything but the groceries, and normally, when he said he didn't think so, she'd go along with it. It occurred to him now that there must have been hundreds of times that she'd wanted something he'd vetoed. With some reluctance, he remembered a time recently when Ellen had shown him a watercolor she'd wanted. She'd seen it in a tiny store in their neighborhood the day before, and had asked him to come and look at it with her. He'd gone, but he'd hated the thing, had realized from a few feet away that he wouldn't want to buy it: apricots in a green bowl, really. He'd wrinkled his forehead and said, "Are you kidding?" And Ellen had looked quickly at the store owner, apologized, and walked out. He'd followed her, saying, "Well, come on, Ellen, you didn't really like that, did you? I mean, if you **really** liked it, let's go back and get it." Ellen hadn't looked at him when she'd said, "Forget it. Let's go and eat." **"Did** you really like it?" he'd asked again, and she'd said nothing. They'd gone to eat at a restaurant he chose.

Well, so maybe he was having a bad day. People had bad days! People made mistakes, were sometimes insensitive! She could have said something, she **should** have said something! All those times he now knew about, when she was feeling sad, or angry, or whatever the hell it was, she could have told him. He was not an idiot. He was not without compassion or empathy. She didn't give him a chance.

He went to the wall phone in the laundry room. **Ellen,** he'd say. **Jesus. I just realized.** He would apologize in a general way, tell her that if she came back, it wouldn't be like that, he would make room in the relationship for her half of things. But he would also tell her to own up to her mistakes. Yes, this would get things going in the right direction. Fair was fair; truth was truth.

The line was busy. Didn't she spring for call waiting? He'd pay for her to get call waiting—it was a necessity. He dialed again—she might have just been finishing her conversation, and had now hung up. Busy. He tried the cell phone, but there was no answer. He stood thinking about who she might be talking to, dialed yet again. Busy! Damn it, didn't she realize that there might be some emergency? Who the hell was she talking to?

But maybe it was Zoe, talking to Grace, her new hobby. Yes. It could be Zoe. Only probably it was not. Probably it was Ellen talking to Peter, who was acting as if everything she said was of great interest to him.

He went back to the box and continued to unpack. Here were the ornaments that Ellen and Zoe had made together out of bread dough—Zoe's big-headed Santa, her gigantic yellow star, Ellen's miniature Christmas tree, decorated with cinnamon candy. He went to the phone again, dialed determinedly. But when it rang, he hung up. He had too much to say.

Back at the box, he stood still, unwilling to take

anything else out. It was unbearably sad, he couldn't do it alone. He'd have Zoe help him; she'd make it fun. He closed the box back up, stashed it in the corner, then thought of Ellen or Zoe answering the phone only to hear a hang-up. Maybe it had frightened them.

He dialed the number again, and when Ellen answered, he said, "That was me, just now. That hung up. That was me. I didn't want you to be scared, thinking it was some . . . I just decided not to call. Because, you know, it was nothing important. It could wait."

"Griffin?" She wasn't afraid; she was amused.

"Yeah. I started to call you, but it can just wait. It was nothing, really, so I hung up. But I thought it might scare you, a hang-up. . . . I'm repeating myself, aren't I? You know what? You know why I think it is?" He laughed. "I think I'm nervous!"

"It's okay." Her voice was warm.

"Who is it?" he heard Zoe ask, in the background. His daughter, at his wife's house. It was impossible.

When Ellen told her it was her father, Zoe said, "Let me talk to him!"

And then there she was, breathing into the phone. "Dad?"

"Hi, sweetheart."

"This is Zoe."

"I know. How are you?"

"Dad, guess what?"

"What?"

"It just started snowing, and it's going sideways! Did you see it?"

"Not yet. I'm in the basement. I was getting out some Christmas decorations, but I think I need some help. I think I'll wait for you."

"Okay. Are we getting a tree?"

"Of course!"

"Because Mommy's not."

"Well, she can share ours."

"Are we getting it soon?"

"Absolutely."

"Okay." She breathed into the phone again, then asked, "So what are you doing now?"

"Well, I thought I'd watch a little TV, maybe go to bed early."

"Oh." A pause, the breathing. And then, "I'm going to meet a friend of Mommy's tomorrow."

Not this. Not now. "Okay, good, Zoe. So, I'll see you soon!"

"Do you want to talk to Mommy again?"

"No, not necessary."

"Don't you want to say goodbye?"

"You say it for me, okay?"

He heard the phone drop and Zoe yelling, "Moooommmmy! Dad wants to say goodbyyyyyye to you!"

When Ellen came to the phone, Griffin said, "You know, I was just unpacking some of the Christmas decorations."

"Uh huh." She waited.

"And I . . . Well, I found the wreath I gave you such a hard time about buying."

"Yes. You did give me a hard time about that."

"I want to tell you that I'm sorry about that. It really is a nice wreath."

"Yes, it is."

"And I'm sorry I made such a big deal out of it."

"Oh, Griffin, what— Okay. Apology accepted."

"I'm going to hang it up on the front door."

"Good."

"Ellen?"

"Yes?"

"I'm glad your hair is back. I mean, I'm glad you stopped coloring it. It isn't you."

"Isn't it?"

Was she challenging him? Or really asking?

"I don't think it's you," he said.

She sighed. "It's just a rinse. It washes out. You have to keep putting it on all the time, and it's expensive."

"You don't need it. Because you're beautiful. Do you know that? You are so beautiful."

"I have to go, Griffin. Thanks for everything." She hung up.

He turned out the basement lights, and went back upstairs. He could not stay here. He couldn't breathe. He'd leave money for the pizza in an envelope, tell the person delivering it to eat it himself. Then he'd head for the mall. He would buy Zoe a Christmas present. He would buy Ellen one, too. She was still his wife.

Even from the parking lot, the mall looked beautiful. Through the glass doors, he could see people bustling about. It would be warm and busy and full of distractions—he would feel better. He'd buy some lights for the tree; they needed more. Maybe all white this year. But Ellen liked the colored ones—he'd get more of those. Last year, Ellen had strung the lights on the tree, then plugged them in and discovered that half of them didn't work. She'd taken them off the tree and spread them out across the rug, waited for Griffin to come home and diagnose the problem. As he'd walked over to take a look, she'd said, "Maybe you plug it into itself."

He'd looked up. "Pardon?"

She pointed to the plug at one end of the strand, the outlet at the other. "Maybe you plug it into itself."

He was astonished. He'd looked at her to see if she was making some kind of joke, but she wasn't. She was staring at the lights, ready to test her theory. He knew if he said, "Okay, let's try it," she would, and then she would wait to see if the lights came on. "Ellen," he'd said, "that is there in case you want to plug another set of lights into it. To make it longer."

She'd looked up at him, embarrassed; she'd laughed. "Oh, God. That's right. You need a source of power, don't you?"

"Yes," he'd said, and he remembered saying it with a great deal of contempt. There hadn't been any need for that.

Though it was true that her ignorance about things like electricity was astounding. She had taken a required chemistry class in college, and Griffin had helped her every night in order for her to earn the D– she received. It was exhausting. "Now, here," he would say, pointing to a diagram, "is a neutron." And Ellen, her forehead wrinkled, really trying, would say, ". . . Why?"

And yet she had a deep, intuitive wisdom. She couldn't follow maps, but when they were lost, she'd say, "Well, I just feel like it's that way," and she would be right. Griffin would ask how she knew and she would shrug, say she had no idea. She knew what to do when Zoe was angry, or sad, or frightened, or ill. Though she was shy with people in general, she could get recalcitrant people to open up. She was good with weirdos, Griffin always said, though now, of course, he regretted saying it exactly that way.

Once, when they'd gone to the zoo, she'd gone

over to the peacock's cage, where people were calling out for the lone resident, who faced away from
them, to show his feathers. The bird picked at his
food, occasionally looked over with his beady eyes,
but remained impervious to the people's desire for
him to spread his tail.

"Watch," Ellen told Zoe and Griffin, and she
crouched down to stare hard at the bird. He turned
immediately to look at her. "That's right," she said,
and he lurched slowly toward her. Then, standing
directly before her, he fanned out brilliantly. The
crowd murmured quiet appreciation, pressed in
closer. The bird turned himself slightly this way and
that, and when Ellen stood and walked away, he
folded himself back up again and returned to his
food dish. "How'd she **do** that?" a little boy asked,
and his father said, "Beats me." "Mommy!" Zoe had
said, and when Ellen had answered, "Yes?" Zoe had
said, "Nothing! Just Mommy! Mommy! Mommy!"
and he and Ellen had smiled, linked hands.

Griffin walked more quickly toward the
entrance. It was getting colder, snowing a little
harder. He remembered a time he and Ellen had
taken a trip in the winter, long before Zoe was born.
Their car was old, the heater ineffective. Griffin
was driving and Ellen was sitting close beside him;
they'd had a blanket thrown over their legs to keep
warm, sleigh-ride style. It was late at night and very

dark, a thick cloud cover obscuring the stars. From the car ahead of them, a cigarette was thrown out the window. It bounced on the road, sparks flying. Ellen had turned her head to watch, then said, quietly, "I never want to be like that."

"Like what?" he'd asked.

"Every time I see that, you know, a cigarette being flung from a car window, I think about it lying there, the car going on. How if it had eyes, it would see the taillights getting smaller and smaller and then just disappearing. I never want to be left behind. I want to be the one going on."

"You're talking about death," he'd said.

She'd said no, she wasn't. He hadn't understood her then; he'd changed the subject. But he thought perhaps he understood now.

In the crowded toy store, Griffin found a teenage girl standing on a high ladder, stocking board games. "Where are the dolls?" he asked.

"Two aisles over." She was overweight but very attractive, and friendly. "Want me to show you?" She began climbing down.

"Sure," he said. "Maybe you could help me. I'm looking for a certain kind. A ballerina doll."

"Oh yeah, we've got those." She pulled her sweatshirt down lower over her hips, a heartbreaking gesture, serving more to accentuate than to hide her large size.

"Do you have any with blue hair?"

She smiled, as though he were joking. Then, realizing he was serious, she said, "I don't think so. I've never seen that. But we have some with blond hair. You could dye it. Is this for your daughter?"

"No. For my wife."

The girl stopped walking, clasped a hand to her chest. "Oh, that's so romantic!"

"I hope so," Griffin said. The girl pointed him to the ballerina dolls and he picked out a pink-cheeked, delicate-lipped one, eternally **en point** in her box behind her cellophane window. Her dress was white, covered with silver sequins in the shape of stars. She wore a tiny silver tiara, plastic, of course, but convincing, in its way. Her ballet slippers were tied with silver ribbons. This was the one. He'd use food coloring to dye the doll's hair. He'd wrap the gift carefully and buy a present for Zoe, too, tell them they each got to have a present early. He'd get a good softball glove for Zoe. On the way out, Griffin passed a Hallmark store, and went in for gift wrap. Black for Zoe; that was her latest. And for Ellen? He looked for twenty minutes and found nothing he thought was right. Finally, he bought a box of mixed wrappings. The right choice would come to him. And to Ellen.

# Chapter 22

· · · · · · · · · · · · · · ·

Griffin was awakened by the phone ringing. He checked the clock: 6:09. He answered quickly, the anxiety in his voice overriding the fatigue.

"Dad?" It was Zoe. Was Ellen all right?

"What happened?" he asked.

"What?"

"What happened?"

". . . When?"

"Zoe."

"Yeah?

"Is everything all right?"

"Yeah!"

He looked at the clock again. "Are you up already?"

"Yeah, Dad! I'm getting ready to go outside and

build a snowman. But there's probably only enough for a baby snowman."

He yawned. "Well, that's a good kind to make. You get done fast." He sat up, rubbed his head. He wanted coffee. "Zoe, can I call you back? I'm still kind of half asleep, here. I'm surprised you're up so early."

"Mommy got up to make the turkey and the noise woke me up. At first I didn't know where I was!"

"Uh huh." Ah yes. It was Thanksgiving. "So Mommy's making a turkey, huh?"

"Yeah. Her oven is **tiny.** The turkey scraped when we put it in."

"Well, listen. You have fun in the snow, and I'll call you back, okay?"

"Okay. Dad?"

"Yes?"

"I **really** want a brother. I decided."

Griffin half laughed. Now what? He rubbed the stubble on his chin, on his cheeks. "Is Mommy there?"

"She's in the bathroom."

"I see. Well, we'll talk later, all right, Zoe?"

"Okay. But why **don't** we get a brother?"

"I think maybe we should talk about that another time. All of us together. Some time."

He heard Ellen's voice in the background, then

Zoe's telling her it was Griffin she was talking to. Then Ellen's voice came into the phone. "I'm sorry, Griffin. I didn't know she was going to call you. She's been up for a while. I don't think she realized how early it is."

"It's all right. So you're making a turkey, huh?"

" . . . Yes."

"Peter coming over?"

She sighed.

He stood, tucked the phone under his chin, reached for his robe. "Guess so."

"Did you want to talk to Zoe again?"

"No. Not now."

"Okay." A pause, and then she asked, "What are you doing for dinner?"

"Got a date."

Silence.

"Hello?" he said.

"Yes," she said, and then, "Okay! I'll see you later, then. Have a good dinner. But don't be too greedy."

"You started it," he said, and then instantly regretted himself. He was going to say something to mitigate his offhand remark, but she hung up before he could think of anything.

After his shower, Griffin mixed blue food coloring in water, titrating as carefully as if he were searching for a cure for some dreaded disease. Then he undressed the doll and lay her down on the counter with her head over the sink. Hands shaking slightly, he poured the dye carefully over the doll's hair, then stood back to observe the results. The blue was holding, but the effect was streaked. He poured more dye on, but too quickly, so that it ran into the doll's face. He stood her on her head in the sink, and went to get a towel. When he returned, the doll had fallen onto her side. Blue dye ran down the side of her face, into her apricot-colored ear, behind her neck. He wiped at it quickly, removing most of it. Then he massaged more of the mixture directly into the doll's hair. It was blue now, but too light. He took the bottle of dye and squeezed drops directly onto the doll's head. **All for you, Ellen,** he thought, and the phone rang. Was it her? He had a strong feeling it was. Without knowing how, he knew it was. He put the towel over the doll's face and picked up the phone.

"I was just thinking of you."

"Were you!" Donna said.

". . . Oh."

"It's . . . me, Donna."

"Yes, I . . . Sorry, I thought you were Zoe. I was just walking out the door and I . . . Well, I thought you were Zoe." He looked over at the doll. Was the dye spreading onto her face?

"I won't keep you, I just wanted to know what

time you wanted to go to dinner tonight. I hadn't heard from you, so . . ."

"Oh, right. Sorry. Well! . . . You know, anytime." It **was** spreading. Quickly, he said, "Just tell me, and I'll be there."

"Six-thirty?"

"Fine, see you then."

"Griffin, are you all right?"

"I'm fine, I'll see you tonight. Looking forward to it!"

He raced back to the doll, lifted the towel and saw that the stain had spread down onto her forehead. She looked like a freak. If he gave it to Ellen, she'd say, "Why are you always making fun of me?" She'd say, "What is **this** supposed to be?" She'd tell Peter about yet another screwup by her husband, and Peter would console her. In his way. In their way.

He tried scrubbing again, and succeeded only in making the doll's eyelids blue as well. He stood with his hands on his hips, staring down at the doll. "Is this how you're going to stay?" Of course she did not answer. Of course her expression stayed fixed, her eyes closed. And though they were not closed against him, they might as well have been.

At six-fifteen, Griffin pulled up in front of Donna's house. He hadn't remembered whether she'd said six or six-thirty. When she came to the door, he said, "Sorry I'm not on time."

"It's okay. I'm ready." She looked beautiful, was wearing a simple black skirt and sweater, and pearls. Black boots with a high heel. Her hair was loose, curled about her face. But when he looked at her now, he felt no attraction. He enjoyed her beauty as he might a painting's. She had nothing to do with him, really.

He was solidly back in his marriage, even if Ellen wasn't. He was who he was: A boy who sat at the kitchen table and finished his glass of milk each and every night, though he did not like milk. A boy who neatened his laces, zipped his jacket up high, did his homework, endured without complaint the rigors of a paper route in winter. A boy who grew into a man who meant what he said when he took his marriage vows, who wanted to preserve that marriage despite the odds, despite the problems. He never had equivocated when it came to Ellen. Do you love her? **Yes.** How about now? **Yes.** Well, how about **now? Yes, yes, and yes.**

"Come in for a drink?" Donna asked, and he smiled, shook his head no. "Better get going." His hands were shoved deep into his pockets, and she looked at him for a long moment, then went for her coat. In the line of her back, he could see that she had seen.

Estelle's was crowded, but a booth had been reserved for them. It was decorated with an orange plastic tablecloth and scallop-edged paper place-mats featuring dour-looking turkeys staring out at their perpetrators of doom.

When Estelle came out to greet them, Donna admired her low-cut velvet dress. "Yeah, this is my party dress," Estelle said. "Turns me into a sex machine, don't it?"

She lifted her chin at Griffin. "Move over. Let me take a load off."

Griffin slid to the far side of his booth. Even then, Estelle was obliged to squeeze in a bit. Her size was truly awesome. He smiled at her and she stared back at him, then told Donna, "Sorry. He ain't it."

"Estelle," Donna said.

"Nope. I can tell."

"We're just **friends.**"

"Uh huh."

"What's for dinner?" Griffin asked, and she turned slowly to answer him.

"Well now. It's Thanksgiving. What might you think?"

"Bar-b-cued ribs?" Griffin asked, and was grati-fied to see that she smiled, however begrudgingly.

"You want some of the best corn bread stuffing you'll ever taste?" she asked fiercely.

Griffin nodded, and she pushed herself out from

behind the booth and lumbered back into the kitchen.

"I'm sorry," Donna said. "She's a little rude, sometimes."

He looked over at Donna, lovely in this low light. She was looking down, tracing the outline of the scallops with her finger. Her earrings glinted prettily; the part in her hair was perfectly straight; he could smell her perfume from here. He wanted, suddenly, to do everything for her that he knew she wanted: grab her by the hand, take her back to her house, and lie with her on her bed. But he couldn't. Could not. "Estelle is right, you know," he said softly. "I'm not the one."

Donna looked up quickly. "I know! I never . . . Well, that's not true. I did think maybe . . . Well, you're the first man I've been interested in since Michael." She laughed. "Maybe it's because I knew you weren't really available. Or maybe I just . . ." She shrugged. "It's just hard, you know, to . . ." She sighed, looked over at him. "These are tough things to say, Griffin. Help me out, here."

But before he could say anything, Estelle emerged from the kitchen carrying a tray with two platters heaped with food. It smelled wonderful. "Eat hearty and get the hell out of here," Estelle said. "I'm going to need the table again soon. Happy Thanksgiving!"

She went back to the kitchen and Griffin reached over to touch Donna's hand. She raised a finger quickly to wipe away a tear. "Oh, God," she said. "So embarrassing."

"Donna," he said, and she interrupted him, saying, "I know. I'm a wonderful woman, but . . . If there were any way you could, you would. . . . You're really sorry that . . . You hope we can be friends." She looked at him, smiled. "Actually, I would like that. Truly."

"Me, too."

"Well, then . . . Fine. Done. Starting here, starting now, as the song says."

Griffin picked up his fork, and Donna said, "So tell me, friend. Why are your fingers blue?"

When he got home, Griffin went into the kitchen to check on the doll. Her face was only mildly stained, he was pretty sure he could fix it. But he would wait until morning. He was tired, now, his spirits sagging and confused.

He went into the living room and stared out the window. He and Donna had gone downtown to the Drake Hotel bar for drinks afterward, and the evening had remained awkward, full of long silences and then abrupt rushes of conversation.

He went upstairs, lay on his bed, and called Donna. When she answered, he said, "I really am sorry."

"I know, Griffin; you told me so about thirty times." He could hear the smile in her voice.

"I just . . . do you believe me?"

"Yes."

"Can I ask you something?"

"Sure."

"Did you want to get back with Michael after he left you?" Call waiting. He'd ignore it. That would be the last straw: **Be my friend, not my lover. Help me figure out how to get my wife back. Wait while I pick up another call.**

"Oh, of course," she said. "At first, I was desperate to get back with him."

"I feel like if Ellen would just come back home, we could work it out. It's just not that hard."

"Oh, Griffin," Donna said. "Yes, it is."

# Chapter 23

· · · · · · · · · · · · · · · · · ·

Again, he was awakened by the phone. This time, it was Ellen, saying, "Oh. Sorry. Are you not up yet?"

He looked at the clock. Ten! "No, I'm . . . Yeah, I'm up. Well, not up. But awake. How are you?"

"I tried to call you last night, Zoe was really missing you. But it just rang."

He said nothing, at first, and then, "Yeah. I was talking to someone. Didn't want to interrupt."

"Who?"

"Well, Donna, actually."

"Oh. I thought you had a date with her. I thought it was probably her you had a dinner date with. For Thanksgiving." Nervous. Was that a good sign?

"I did."

"So . . . you had a date and then when you got home you called her?"

"Well, yes, but—"

All business now. "Let me get Zoe. She wants to talk to you."

"Ellen, wait a minute."

"Yes?"

"It's not. . . . Well, it's not what you think, okay?"

She laughed, dismissing him, put down the phone and called Zoe.

"Dad?" She was out of breath.

"Hi, sweetheart. What are you doing?"

"I was outside playing. With guess what?"

"What?"

"My puppy!"

"Mommy got you a puppy?"

"No, her friend did. Peter is his name, his neighbor's dog had puppies and I got one! A boy. His name is Nipper, because he bites all the time. But just play bite. He'll stop, Peter said it's real easy to train them not to do that. Wait till you see him, Dad! He's got one white spot on his nose and otherwise he's all black. And he already knows not to do it inside!"

"Well, that's great, Zoe. I guess you'll miss him when you come home, huh?"

"Dad! He's coming **with** me! He's **mine!**"

"I see. Listen, can I talk to Mommy for a minute?"

He heard Zoe tell Ellen that Dad wanted to talk to her, then the low, indecipherable sounds of Ellen talking. And then Zoe was back on the phone. "She said she's busy now, but she'll call you later."

"Busy doing what?"

**"I** don't know."

"Well, let me talk to her."

Again, he heard Zoe tell Ellen he wanted to talk to her, and then there was Zoe on the phone again. "She said she'll call you later, Dad."

"Zoe, let me talk to her. Tell her that Dad needs to talk to her right now."

**"Okay!"**

He heard Ellen say, "Yes, all right, but be sure you keep him on the leash." And then, into the phone, "What, Griffin?"

"He gave Zoe a puppy?"

"Yes, he did."

"Which you intend for me to keep here."

"Well, you do have a fenced-in yard. And there are no pets allowed here."

"Did it ever occur to you to consult with me on this, Ellen? It will be living here. In my house. Did you think for one fucking second about—"

"It was a surprise to me, too, Griffin! He just showed up with him. And Zoe was so happy, I couldn't . . . I mean, maybe it would be nice for Zoe to have something, now. Her ant died." In a way that seemed against her will, she started giggling. And Griffin, despite himself, smiled, too.

"I know," he said, softly. And then, for this one, isolated moment, it was as though they moved back into the relative comfort of **before.** Zoe and her animals. They shared this specific knowledge and history: their daughter's caterpillars in a shoebox, the lightning bugs she captured in a jar to read by at night, then freed in the morning. The parakeet who lived only a month; the fish who died after one day; the gerbil who ate her own young. Slinky, whom they'd had for seven years, who for seven years ignored all of them. It was time, probably, for Zoe to have a pet who loved her back, who came when she called it, who slept on the bed with her.

"Ellen?" In the background, a man's voice.

"Oh, hi!" Her voice fresh and invigorated. "Come on in, I'll be off in a minute."

And then, to Griffin, "So . . . was there anything else?"

"I'll see you Saturday." He hung up the phone. And then walked into the kitchen, took the doll off the counter, and threw her in the trash. This time, the coffee grounds would be on top of her.

Just before five o'clock, he was half reclining in front of the television when the phone rang. It was Ernie, saying, "Listen, if you're not doing anything, how about you come over and have an early dinner with me and the Mrs.?"

Griffin declined politely, automatically.

"What, you got plans?" Ernie asked.

"Well . . . No."

"Then don't be a putz. A quick dinner, that's all it is."

Something occurred to him. Ernie liked Donna, and knew Griffin had been seeing her. "Is anyone else coming?"

"Yeah, the President of the United States. No, no one else is coming, this is just a spur of the moment kind of thing. Get your butt over here, Griffin. Grab a pencil so you can write down the directions."

Ernie's wife, Angie, let him in. "So nice to meet you," she said, in a voice so husky and low she sounded like a man. "Let me take your coat."

She was a good-looking woman, with an olive complexion and widely spaced brown eyes. Black hair barely touched by gray. Somewhat overweight, but in a cozy, attractive way. She wore a white, bib-style apron, and the sight of it made Griffin feel instantly comfortable. Beneath it, she wore a matching blue skirt and sweater.

Griffin was sorry he hadn't dressed up more—he was wearing jeans and a flannel shirt with the elbows wearing thin. Nor had he remembered to bring anything along as a hostess gift—Ellen had always been in charge of that. "I'm sorry I didn't bring anything," he said, and Angie waved her hand. "All we needed was you."

"Smells great in here."

"Oh, it's only meatloaf. But who wants to get fancy the day after Thanksgiving?" She smiled at Ernie, who was coming down the stairs, then disappeared into the kitchen. "Hey, buddy!" Ernie slapped him on the back. "You're going to be in for it when you go to work tonight!"

"Oh?" Griffin shifted his shoulders slightly— Ernie had more strength than he knew.

"They all come out of the woodwork the day after Thanksgiving. I had my picture taken so many times today, I nearly went blind. Remember to look away from the camera, okay? Look **away!**"

Griffin thought of Donna, the editing of her expression that was sure to be there, the awkwardness with which they would now greet each other. He wondered how many people would consider him a fool to let a woman like her go, especially since it was in favor of a woman like Ellen. But the Ellen he saw was not the Ellen others did. And how to explain? There were no formulas to account for the idiosyncratic yearnings of a human heart, no ways to extract from someone feelings that lived as matter-of-factly as blood and bones inside of him. In the end, Griffin thought, we are only who we are.

He followed Ernie into the kitchen, sat at the chair Ernie pointed to. "I'm actually looking forward to being busy."

"Yeah? Talk to me when your shift is over. I got **bit** today!" He showed Griffin the marks on his hand, the faint pink semicircle of injury. Angie, mashing potatoes at the stove, turned around to shake her head, sighed, then went back to work.

"How'd that happen?"

Ernie reached into the refrigerator for drinks, handed Griffin a soda. On the top shelf, Griffin saw a chocolate cake, decorated with walnuts. Reflexively, his spirits lifted.

"I'll tell you something," Ernie said. "When a kid doesn't want to sit on your lap, he doesn't want to sit on your lap! The little guy kicked me, too!" Then, seeing Griffin's worried face, he said, "Aw, you know. That's not what usually happens. It's made up for by all the good kids you see. Had a little girl today about five years old tell me that what she wanted was a tea set, a wedding dress, and an ATM machine. Wanted the machine in her bedroom so her mother could come there and get money whenever she needed it."

"That's pretty smart thinking. Like on your third wish from the genie, asking for more wishes."

"Exactly." Ernie took a long drink from his soda can. "Another kid wanted me to get his dad out of jail. Those are always the tough ones. Get my dad out of jail, take away my grandma's cancer. Those are tough."

He leaned back to make room for Angie to put platters of food on the table. "Once a little girl asked him for a new house," she said. "Turned out it was because hers had burned down."

"So what did you say?" Griffin asked.

Ernie shrugged. "What **can** you say? 'Santa can't do everything, but he'll try to make your Christmas merry.' Some crap like that."

"Is this your first year, Griffin?" Angie asked.

"It is."

"How does your wife like your doing it?"

Griffin swallowed, saw in the panicked look on Ernie's face that he hadn't told her. "I'm . . . separated," he said. Odd word. An invisible finger seemed to appear and point itself at him, to hover directly over his head, where it would stay as he reached for meatloaf, as he leaned back in his chair, as he tried to make conversation about anything but what occupied him most. "It's not my fault we're separated," he wanted to say, but did not. Could not, in fact.

After dinner, Ernie walked to the corner store for vanilla ice cream, claiming Griffin could not eat chocolate cake without it. Griffin sat at the table talking to Angie, who had refused his help in cleaning up. "I'm an old-fashioned gal," she'd said. "Men doing things in the kitchen make me nervous.

"I'm sorry I asked you about your wife," she said now, her back to him. She was rinsing the plates in hot water, and the steam rose up in loose billows. "Ernie never told me. It's just that I'm always interested to know how wives like their husbands being Santas. Some of them love it, and some of them really don't—they resent the time it takes. I guess I just always assume everyone's married." She turned around to look at him, laughed. "Even animals! Ever since I was a little girl, I've made couples out of everything—pigeons in the park, the rabbits that used to live under our porch, animals in the zoo. I liked to think about everybody bedded down for the night, lying next to someone else. I guess it made me feel secure to think that everyone grew up and had their someone. Too many fairy tales, probably. But I need to stop assuming!"

"It's all right."

"Especially when divorce is so common now." She said this in a way that he supposed was meant to comfort him.

"How long have you and Ernie been married?"

She came over to the table, wiping her hands on a dish towel. "Forty-two years."

"Bet you never thought of divorce, huh?"

She smiled, sat down on the chair across from him. "Yes, I did. Oh, yes, I did. There was a time in our marriage when I thought about it every day." She looked down at the tablecloth, traced the outline of one of the embroidered daisies. "Ernie never knew. But I used to spend hours a day planning on how I would move back in with my mother, save some money, and then get a little studio apartment of my own. I was going to get a job selling clothes over at Marshall Field's. And I was going to keep a little lamp in my window so when I came home at night it would be there to look up at. **My place.**" She looked away from Griffin, stared into space. Then, looking back at him, she said, "He never knew. He thought I was just mad about something for a while. Thought he'd mind his own business and wait for it to blow over."

"Were you?"

"Was I what?"

"Were you mad about something?"

"I **was** mad about something. But it wasn't really him. It was something else that I could never put into words. Couldn't then, and couldn't now, either. But it was . . . You know, in those days, it was rare for a woman to be on her own. I didn't think of it as a possibility for me—I told you how I used to make couples out of everything! But at the same time that I thought I knew my destiny, knew what I wanted, there was another part of me that felt like I was drowning after I got married." She looked at him. "You know that old Peggy Lee song, 'Is That All There Is?'"

Griffin nodded.

"Well, that's what it was, I suppose. I was young, I thought I was in love, I got married, and then I woke up one day and thought . . . Wait a minute. **Do** I love him? Is this really love? Is this what marriage is supposed to be? You know, **Is that all there is?** And of course Ernie and I couldn't have children, I think that was a big thing." She waved her hand, settled back in her chair. "Oh, listen to me telling you all this. You won't tell Ernie, will you?"

"No. I promise."

"I think I just had too much time on my hands, a woman staying home with nothing to do but housework. I think that was it."

"But you didn't leave," Griffin said.

She smiled. "No. I didn't."

"Why not?"

"It was such a different time. Divorce was risqué. But also . . . Well, I think it was because of Ernie, that I stayed, even though it was also because of Ernie that I wanted to leave. I thought about being without him and I thought, Oh, I'd just end up telephoning him every day. Asking his advice about this or that. Wanting to know if he was all right, what he was doing. If that was so, why not just stay?" She pointed to a tray on the table, holding about a dozen vials of pills. "Those are all Ernie's. You'd never know it to look at him, but he's quite ill. He's got . . . Well. Let me just say, I'm so glad I stayed. So that I can be here now. Everybody thinks the best time to be with someone is when they're at their best. But for me—"

The door opened and Ernie walked in. He pulled out a half gallon of premium vanilla. "So much?" Angie said. "Ernie, you know you're not supposed to have ice cream."

"Oh, take it easy, this is all for you and Griffin." He opened the carton, peered in. "Maybe I could have a taste, though." He looked over at his wife, sighed. "I know, I won't. But I **am** going to have a little cake!"

She said nothing.

"Aw, come on. I'm Santa Claus, for Christ's sake."

She laughed, went over to a drawer, and took out a knife. "All right, all right. But a small piece." She came back to the table, kissed Ernie's forehead, and began slicing the cake.

"Ball and chain," Ernie said, but these were words of love. And though he was talking to Griffin, he was staring at his wife with such obvious affection, it was as though the sentiment were another person in the room.

Angie nodded at Griffin, smiled a small smile. **You see, then.**

And Griffin nodded back. **I do.**

# Chapter 24

· · · · · · · · · · · · · · ·

Staring into the dressing room mirror, Griffin put on his hat, then his white gloves. The Santa on duty before him came into the room, unfastening his belt. "Whew!" he said. "Busy! Your turn, pal. Make sure they give you a lot of water—it's hotter than hell up there."

"I will, thanks," Griffin said, and, making a final adjustment to his beard, he went out into the mall. He was spotted immediately by a Hispanic girl coming out of a shoe store, holding onto her mother's hand. **"Hola,** Santa!" she yelled excitedly. And then, **"Mami!** Santa!"

The mother smiled and waved shyly at Griffin, and he waved back, then discreetly hiked up his belly.

There was a long line waiting for him. Griffin nodded at Donna and her elf assistant, then took

his place in his gigantic chair. A boy around seven
years old was first in line, and he walked slowly up
to Griffin, then stood silently before him. He was
wearing a buttoned-up coat and a stocking hat
pulled low over his forehead. "Hello there!" Griffin
said.

"Hello," he said dully.

"Aren't you warm?" Griffin asked.

The boy shook his head, then asked, "So, come
on, are you real or not?"

"Pardon?" Griffin asked, buying time.

"Are you real? I heard you're not real."

"Who said that?"

"Ethan Wendell."

"Oh, well, Ethan. You know how he can be."

"Yes."

"I wouldn't pay too much attention to Ethan if I
were you."

"Okay."

Griffin sat back in his chair. "Want to come sit
up here with me?"

Again the boy nodded, then stood stiffly as
Griffin pulled him onto his lap. "Now," he said. "Do
I or do I not feel real to you?"

A tiny smile. "Real."

"So. What would you like for Christmas?"

The boy took a big breath in. "One best thing is a
microscope. And I want a number seven submarine

sandwich. And a car that is **not** like anyone else's that has a horn and headlights. You can build it so that it is not like **anyone else's.** I could use a German shepherd. And I would like more LEGOs and some disappearing ink and some magic tricks, especially the dollar bill maker. And a hockey stick." He paused, looked at Griffin. "Do I just keep going?"

"Well, I might not be able to bring you everything. But you can **tell** me everything."

"I know. My mom said if I ask for too many toys, the sleigh might tip over."

"Something to consider," Griffin said, and then, seeing Donna signaling him, he said, "Say. How about we have our picture taken together?"

"Yeah," the boy said. "And then we send it to my grandmother. Which you probably know."

"And she really likes it, doesn't she?"

The boy shrugged. **"I** don't know."

"Well, how about you smile right at that pretty lady over there?"

After the flash, the boy hopped off Griffin's lap and saluted smartly. "See you," he said.

A baby was next, a charmer in a pink ruffled dress who smiled engagingly and then quietly vomited on him. Donna rushed forward with a handful of paper towels, and she and Griffin laughingly reassured the embarrassed mother.

Next came a little girl around three, who cried hysterically when put on Griffin's lap, then instantly quieted when her mother sat on Griffin's other knee. "What would you like for Christmas?" Griffin asked the woman, and she said, "Sleep."

"No!" the girl shouted. "She wants diamonds!"

"Only from Daddy, sweetheart," the mother said. "But why don't you tell Santa what you want?"

"He knows."

"How does he know?"

"Remember we sent him that letter?"

"Ah, yes," the mother said, winking at Griffin. "Well, we can remind him."

"Easy-Bake Oven and a call girl suit," the girl said. She wiped her hand across her nose.

"Pardon?"

"Easy-Bake Oven and a **call** girl suit. With a holster and a hat and boots."

"Oh! A **cow**girl suit!"

"Yes!" the girl said.

"I'll do my best."

After they posed for pictures, the girl climbed off his lap and said, "I'm going to leave cookies for you, you know. And coffee and toast for the reindeer."

Griffin handed her a candy cane and antlers. "Thank you."

"Know what?"

"What?"

"I LOVE YOU!!!!"

"I love you, too," he said, and reached for his mug of ice water. "Why don't you call me sometime?" she asked, and her mother said, "Okay, honey, that's enough, let's go."

When Griffin put down his mug, he saw a few feet before him a boy large in size but about six years old, as evidenced by his missing front teeth. He was wearing camouflage pants and a bright orange T-shirt, high-top sneakers, unlaced. He had stuffed his jacket between his knees.

"Come on up," Griffin said.

The boy approached solemnly, then sat down heavily on Griffin's lap. His weight was equal to an adult's and Griffin tried subtly to twist his leg into a more comfortable position.

"How are you?" Griffin asked.

"I only got one thing," the boy said.

"What's that?"

"Can I tell you in your ear?"

Griffin leaned his head down, and the boy whispered, "Can you take away my breasts?"

Griffin leaned back, stared into the boy's eyes in an effort not to stare directly at his chest. But the boy was right—there they were.

"Well," Griffin said.

"Can you?"

"What's your name?"

"Estevan."

"And you're how old?"

"Six."

"Well, here's what I can promise you. You are going to grow and change a lot, Estevan. In your body and also in your mind and in your heart. And the way you are now is not the way you'll always be. Okay?"

"Okay." His face still full of sadness.

"Any toys you want this year?"

"Not really. Well, I want a puppy, but don't bring me that, because my dad, he said he'd take him out the Kennedy Expressway and leave him. So don't bring me one."

Ernie was right. Some kids broke your heart. "How about something else?" Griffin asked.

"Well, you usually forget. So . . ."

"Well, here's a gift I'll give you now," Griffin said. "I'll tell you that I can see what kind of man you could be when you grow up. I believe that if you just try, you'll be a great man."

". . . I don't know," the boy said.

"I believe you have a lot of power inside. You can feel it sometimes, can't you?"

There, a light in his eyes. "Yes. Sometimes."

"I want you to trust in that, okay?"

"Okay."

"And here are some orders. I want you to take good care of yourself, every day!"

"Okay!"

"I want you to eat your vegetables!"

The boy giggled. "Okay!"

"Now. Who's your best friend?"

Uh oh. Bad question. The boy shrugged, stared at the floor.

"I'll tell you something in **your** ear," Griffin said. And as the boy held still, he whispered, "I'll be your best friend. It's our secret, okay?"

The boy smiled, nodded.

"How about a picture of you and me together?"

The boy looked over at his mother, an unhappy looking woman standing off to the side. "I can't," he said. "She said we can't pay for that."

"This one's free," Griffin said. He would pay for it. "I'll let my friend over there know that this one's free. And you take the picture home and put it somewhere special, will you?"

The boy turned to look into Griffin's eyes. "Yes, sir." He stood up, then turned back to say, "Can I have your autograph on my arm?" He handed Griffin a pen, and, after he signed, whooped and ran down the steps toward his mother, who was smiling now.

The line stayed long until Griffin's shift was up. Finally, exhausted, he said goodbye to the last child and stood up from his chair. He was filled with a sadness he couldn't explain. He walked over to Donna to say good night, and she looked up at him, smiling. Then, seeing his expression, she asked, "What's wrong?"

"I don't know. Tired, I guess. My arms are killing me."

Donna called out to her assistant that she'd be right back, then walked with Griffin as he headed back to the dressing room. "It's . . . this **belief** they have," he said. "And the things most of them want. I thought they'd have lists six miles long. But they don't. Most of them don't ask for much at all."

"And you wish you could give every single one of them what they want, right?"

He smiled at her ruefully. "Actually, it's more selfish than that. I wish **I** could buy a video game and have it fill the void."

"That doesn't fill it, not even for them," Donna said. "Come on, you know that. We're full of false bottoms from the day we're born."

He reached the door of the changing room, and turned to Donna. He started to speak, then stopped.

But she heard him anyway. "Why don't you just ask her to try again, Griffin?"

He said nothing.

"What have you got to lose?"

"I don't know."

"Ask her."

She touched his hand, smiled, and walked away. In the air, the lingering scent of her perfume, like a last kiss.

# Chapter 25

· · · · · · · · · · · · · · · · · · ·

Griffin pulled up outside of Ellen's apartment, turned off the engine, and sat quietly, thinking. He could hear the **tick-tick-tick** of the engine as it cooled, the sound of the traffic at the busy intersection on the corner. Her lights were on, and he watched for a while to see if he could see anyone moving about. No one.

He opened the car door, stepped out, and saw his shadow against the sidewalk. He'd forgotten that he hadn't changed out of his costume, and he was startled, at first, by what he saw on the ground. Then, enjoying the unexpected sight of his alternate persona, he tipped his hat to himself.

He didn't want to knock on the door and risk being unwelcome. He wanted only to see her. He crept silently up to the living room window. She was on the sofa, talking on the phone. Zoe was nowhere in sight—asleep in the other room, Griffin supposed. Ellen's face was serious, and the responses she was giving were brief. Who was she talking to? When they lived together, he could mouth this familiar, domestic question, and she would mouth back the response. Now it was no longer his business. Her face grew angry, she said a few words into the phone and hung up, then sat with her forehead in her hands.

This could be good. This could be very good. It had to be a fight between her and Peter. Griffin's spirits lifted, and he became emboldened—he would let her know he was here, after all. He would knock on the window rather than go to the door. That might be romantic. Ellen would like that. He raised his hand to knock, but then Ellen picked up the phone and dialed. Now her face was soft and conciliatory. **Come over,** she'd be saying. **I'm sorry.**

He sat down on the ground and sighed, his back against the house. But it was cold and uncomfortable, and he got back up and looked through the window again. She was still talking, smiling now. He watched her for a while, nodding, listening. **Yes,** she was saying. Another nod. **Yes.**

Damn it. He reached up and knocked at the window. Ellen jumped, pulled her sweater tighter around her, said something into the phone. Then she lay the receiver down and moved cautiously to the window. She was frightened; her eyes were wide, her fists clenched.

Griffin took his hat off and pointed to himself. "It's only me," he said loudly.

She opened the window. "Griffin! What are you **do**ing?"

"Are you on the phone?"

"Well, I guess if you've been standing there watching me, you know that. What are you doing? You scared me to death!"

So much for his ideas about her ideas about romance. "Who are you talking to?"

She sighed. "My mother. We had a little fight. Now we're making up. If you must know."

His feet were cold, and the tips of his fingers. "Can I come in?"

She stared at him. "Why? What do you want?"

He shrugged. "Cold out here."

"Oh, all right, come in."

After she opened the door, she went to the phone and said, "It was only Griffin, Mom. I'll call you tomorrow." A pause while she listened, and then, "No. Goodbye."

"What were you fighting about?"

"Nothing. What are you doing here, Griffin?"

"I was in the neighborhood. Is Zoe asleep?"

"Yes. Why are you still dressed up?"

"I don't know. Didn't feel like changing."

"Well . . ." She held her hand out. "Give me your coat. Would you like some tea?"

He followed her into the kitchen. "Sure."

She filled the kettle, stood on tiptoe to reach the box of tea in her high cupboard. She set out two cups, then sat opposite him, folded her hands. "I'm glad you came over. I have something to tell you."

**Oh, Jesus.** They were getting married.

"Peter and I are . . . over."

At first, expecting the news he had, what she actually said did not register. But then it did.

"You're kidding."

She looked down into her empty cup.

"But . . . he's why you left!"

She looked up. "No. He's one of the reasons I left."

He searched her face. What did this mean? "So . . . are you sure, Ellen?"

"Oh, yes. Yes, I am. I am quite sure."

"Well . . . who got the puppy?"

"Zoe did. He's in there sleeping with her. They ran around all day—they're both just zonked." She looked at Griffin and her eyes filled. "I'm tired, too. I'm so amazingly tired."

"I can see that."

She put her face into her hands. "And I don't know what I'm doing."

He wasn't sure he could touch her. He reached out a hand toward her, then pulled it back. "Ellen."

She looked up suddenly, dry-eyed. "I honestly don't know what I'm doing." Behind her, the teakettle whistled, and she went over to turn off the flame. "Do you really want tea?"

"No."

"Me either." She sat down again. "See? I knew that."

"I know you did."

Silence.

And then she said, "I wake up a hundred times every night. And every day, hours before I go to work, I clean. Isn't it clean in here?"

Griffin looked around. "Yes, it is."

"That's right, because that's what I do, is clean."

Silence again, but for the dripping of the tap. And then she said, "All of my clothes are organized according to color."

He stared at her blankly. What did she want? "Uh huh."

"I clean my **cleaning** products, Griffin. All the bottles and cans, I wipe them all off."

". . . Why?"

"I don't know. I don't know! I think I'm like Lady Macbeth, trying to wash the guilt away."

"Ellen. Do you want to come home? Let's get Zoe and go home."

"I can't do that, Griffin."

"Why not?"

"I can't **do** that. Something **happened.** I can't just come home."

"You can."

"Well, I **won't** then. Put it that way."

Griffin closed his eyes, rubbed his forehead. What was on TV tonight?

"Do you want to know what happened with Peter?" Her voice was soft, itself again.

"I don't know. . . . I guess. Fine, what happened?"

"He's not what I thought. I was so wrong about him. I thought he was part of what I needed to move toward. To become. And then as soon as I moved here, everything about him was wrong. He got up and ate in the middle of every night like a weird person. He doesn't understand children. He pretends to, but he doesn't. He . . . He . . ." She began to cry again. "Oh, Griffin, I just don't know how I can ever . . ."

"Ellen. You screwed up. I screwed up, too. Just come home. Come on. We'll work this out."

"How can you say that? How can you even stand me anymore?"

"I feel bad for you. I think you made a mistake. I think it's okay to forgive someone who makes a mistake."

"But there were things wrong with us, Griffin,

and those things are still there, they will still be there!"

"Well, then we'll fix them together."

The door to the bedroom opened, and Zoe came out, followed by a small black puppy. "Dad?" She rubbed her eyes. "Hey. You're in your Santa suit. What are you doing here, Dad?"

Ellen scooped up the puppy. "I'll take him out," she said.

"Stay here," Griffin said. "I'll do it."

She hesitated, then nodded. "Okay. Thank you."

Griffin took the puppy out to the yard, stood with his hands in his coat pockets while the dog sniffed, took a few steps, and then sniffed some more. "Come on," Griffin said, and, as though on cue, the dog squatted, then rose and ran toward the house.

"Good boy!" Griffin said, picking him up and petting him. He would be very good about not holding anything against the dog. He would be very fair.

When he came back inside, Ellen said, "She's back in bed. She wants you to tuck her in."

Zoe lay with the covers pulled up to her nose. Griffin sat on the small bed—it wasn't much more than a cot, really—and put the puppy into her arms. "Looks like you got your brother, huh?"

"What are you doing here, Dad?"

"I came to visit. Is that okay?"

"Yes. But I'm coming home tomorrow."

"I know you are."

She stared at him, yawned hugely, then said, "Dad? Can you get me a drink?"

He went into the kitchen, took one of the empty mugs from the counter, and filled it with water. By the time he gave it to Zoe, she was half asleep again. "Thanks." She turned over, and was out.

Back in the living room, Griffin sat on the sofa beside Ellen. "I'm so ashamed," she said quietly. "I can't imagine how all of this came about. One thing, then another, then this awful kind of momentum . . ."

Griffin said nothing, stared at his hands on his knees.

"And now I've gone and screwed Zoe up, too."

"She's not screwed up. She's stronger than that."

"I think she's just being careful. To not let us see. I think she's trying to take care of us. And that just kills me, Griffin."

"Well, if you don't want to come home, what do you want to do, Ellen?"

"I don't know. Griffin? How long since you stopped wearing your ring?"

It occurred to him to lie to her about what he had done. But he didn't. He told her. He also told her that he'd regretted it, and had tried to find the ring, but could not.

"I see," she said. And then, "Maybe you'd better go, now."

"Ellen—"

"I want you to go, please."

He did not look at her on the way out, nor did he look back at her apartment as he pulled away. He wanted a psychic shower, a feeling of all of her sliding off of him and heading down a drain.

# Chapter 26

• • • • • • • • • • • • • • • • • •

In the last days before Christmas, Griffin volunteered for more hours than he'd been scheduled
for. He and Ellen continued to "share" Zoe, and
the evenings when his daughter was gone were better
spent in the company of other people. Otherwise, it
was hours of mind-numbing television, bowls of
potato chips and bottles of beer, and visits to the bedroom with the Victoria's Secret catalogue in hand—
the mild elevation of mood going in not worth the
empty despair he felt coming out, and certainly not
worth the abject foolishness he felt washing up. All
things considered, better to impersonate a saint.

Daily, the lines of children stretched around the
corner, until, from his vantage point, he could
never tell anymore how many were waiting. Babies
cried and flirted, siblings fought, and parents bent
over to whisper admonitions between clenched

teeth. Legions of small, solitary figures of varying heights stood quietly holding their jackets, staring straight ahead. Many parents fussed and carried on, preparing their children for the photos—"Smile like we **talked** about, honey; remember what we said?"—but most grandparents relaxed and let the children have a good time. A woman brought her toy poodle, decked out in red ribbons and green nail polish, to be photographed with Santa; Griffin held the perfumed creature while "Mommy" brushed her just one more time.

Three days before Christmas, Griffin drove to Ellen's apartment to pick up Zoe. It was five o'clock and he was starving—he'd skipped lunch. He wished he hadn't promised Zoe she could help make dinner that night—he wanted to stop at the Cozy Corner and eat quickly. But in the overly solicitous way of single parents, he decided not to risk doing anything that would disappoint Zoe.

He and Ellen hadn't talked much since he'd last sat in her kitchen with her. They had exchanged only necessary pieces of information regarding logistics. He didn't want to intrude, but he was worried about Ellen. She was pale, too thin. Last time she'd leaned over to put Zoe's head between her hands and kiss her goodbye, he'd noticed her hands were shaking.

Zoe answered the door when he knocked, then put her fingers to her lips. "Shhh! Mommy's sleeping." Ellen was stretched out on the couch, an old sweater covering her.

"I'll get my stuff," Zoe whispered. "Don't wake her up; she's really sleepy."

Griffin waited, his hands in his pockets, while Zoe collected her things, leashed the puppy, and put on her coat. She tiptoed over to the sofa, pulled the sweater up higher over Ellen's shoulders, and nodded at Griffin. "Ready," she whispered.

"I'm going to tell her we're leaving." Griffin said. "Shhhhhhh!"

"No, Zoe, we have to tell her. Otherwise she'll wake up and you'll be gone and she'll be worried."

"No, she won't! She knows you're coming!"

Their argument was settled by Ellen awakening, sitting up quickly, and pushing the hair off her face. "Oh! Oh, I must have . . . I fell asleep! Is it time already?"

Griffin nodded. "Yeah. Hi."

"Hi." That little slice of shyness. She looked around the room. "Do you have all your things, Zoe?"

"Yes. And I **told** Dad not to wake you up. Twice."

"It's okay." She smiled at Griffin. "How are things at the North Pole?"

"Busy. Tomorrow's my last day."

"Well, I'll be here all day—bring Zoe back whenever you want."

"What are you doing for Christmas?" Griffin asked.

"I . . . don't know. I'm not sure."

"Zoe," Griffin said. "Can you wait for me outside? Give Nipper a chance to go out before we put him in the car?"

"I know," she said. "You can't fool me."

"What?" Griffin asked.

"You're going to talk about my presents!"

"How do you know?"

She pulled her stocking hat low on her forehead. "I have my sources."

"Take the dog out, and after he goes, get in the car and wait for me. It's warm in there."

"I don't get cold," Zoe said. "I am reptile woman. I shall play in the snow with my companion until you report to me." She ran out the door with the puppy at her heels.

"Guess we should have gotten her a dog a long time ago, huh?" Griffin said.

"He's been good for her."

"You know, I haven't gotten her anything yet for Christmas. I was thinking of an aluminum bat."

Ellen nodded. "I was, too. But I'll get her something else."

"What are you doing for dinner tonight?" he asked. God, she was thin.

"Oh, I don't know."

"Come eat with us."

"I don't think so, Griffin."

"It's not against the rules."

"I think it would be confusing."

"Just come and eat. Drive yourself—you can leave right afterward, or whenever you want. Come on, Zoe's making meatballs."

She looked out the window, her arms crossed tightly over her chest, considering. Then she said, "All right. I'll be there in an hour."

Zoe prided herself on making each meatball exactly the same size. She lined them up on a cookie sheet as she prepared them, inspecting them from above and from the side at frequent intervals.

Griffin made a salad and some marinara sauce, tried to quiet the nervous feeling that had settled in his stomach. He had just put water on to boil when the doorbell rang.

Ellen stood before him when he opened the door. "What, you ring the **doorbell** now?" he said. Then, when she pulled flowers from behind her back with a flourish, he felt bad. She had only wanted to surprise him.

After she hung up her coat, she went to one of the high kitchen cupboards for a vase. It was odd, seeing her perform this familiar chore when she no longer lived here. It tore at him and it pleased him.

"Smells good!" she said, sitting at the table. And then, to Zoe, "Well. There's some nice work."

"Wine?" Griffin asked.

"Yes, please," Zoe answered, then laughed at her own joke. "Hey, Mommy," she said. "Do you notice anything about these meatballs?"

Ellen took a long swallow from the wineglass Griffin handed her, then said, "Uh huh. They look delicious."

"But do you notice anything?"

Ellen looked carefully. "Ah. They are all the exact same size."

"Yes!" Zoe said. "And now, for your grand prize, I will be right back."

As she ran upstairs, the phone rang. Ellen started to move reflexively toward it, then sat still as Griffin answered. "Zoe!" he called. "It's Grace!"

He listened until she picked up the phone, then hung up. "She's got a girlfriend, did you know that?"

"Yes. I'm glad."

"Could be the beginning of the end."

"Oh, it's nice. Grace makes her play dolls a little and Zoe makes Grace play hockey a little."

Griffin dumped the pasta into the boiling water, then came to sit at the table with Ellen. "Tell me something. Are you okay? Because—no offense, but you look like shit."

She laughed. "Thank you very much."

"Seriously, Ellen."

"I'm fine. I've just been doing a lot of thinking. A lot."

"And?" He swirled the wine in his glass. This was a nice cabernet.

"Oh . . . you know."

He looked up. "I don't."

"Well, I've been trying to understand why I . . . I've just been trying to understand some things, that's all."

"And how is that going?"

"How that is going is that I don't understand much, all right? Except that there is a lot wrong with me." She nodded as though agreeing with herself. "There really is."

Silence but for the nearly conversational bubble of the pasta water. And then he said, "Come home, Ellen."

She sighed. "See, Griffin? You didn't even hear what I said."

"I did hear you. I don't feel the same way about those words that you do, that's all."

"What do you mean?"

He leaned forward, took one of her hands in his own. "Ellen. Did it ever occur to you that part of the reason I love you is **because** of your flaws?"

She pulled her hand back. "Oh, Jesus."

"Just listen. If you would only—"

Zoe clattered down the stairs and bounded into the kitchen. "Here," she said to Ellen, "is your most excellent present!" She handed her mother a small package, wrapped in the Sunday comics and tied with red yarn. "Open it!"

"Should I?"

"Yes, I **made** it!"

Ellen unwrapped what appeared to be a ceramic plaque. Griffin could only see the back of it, but whatever was on the front was having a strong effect—Ellen, her smile frozen, her eyes bright with tears, hugged Zoe, saying, "Thank you. This is beautiful." She held the plaque up for Griffin to see. A simple message, written in exuberant script, **Welcome home!!!!**

"I **told** you I was learning cursive," Zoe said. "And this is for you, because you're coming home at Christmas, right?"

Nothing. "Mom?" Zoe said quietly. "That's what you said, remember?"

"Yes, I do remember," Ellen said. And then, to Griffin, "Are we about ready to eat? Because I'm starving!"

"But do you like your present?" Zoe asked. She leaned onto the table, pressed into her mother.

Ellen kissed the top of Zoe's head. "I love my present. And I love you."

"And you love Daddy, right?"

Ellen looked quickly at Griffin, and haltingly said, "Oh, now." A nervous laugh.

"Zoe," Griffin said, quickly. "Get some plates out of the cupboard, will you?"

"I love Daddy," Ellen said. "Zoe? I love Daddy." She put her fingers up to her mouth, cleared her throat. Then, her hands folded before her on the table. "So."

Griffin did not speak, nor did he move at all; and then Zoe, giggling, said, "I **know.**"

"Will you get some plates, Zoe?" Griffin asked, nearly whispering.

She sighed. "Do I have to do **everything** around here?"

Apparently, she did.

Ellen stayed until Zoe's bedtime, then tucked her in. When she came downstairs, Griffin had started a fire, and he patted the sofa cushion for her to sit beside him.

She leaned back, sighed deeply. "This is nice. Thank you."

"You're welcome."

They sat silently for a while, listening to the crackle and hiss of the fire, and then Ellen said, "Griffin, you know what you started to say before, about loving me because of what's wrong with me?"

"I didn't exactly say that. I said that your flaws were one of the things I loved about you."

"Well, Griffin. With all due respect, that's idiotic."

"It's not."

"It **is.** I mean, I don't want to be taken home because I'm the ugliest puppy in the box."

He looked at her. "All right. I'm going to try to tell you something, here. Don't interrupt."

She nodded. "Okay."

**"Don't** interrupt."

"Okay!"

"I think that loving someone for their flaws—"

"I think you said, **along with** their flaws."

He sighed. "Ellen. Jesus."

"What?"

"You're **interrupting.** Shut **up. Listen** to me."

She moved away from him, turned to face him. "Sorry."

**"Listen.** Don't say anything until I tell you you can talk. Okay? We'll take turns. I talk, then you talk. Okay?

She nodded.

"Good. Good. Now . . . Damn it, I forgot where I was."

She raised an eyebrow, permission to speak, and he said, "No! I'll remember. In fact, I do remember, exactly. Loving someone for their flaws, that's what

I said. That's what I started to say. But I believe it makes sense. Because, Ellen, we are all flawed indi- viduals. What people want, I think, is to be known completely. Didn't you say something like that about Mr. Wheels?" She started to answer, and he held up a hand. "That was a rhetorical question, Ellen. I will tell you when it's your turn. You'll know, because I'll say, 'It's your turn.' "

He drew in a breath. "Now. I know you can love, Ellen. I've seen how you love Zoe, everyone who knows you sees that. I've seen how you love fucked- up people like Dan Swaylow, remember that burnout case you were so nice to in college? The guy with the fried brain, who cried all the time? You were wonderful with him. But the danger for you, Ellen, is when someone your own size wants to love you back. So to speak. You're so afraid. But you're also so full of love, Ellen. I know it.

"Not everyone does. You're a pain in the ass. Most people would wonder why I bother with you. Why I bother with you is I know what **else** you are. I see you, Ellen. You don't have to hide here, don't you see that? You're home."

She blinked once, twice.

"What I've learned since you've been gone is that there isn't a bad guy and a good guy when people in a relationship have trouble. There are two bad guys. And I have come to understand my own part in our . . . undoing. And I want . . ." His throat tightened, and his voice hoarsened. "I want you to come home now and for us to have our little family back, and I want us to do it right this time. I want us to wake up. To be careful. To pay attention. To offer each other a kind of respect that was missing from both sides before. I want you to go upstairs and get into bed with me, Ellen, and I want you to look at me and see me. And in the morning, I want you sitting across from me. And the next morning and the next morning after that until one of us croaks. Come back home, Ellen. Please. Don't . . . waste this. Don't lose it."

She sat staring into her lap, unmoving. "You can talk now," he said.

She looked up. "You know, you talk about listening. But I don't think you heard what I said, about not wanting to be loved for my flaws. I want to be loved for the good things about me. But I . . ." She swallowed. "I can't find too many. I don't think I do anything well but love Zoe. And even that . . . Oh, I **can't** just come back and let you love me when I have so little respect for myself, Griffin. I can't respect **you,** that way. I have so much work to do before I . . ."

"Why don't you do it here?" he said. "Wouldn't that be convenient? Wouldn't that be good for Zoe?"

"What would be good for Zoe is to have two good parents who are happy to be with each other."

"And you don't think that's possible for us."

"Oh, Griffin. I don't see how you can ever really forgive me. So much has happened, I don't know if we can . . ." She sighed. "I just don't know."

He leaned back, rubbed his neck. And then he said, "Wait here. I have a present for you."

"No," she said, but he was up and gone to the basement. When he came back into the living room, he handed Ellen a box wrapped in silver paper.

"Open it," he said. "Please."

She took the box from him, carefully unwrapped it. "Oh, my God," she said. "Where did you . . ." She smiled and held up the ballerina doll, touching her dress, her blue hair, her stained forehead. "You dyed her hair!"

He shrugged. "Well. Yeah, yeah, I did."

She laughed out loud. "I can't believe you did this! Thank you!"

"You're welcome."

"But I don't have anything for you!"

"It's okay."

"No, it isn't." She looked at her watch. "Oh, God, Griffin. I've got to go; I have to get up so early tomorrow. And I've been so tired."

"Why don't you stay for just a while longer?"

"I can't."

He walked her to the door, kissed her cheek. "Thank you again," she said, and closed the door softly behind her. He watched her walk to her car, watched her taillights disappear, and then went to the fireplace to stare into the flames.

Upstairs, he checked on Zoe, who slept soundly, all of her covers on the floor. He covered her back up, then went into the bedroom and lay on his own bed, his hands laced over his belly. Well, what had he expected? That everything would be neatly resolved in an evening? That, like the children who sat on his lap believed, he was capable of miracles?

If only it were so. He got up, stretched, and contemplated what he should do tonight. Read? Watch some cable show?

On the dresser lay his Santa beard, and Griffin put it on, then added his hat. He looked at himself in the mirror, saw the stubborn transformation. When he was dressed like this, everything really did change. He put on his wire-rimmed glasses and headed downstairs. Santa would clean up the kitchen, then surf the 'net for baseball memorabilia for Zoe.

In the living room, he drew the curtains, turned off the lights, and made sure the fire was out. He locked the front door, put the chain lock on. In the kitchen, he turned on the radio and began rinsing dishes. "Because we **need** a little Christmas, right this very minute," he sang along. His glasses fogged, and his beard seemed to grow heavier with the rising steam.

And then he heard a noise at the front door. He turned off the water and stood listening. Yes. Someone was out there, trying to break in. Only a week ago, someone had broken into a house the next block over and stolen nearly everything of value, including Christmas gifts.

Griffin moved quietly to the front door, reached into the closet for Zoe's wooden baseball bat. He reached up to wipe off the perspiration that had formed on his forehead, and realized he was still wearing his costume. Well, Merry Christmas, asshole. Here's your gift: a concussion.

The door creaked slowly open, and Griffin took in a breath, raised the bat up high. When the door stopped because of the chain lock, he heard someone whisper, "Damn it!" It was a woman he was hearing. Ellen!

Relieved, he put down the bat and peered through the crack in the door. "What are you doing!"

"I was . . . I wanted to surprise you! Hey. You're in your costume."

"Just . . . neck up." He undid the lock, opened the door fully. "Come in."

She stood still. "I had this whole thing planned. I wanted to surprise you!"

"Come **in,**" he said.

"No. Just leave the door open, and you go back to whatever you were doing. What were you doing?"

"Washing dishes."

"Well, go back and do it."

"Ellen . . ."

"Please. Please?"

"Oh, all right." He shut the door, went back to the sink, and began rinsing the silverware. And then, in the window glass before him, he saw the reflection of Ellen, standing there and holding out a gift.

"Merry Christmas," she said.

He turned around, wiped his hands on the dish-cloth. "Considering the way I'm dressed, I'd say this is backwards."

"Well, I'd say it's about time."

She handed him a small white box, wrapped with green ribbon.

"You didn't have to go get me something, Ellen."

"I had it, already. I just had to go get it. Open it."

He took the lid off the box and saw, lying on a folded square of a paper napkin, his wedding ring.

With some difficulty, he asked, "How did you find this?"

She sat down at the kitchen table, smiling.

"After you told me what you did with it, I went and looked for it. It wasn't easy, even with so little snow! I must have walked back and forth in that field forty times. The guy that drives around in the security car asked me what the hell I was doing, and then he helped me for a while. But he gave up. I found it just as I was ready to give up myself—the sun was going down and I was so cold."

He put the box on the table. "Well, thank you, Ellen."

She looked at the ring, then up at him. "Aren't you going to put it on?"

"I'll put it on when I'm married again."

"We're still married!"

"You know what I mean."

"We're still **married.**"

He stood still for a long time, listening to the sound of his own breathing, then slipped the ring back on his finger. It was cold, at first; but then it warmed against his skin.

She stood. "Okay. Well, I'm glad you have it back."

"Are you . . . What are you doing, Ellen?"

"I thought . . . Look, I want to tell you something. I want to try. On the way home, I thought about everything you told me tonight, Griffin. And here's what I want to say back. Two things. One is, I think our marriage was like a house we stopped using. I mean, you know, you move in, and there are all these terrific rooms, and you think about how you're going to read in the living room, and write nice little notes on the dining room table, and have tea over there in that corner, and naps over there, and then you just end up being in the same two rooms all the time. And after a while it just feels odd to be anywhere else, even though you'd **like** to be somewhere else. You begin to feel as though you **can't** use the living room because you're never there. I think you and I stopped ourselves from doing so much. We got swallowed up by a domestic routine that didn't leave room for us as the individuals we are. I think I gravitated toward a . . . Well, toward a love affair, because I thought it would free me, it would let me be all these wonderful things that I couldn't be with you. It would make me be someone I would like. I felt like somewhere in me was this wild and beautiful thing, capable of so much more than I was being, and I needed this exotic love to let myself out of a jail I thought you had put me in. But I know now that I was the keeper of the keys. I've learned that, Griffin, and now I have to do some things about myself. And I just don't know how it will go if I try to do it in your presence. I don't know. It might not work."

He nodded. He couldn't force her. He'd said all he could.

"But anyway, I thought I'd give you the ring, and . . . Well, we'll see."

"Okay."

"I'm going out to the car."

". . . Okay."

He sat at the table, staring at his ring, listening for the sound of her car to drive away, wondering how long it might take for her to make another move toward him. Or away. He thought of his mother, saying how, after her husband had died, she still listened for his car. Griffin's father had had a heart attack in the middle of the night, and the day after the funeral Griffin had sat with his mother on the sofa in the living room, the blinds drawn, holding her hand as she wept without speaking for nearly an hour straight, the racking kind of sobs that hurt the observer nearly as much as the one weeping. Then, abruptly, she had stopped. She had blown her nose, sighed hugely, and stood up. She'd said, "I am going to lie down on my bed, under my blue satin quilt, for a day and a night. Do not disturb me. Do not ask me anything, and do not ask me for anything. I'm going to remember every good thing I can think of about your father, and I am going to remember every bad thing. And then I'm going to come down to the kitchen and make some eggs and fried potatoes, and start living what's left of my life." He remembered how he'd felt, witnessing that moment of extreme sorrow and strength.

And then he heard the door opening again, heard what must have been Ellen's suitcase banging into it. That suitcase was heavy; it was always hard for her to handle. He started to get up to help her, but then did not. Rather, he did not move at all. He surveyed his surroundings: the wooden table where he sat, the four ladder-back chairs grouped around it. The fruit bowl over on the counter, low on bananas; he'd get more tomorrow. He looked at the cupboards, thought about how he now knew where everything was: the wok, the pie plates, the allspice, the plastic wrap, the small stash of Band-Aids bound tightly together with a green rubber band, the little calendar that kept track of doctor's and dentist's appointments. He looked up at the black square of kitchen window, and saw the reflection of the top of his costumed head. He stood, the better to see himself wholly, and then, with a feeling of a soft turnover at the center, gave a small wave. Goodbye to this costumed self; and, in fact, to all manner of disguise. He was himself for her to take or leave; either way, he would be all right.

"Griffin?" Ellen called softly.

"In here." He sat back down and took off his beard, his glasses, and his red hat, put them on the kitchen table. And then he leaned back and waited for her to come to him.